Tyler Keevil grew up in Vancouver, Canada, and in his mid-twenties moved to Wales, where he now lives. His short fiction has appeared in a wide range of magazines and anthologies and has also won several awards, most notably the Writers' Trust of Canada Journey Prize. His first two novels, *Fireball* and *The Drive*, were both nominated for the Wales Book of the Year and both received the Wales Book of the Year People's Prize. He has worked as a tree planter and ice barge deckhand, as well as in factories, restaurants, video stores, and shipyards; he currently lectures in Creative Writing at the University of Gloucestershire.

Praise for *Burrard Inlet*

'Beneath the deceptively calm surface of these spare and beautiful stories, mad passions boil. There is a transatlantic tradition of studying the interaction between men and nature, in such figures as Hemingway, Carver, McGuane; now Keevil extends and enriches that lineage. He truly is that good.'
     – Niall Griffiths (author of *Grits*, *Runt*, and *Kelly & Victor*)

'Keevil's "Tokes from the Wild" is an assured story of a city boy who follows his friend into the countryside to spend a summer tree planting, which soon degenerates into a mess of weed smoke and recriminations.'
     – *The Short Review*

'Tyler Keevil's "Carving Through Woods on a Snowy Evening" tells of a snowboarder, missing on a mountainside not long after an accident, being tracked by hopeful rescuers. "Carving" has... storytelling rich in symbolism; subtle plot devices; and an ending that opens and sings.'
     – *New Welsh Review*

'There's real quality in Tyler Keevil's gripping tale of mountain rescue, "Carving Through Woods on a Snowy Evening".'
     – *The Western Mail*

'I read Tyler's amazing story "Sealskin" and was blown away. Beautiful writing...stunning'
     – Miriam Toews, author of *All My Puny Sorrows*

'Vividly told in muscular prose, Keevil's stories are compelling evocations of isolation and strength in an often unforgiving landscape.'
     – Carys Bray, author of *A Song for Issy Bradley*

'*Burrard Inlet* is, first and foremost, a collection of short stories that tries to recognise the relationship between humans and nature through separate human identities...This is a piece of work that, without a doubt, should be added to a book-shelf of short-story lovers and novel aficionados alike.'

– *Wales Arts Review*

'The masculine, often unforgiving scenarios which unfold here are a suitable fit for Keevil's economical – if elegant – phrasing, but a strong moral core is ever-present, and sometimes vindication for the downtrodden.'

– *Buzz Magazine*

'"Sealskin" is a stunner: straightforward and unadorned, but humming with subsurface power. Possessed of a sturdy narrative backbone and unrelenting forward momentum, the story explores familiar themes – alienation, humanity's relationship to nature, coming of age, and loss of innocence – but does so in a way that seems fresh and vibrant. Strong physical details adjoin keen psychological insights, and Keevil handily builds scenes that reverberate with insight and potency. Keevil has accomplished something rare: a story about rough masculinity that brims with emotion and pathos.'

– The Journey Prize judges

'Keevil's writing has been compared to Raymond Carver's and I can understand the comparison, although the voice is most definitely his own. As with Carver, Keevil's stories are like ink on wet blotting paper – there's a dense dark core of story arc, spare but telling detail and dialogue, yet around that dense mass is an aureola of implied back narrative and a sense of a continuum past the final full stop.'

– *CCQ Magazine*

Praise for *Fireball*

'*Fireball* pushes beyond the bounds of its genre, capturing the dynamics of friendship, seduction, and loss to impressive effect... confirming Keevil's flair for evoking empathy with the extreme in this breathlessly readable and confident debut.'

– New Welsh Review

'This is a truly accomplished novel: funny, gripping and touching in turns, with a conclusion that continues to resonate long after the book is over. Keevil's skill as an author is everywhere evident: in the quirky dialogue, the lucid prose, and the skillful interweaving of multiple and non-linear narrative strands. This is clearly a novelist to be reckoned with.'

– Planet Magazine

'The author stretches time and builds his story in layers, achieving a sort of restrained tension. It's absorbing, moving, tragic and sometimes funny. *Fireball*, one of four novels that heralds Parthian's new Bright New Things series, is a brilliant and memorable first novel from a writer who grew up in Vancouver and now lives in mid Wales.'

– The Western Mail

'[A] fragmented narrative technique that circles and worries around the events of that summer...effectively rendering Razor's troubled, obsessive state of mind and the gradual process by which he attempts to make sense of the death of his friend. There's also a real sense of loneliness and loss behind this story, and the insecure, virginal Razor speaks to the troubled teenager in all of us.'

– The Guardian

'Sylishly written and immensely readable, *Fireball* gives notice of an impressive new talent.'

– Jem Poster

'This book deserves to be a cult hit.'

– David Christopher

Praise for *The Drive*

'Along the way, [Trevor] survives scrapes with mescal-swilling bikers and cannibalistic chefs, gets high on peyote and inadvertently shoots a bald eagle...the narrative is packed with with so many quirky diversions and oddballs that, by the end, you're happy to have joined him for the ride.

– The Financial Times

'Keevil's prose is blisteringly honest and, despite the novel's length, spare. This is an epic journey by anyone's standards but the short chapters, snappy dialogue and pure and simple crazy situations keep you firmly gripped to the back seat.'

– We Love This Book

'His journey into the American West is hilarious, his journey into himself revelatory, and you'll be glad to have gone along with him for the ride...Enjoy.'

– Nye Wright, Waterstones Blog

'The heightened cartoon touch drives the action along at a snappy pace and the humour and vim with which each scene is setup helps illuminate this half-innocent, half-demented take on the world.'

– Litro

'Keevil is such an accomplished and confident stylist – inventive, engaging, casually hilarious – he never loses the reader for a second. When he wants to, Keevil can set his charm to stun...From postmodern doubt to full-on emotional commitment, not least in terms of literary miles on the clock, Keevil's second novel is quite a trip.'

– New Welsh Review

'If you're up for a coming-of-age-finding-yourself tale with a heavy dose of booze, weed, endless stretches of road and a smidge of magic, give *The Drive* a read. I thought it was better than *Fear and Loathing in Las Vegas*, and that's saying something!'

– The London Diaries

Burrard Inlet

Tyler Keevil

PARTHIAN

Parthian
The Old Surgery
Napier Street
Cardigan
SA43 1ED
www.parthianbooks.com

First published by Parthian in 2014
This edition published 2015
© Tyler Keevil
All Rights Reserved

ISBN 978-1-910409-97-8

The publisher acknowledges the financial support of
the Welsh Books Council.

Edited by Claire Houguez

Cover design by Robert Harries
Cover image: *Burrard Inlet* © Jianwei Yang www.jianweiyang.com
Typesetting by Claire Houguez

Printed and bound by Gwasg Gomer, Llandysul, Wales

British Library Cataloguing in Publication Data

A cataloguing record for this book is available from the
British Library.

For the old man

Contents

Snares

As usual, Roger's up before me – looking for his ducks.
When I cross the breezeway from the bunkhouse to the cabin,
I find him standing at the window with his back straight and
his legs apart, like a sentry on duty. He's even got a pair of
binoculars trained on the stretch of water between our barge
and the shore. The morning sun has already hit the inlet,
setting off crescent-shaped flickers. I know what he's doing, but
I also know he doesn't like me to directly mention the ducks, so
instead I ask, 'See anything out there?'

He grunts. 'No – not yet.'

I walk over to stand beside him, shoulder to shoulder. I'm
six-one and he's still got an inch on me. He's got the weight,
too – all top heavy like an old bulldog. Muscled arms and thick,
scarred fingers. Nine of them. He lost the other one in a net,
during his days on the seine boats.

'Here, you have a look. You got younger eyes than me.'

I accept the binoculars, which are heavier than I expect,
and peer into the eyepieces. It takes me a moment to find the
place to look – among the rocks and kelp beds and murky

water swirling beneath our dock. There's no movement, though. No ducks. I study it awhile longer, listening to Roger breathe beside me, before I give up.

'Nothing doing,' I say.

'Ah, well – it's still early, yet.'

He means in the year, not in the day. The truth is, though, we usually see the ducks by mid-April, and it's getting close to May, now. He takes the binoculars back from me and fiddles with the focus wheel, as if he's hoping they might be broken or faulty in some way.

'Better get some starter fluid in you, greenhorn,' he says.

I head into the galley, where the coffee pot is warbling steam, and pour myself half a mug. Roger makes it strong and bitter as crude oil, and I always top mine up with milk to mellow it out. I'm in the process of putting the milk away when Doreen breezes into the galley, her brown dressing gown flapping about her like the wings of a bat. A grey nightie underneath. Pink curlers in her hair. Varicose veins bulging on the backs of her calves.

'You boys sit down,' she says, yanking open cupboards. 'I'll fix you some grub.'

'Get some clothes on, woman!' Roger says. 'You can't go wandering around like that. You're likely to scare this poor boy half to death.'

He always says this, and Doreen always gives the same answer: 'Oh – Alex is family, now.'

During the herring season, she would never have appeared in the galley half-dressed. Her cook's uniform of jeans and blouse and apron was as standard and consistent as my deckhand's coveralls. But it's different now that the others are gone, and it's just the three of us. The curlers and nightie are simply part of the routine – the same as the ducks, the coffee. The same as

2

the scrambled eggs Doreen whips up for us. We sit down at the table together, Roger and Doreen on either end and me in the middle. I only take a spoonful of egg, and smear it across one piece of toast. This early in the morning I never have much of an appetite, which is something Roger doesn't understand.

'Better eat more than that,' he tells me. 'We got work to do.'

Roger makes sure that there's always work to do on the barge, even at the end of season: swabbing the decks or scrubbing the walls or cleaning the engine or replacing pipes in the ice-making machines. Today the two of us will be shovelling out the ice bins. It's a job I don't like, because of the ice rakes – but I've never told Roger this and I never will.

'Don't push Alex too hard, now,' Doreen says, 'or he might not come back next year.' She's smiling as she says it, and I chuckle politely, as if the idea of me not coming back is crazy, absurd. Totally ridiculous. 'By the way, do you think you boys could finish by two o'clock today?'

Roger stares at her like she's asked him to scuttle the barge. 'We got a full day to put in.'

Doreen purses her lips. 'Well, I'm only asking because Beverly's stopping by with little Josh, and I thought it might be nice for us all to have coffee and cake together.'

She says this carefully, letting the significance of the words sink in. Roger considers her proposal while lathering butter on a piece of toast. 'Suppose we could skip lunch, grab a sandwich on the go instead.' He glances over at me. 'That sound okay to you, Alex?'

'Sure. Sounds fine.' Beverly is their granddaughter – the one I haven't met. The oldest, I think. 'We should be able to get the first bin done by then.'

Roger nods, having decided, and bites into his toast. He

likes it almost black, and as he chews I can hear it crunching between his teeth.

We put on gloves, take two snow shovels from the breezeway, and clomp out onto the back deck. Our barge, the *Arctic King*, is as big as the ferries that chug to and from Horseshoe Bay, except instead of cars and passengers it carries ice, which we deliver to the seine boats during herring season. When the fishery ends we moor up here, at a sheltered dock near the Westco shipyards in Burrard Inlet. Out on the water I can see a floatplane coming in to land, its fat pontoons skimming the waves, and in the distance the thin arc of the Second Narrows Bridge hums like a superconductor. Roger leads me down the steel stairway to the lower deck, moving heavily, getting slow in his old age. As we descend, he can't help but glance to his right, towards shore. But there's still no sign of his ducks.

At the bottom of the stairs, he asks me, 'Port or starboard?'

'Maybe starboard – we're listing that way so it'll level us out.'

Our barge was built to house the ice bins. There's two of them, about the size of tennis courts, running bow to stern. Each has its own freezer-style door, accessible from the back deck. A sign on the starboard door shows this diagram of a helpless stick man, all bent and mangled, caught up in the bars of the rakes. The warning reads, *Do Not Enter Ice Bins Without First Raising Rakes And Shutting Off Power*. I'm sure Roger's done this – he's very particular about safety – but that doesn't make me feel any better about stepping inside.

Our boots crunch on the leftover ice resting at the bottom of the bin. It's dense and compressed, about six inches thick. Roger tests it once with his shovel, to make sure it has thawed enough, before going to fetch the wheelbarrow. I'm left alone in the frosty darkness, alone with the rakes. I can see them glittering overhead – long girders fitted with talon-like steel hooks. During herring season, they rest atop the ice that fills this bin. When we service a boat, the rakes sweep the ice into an auger, which pumps it out our delivery hose. The rasp of rakes across flaked ice is a constant background noise to our weeks at sea. The noise doesn't bother me, but the nightmares do. Night terrors, almost. This recurring dream of being caught in the rakes and dragged towards the auger. It always starts like this – with me standing alone in the bins. Then the door slams shut, and the rakes lurch into motion. As they descend, I batter on the door, scream over the rumble of the generator. There is nothing I can do, except wake in a tangle of sheets and lie there sweating, heaving, waiting for dawn.

'Give me a hand here, will you Alex?'

The wheelbarrow is stuck on the lip of the freezer door. I go over and help Roger lift it clear. We lay down a piece of plywood to make crossing the threshold easier. Then we run an extension cord in from outside, plug in a work lamp, and hang it on one of the rakes.

'Well,' he says, 'this ice ain't going to walk out of here.'

He grips his shovel with both hands and drives it straight down. The steel blade crunches into the ice. Levering a chunk free, he dumps it into the wheelbarrow. I walk around to the other side, so we each have room to work. We fall into a steady rhythm of shovelling, lifting, and dumping, like clockwork men keeping time together. When the wheelbarrow gets full, Roger seizes it by the handles and trundles it out on deck. I stand in the doorway to watch him tip it off the starboard side. The ice slides out and hits the water with a satisfying splash.

As he wheels it back he says, 'Best to dump away from shore.'

I nod. The next time the wheelbarrow fills up, it's my turn to empty it, then Roger's, then mine. As we work we pause every so often to lean on our shovels, exhaling clouds of frost. We talk about the season just past, which was bad for herring roe, and we talk about our plans for the summer. Roger's going up to his family cabin in Sicamous, to hunt and fish. I'll be working as a landscaper – cutting lawns and pruning trees and laying paving slabs.

'You take to that work?' Roger asks.

'Not like being at sea. But I need the money.' I pump the handle of my shovel back and forth, prying loose a piece of ice. 'I got to save up if I want to see my girlfriend again. Out in Wales.'

Roger makes a sound in his throat. I know he doesn't understand it, this situation I've got myself involved in with a Welsh girl. It's not like in his day, when people stayed close to home, settled down young, got married. There was no such thing as a long-distance relationship. When I used that term around him, he looked at me as if it was an oxymoron.

'I'd take you out for salmon,' Roger says, 'but you know how it is.'

I nod. He only gets one deckhand for salmon season, and the union would raise hell if he picked me over some of the other guys who have more seniority.

'But next year herring should be good,' he says. 'Make up for the mess they made of it this time around.'

'You'll be going out?'

Roger's sixty-seven, two years past retirement age. He's talked about quitting since my first day on the barge, but each year the company lures him and Doreen back with a one-off contract. 'Don't rightly know,' he says. 'Man's gotta retire sometime, but I sure ain't gonna let this girl fall into the wrong hands. Besides, we have fun out there, don't we?'

I know I've got to tell him. Tell him there's a chance I might not be back next year. A chance I'll be moving to Wales, to be with her, if I get this work visa sorted out. I've been meaning to tell him and Doreen all season, but haven't found a way to bring it up.

So instead I say, 'Sure, Roger. You know it.'

And I listen to him go on about next season, about how it's going to be a big catch since the company didn't make their quota this year. He says he'll bring out his lobster pots for us to fix up and use. He's got a new lathe and scroll saw, too – so we can do woodwork during the lulls. And that's how we while away the morning, one wheelbarrow at a time. Our shovels shearing back the layers of ice, revealing the fibreglass floor beneath.

Just before noon, Doreen brings us down sandwiches and pop. She's dressed, now – in her trademark jeans and blouse, her grey hair carefully curled and her face grainy with make-up. I go to fetch the tatty lawn chairs from the storage compartment on the back deck. During our nights on watch, we'd sit in these, wearing our parkas and rain slickers, waiting for a fishing boat to materialise out of the dark. Today we set up the chairs in the sun, facing the shore. This is so we can keep an eye out for the ducks – though of course we don't say that.

Roger and I take off our gloves and unzip the top half of our coveralls, letting them drape down the backs of our chairs like discarded skin. The sun immediately starts steaming sweat from our undershirts. Doreen has made pastrami, pickle and mustard – her staple – and for a time we sit and chew in silence, listening to waves slap against the side of the barge.

Then Doreen says, 'Stanley called. Wanted to know when payday is.'

Roger chuckles. Stanley's one of the other deckhands. Fortyish. Big and blubbery. Likes sleeping in and drinking beer. Even though Roger keeps a dry boat, Stanley always hides bottles of Molson beneath his bunk, to suck back in secret after dinner.

'He'll be lucky if he ever gets paid,' Roger says, shifting around in his chair. 'The amount of work he done for us.'

Doreen says, 'We should give his cheque to Alex.'

'That would be fair.'

I crack open my can of cola and say, 'I sure could use it.'

We all laugh, enjoying our bit of mischief. Roger's no dummy. He sussed out Stanley the moment he set foot on the barge. He told me, 'That fat old hound is sniffing around after my job.' If he'd had a choice, Roger wouldn't have taken him on. But the barge belongs to the company, and they dropped Stanley on us like a hunk of ballast at the start of last season.

'I'll be damned,' Roger says now, gazing off the port side, 'if I'm going to let him take over this girl. They'll have to crane me off in a coffin, first.'

'Oh, Roger,' Doreen says.

There's some splashing in the river, which makes us all lean forward. Roger even half-rises out of his chair – that's how excited it makes him. Near the rocks, I spot the bird: it's got a dirty white body, grey wings, and a hooked yellow beak.

'Damn,' Roger says. 'Just a herring gull.'

The three of us settle back into our chairs, frowning.

'Don't you worry,' Doreen says. 'Your Mallards will turn up.'

It's the first time any of us have mentioned the ducks,

and Roger actually winces, like he does when his arthritis is acting up.

'It's not safe out here for them,' he says.

'They're okay. They're survivors.'

'A lot of idiots in motorboats, these days. Not paying attention.'

'Ducks are fast, honey. They can fly.'

'Not the ducklings.'

'No, not the ducklings.'

'Then there's the Chinamen,' Roger says, 'with their snares.'

I take a big slug of cola. Roger's convinced that chefs from restaurants in Chinatown set snares in the grass along the shore, to catch ducks to serve on their menus. Saltwater duck is a delicacy, he says. I don't know if that's true, but I'm anxious about the ducks all the same. Doreen is, too. At first we only worried because Roger worried. Now, though, it's gone way beyond that. They've been a part of our routine each year, and we've never had to wait this long for them. It's like those oddballs in the States who wait for the groundhog to appear – and if he doesn't, it feels like spring might never come.

After lunch the pastrami is sitting in my belly, weighing heavy, slowing down the motion of my shovel. We're like two prisoners on a chain gang, Roger and I, digging and lifting with sluggish resignation. I can feel the ache in my lower back from stooping, and the burn in my biceps from all this lifting. I don't complain about it, though. I never complain around Roger. I figure I don't have the right, really – with him being nearly three times my age.

As we work, I ask him about this girl we'll be meeting later. His granddaughter.

'How old is Beverly, again?'

'About your age. She's Jim's daughter.'

Jim is Roger's youngest. A portly guy with a bristle-brush moustache. He visited us on the barge at the start of last season. He had a habit of fiddling with things: the tools in our gear locker, the dials in our engine room. He kept that up until Roger yelled at him about it, in front of the crew. Nobody gets preferential treatment on Roger's barge. Not even family.

'And Josh is her son?'

'That's right,' Roger says, sticking his shovel in.

For a second neither of us says anything. Roger is struggling with this chunk of ice, more solid than the others, that won't come free. He leans his weight on the shovel, using it like a crowbar, and finally the ice cracks loose.

Then he says, 'She's not married. Had the baby out of wedlock.' He says it all at once, quiet and defiant, as if he's confessing something. 'This fellow got her in a family way, and then refused to stand by her. Turned yellow-belly and took off some place.'

I didn't know people still said things like 'in a family way' until I met Roger. And I can tell he's worried I might think less of this girl – maybe even of their whole family – just because she's a single mother. Keeping my head down, I scrape up another scoop of ice.

'That must have been tough,' I say.

'Sure was. But you know what the kicker is?' He's scowling now, shovelling faster. Like he needs to get this off his chest. 'After Josh was born, this fellow all of a sudden reappears. He's decided he wants to be 'part of the baby's life.' That's what he said. Can you believe it? This is months since the birth, mind you. God knows where he's been in that time. Living down in Mexico, apparently. Smoking dope with his hippy friends.'

'Had a change of heart, eh?'

Roger grunts and brings his shovel down hard, as if he's imagining splitting this hippy's head in half. 'Don't your worry,' he says. 'Me and Jim went down to his place and told him what we thought of that little plan. No way I'm letting my grandson grow up in a dope-house.' Roger smiles mischievously. 'Haven't seen hide nor hair of him since.'

Imagining the confrontation, I can't help but smile, too. 'Well, it sounds like she's better off without a guy like that.'

'Damn straight. Better off by a mile. If there's one thing I can't abide, it's a man who shirks his responsibilities.' He breathes out hard, making his lips flap like a horse. 'I just don't know, Alex. I don't know what's going on these days. Everybody seems to be gallivanting around the place. All airy-fairy. Not sure what they want or what they've got.'

I grunt in agreement. I'm thinking of my girlfriend, and this relationship I have. A voice on the phone. Sporadic emails. Letters postmarked from Britain. Vague and fading memories. Like I'm in love with some kind of ghost. Then I heft my shovel and say, 'It's a different world, I guess.'

'You can say that again.'

So I do say it again – just to rib the old guy. He gets a kick out of that.

By quarter to two we've finished the starboard bin. Rather than tackle the port side, Roger calls it a day. We head upstairs to wash up before our company arrives. There's a decent bathroom in the bunkhouse, with a full shower and toilet and sink. Roger likes to lather his hands in soap and rub them over and over, cupping one inside the other. He can never get them quite clean – the creases in his palms are stained black by years of dirt and engine oil.

'I think I might put on a shirt,' he says, stepping aside to dry his hands. 'Tidy myself up a little. It's not every day we have guests, eh?'

I can tell he's suggesting I do the same, so when he goes back across the breezeway I shuck off my coveralls and dig around beneath my bunk. I don't have many fancy clothes, but I've got this one pair of jeans and a collared shirt that I save for when we have shore leave. I hop into that outfit, slap on some deodorant, and run a comb through my hair. Then I check myself in the mirror. There's a long crack in the glass, running slantwise across my reflection, so it looks like I'm split in two. Roger's going to replace it during the off-season.

When I cross the breezeway, the galley is empty. The counters are dusted with flour and the air smells fragrant as a bakery. I hear voices coming from the lounge, so I head that way. Roger and Doreen are sitting on the couch beside the window that overlooks the shore – our duck-watching window. Opposite them, on the smaller couch, is this girl in a red dress. Her dark hair is pulled back behind her ears and pinned in place with barrettes. A baby boy is standing on the floor in front of her. He's not old enough stay up on his own, so she's holding him by the hands to keep him balanced.

The three adults look my way as I come in.

'My,' Doreen says, 'don't you look like a catch.'

I laugh at that, because I'm expected to. Beverly and I don't get formally introduced. We just skip that part. The only seat is the one next to her on the couch. She shifts down to make room for me but it's still a tight fit. Our knees keep touching, and it's hard to get comfortable. The couch has a dip in the middle that eases us towards each other.

Doreen says, 'Isn't little Josh the sweetest thing?'

'He sure is.'

The four of us stare at the baby, because it's easier than looking at each other. He's wearing these blue overalls and underneath them I can see the puffy shape of his diaper. His mother is still holding him by the hands. When she lets go, he totters on his own for a second or two before sinking to the carpet. He gazes up at me from down there, uncertain.

'Hey, big guy,' I say, and prod him in the belly. 'How you doing?'

He giggles and makes a grab for my finger. I pull it away.

'Oh – you like that, do you?'

He likes it. They all do. The two of us play like that for awhile, making everybody laugh. When the game gets old, Beverly picks him up and rests him on her knee. He sucks on his hand, still staring at me, his chin glossy with drool.

'And how did it go today?' Doreen asks.

It's hard to tell whether she's asking me or Roger, because she's still gazing at the baby. We all are, as if we're afraid he might disappear the moment we look away.

'Oh, pretty good,' I say. 'We finished the starboard bin.'

'What were you doing?' Beverly asks.

I tell her about shovelling the ice, about how the rakes can't empty the last six inches and so we have to do it by hand. As I explain I glance at her every so often, but my eyes keep sliding away, not knowing where to rest. Her dress has these wide straps that meet behind her neck in a little bow. I can see a sprinkling of freckles on her bare shoulders.

'What about you?' I ask. 'What are you up to these days?'

I say it as if we've met before, but nobody seems to notice.

Doreen says, 'Beverly is going back to school. Isn't that right, darling?'

Beverly nods and wipes the drool from Josh's chin. 'I'm training to be a nurse.'

We nod and listen as she tells us about her course, which she's taking out at Langara College. The whole time, Josh is sort of waving and pawing at my shoulder, struggling against his mother's grip. Eventually he breaks free and squirms right into my lap.

'Oh, isn't that the most darling thing?' Doreen says. 'We should get a photo.'

She disappears into their bedroom, and comes back with a camera – an old film camera with the kind of flash that takes about two minutes to charge up.

'Okay, smile you two.'

Beverly leans in towards me, and I make sure Josh is facing the camera. The flash goes off, catching us clean. Doreen takes a few more photos, and the whole time Roger just sits there, smiling and content, his fingers laced together over his belly like Santa Claus.

When the photo shoot is done, Doreen looks at him and says, 'Now I think it's about time I checked on that date cake, Roger.' She slips around the corner into the galley. We listen to her puttering about in there, humming to herself, opening and closing the oven. 'Oh, Roger,' she says, a bit too loudly, 'would you fetch me some cream from the downstairs fridge?'

I volunteer to get it, but Roger is already up. He motions for me to stay put.

'You just have a sit, there. I need to stretch the old legs before I doze off.'

I hear the deck door slide open as Roger steps outside. Then it's just Beverly and I, sitting thigh to thigh, with me cradling her baby on my lap. We're both real quiet. Even the baby's gone quiet. So I start talking. About anything. Mostly I ask her about herself: where she grew up and which high school she went to and what she does for fun on weekends. I tell her it must be hard, having to balance work and school and trying to be a mother at the same time.

'What you end up missing is your personal life. You don't go out with your friends, don't get a chance to meet people. I haven't really dated anyone since Josh's dad.' She lowers her eyes from me to him. 'But I suppose Roger told you about that.'

'Some. He told me some.'

'What about you?' she asks. 'Are you involved or whatever?'

I don't know how to explain my situation. My long-distance situation. It seems sort of airy-fairy, as Roger would say. Inappropriate, even. So instead I sit there and say, 'Well.' Just that, nothing more. Well. And while we're sitting there with that word hanging between us, Josh starts squirming in my lap, stretching his hands out towards his mother.

She sighs. 'Looks like somebody needs a feed.'

Taking him from me, she rests him on her knee. Then she angles her body away from me – but not really far enough to hide anything – and unfastens the tie at the back of her dress. The left side comes down, half-exposing her breast. She discreetly guides Josh's little mouth to her nipple, which is dark and ripe with milk. He fastens onto it and starts to suckle. She turns back to me, smiling, as if it's the most natural thing in the world. And maybe it is.

'What about this summer?' she asks. 'Do you have a job lined up yet?'

I tell her about landscaping, as best I can. I tell her that, if the summer is dry and I can cut lawns quickly, I sometimes make a hundred and fifty, two hundred dollars a day. But I'm stuttering, talking too fast, feeling heat prickle my scalp. In the middle of that, Roger comes back with the cream, and Doreen finally brings in her coffee and cake. She places the tray on the table and hands out napkins. The date cake is cut into neat little squares, all stacked together to form a pyramid, and as she pours the coffee steam twists out of the spout like a genie.

'Ah,' Roger says, trying the cake. 'That sure is tasty.'

I lean forward to take a piece for myself. I eat it slowly, sitting with my elbows on my knees, concentrating on each bite. I'm not looking at the baby, now. Nobody is. We look anywhere but at the baby, and that breast. Roger's talking about next season, again, about how it could very well be his last year on the barge – no matter how much money the company offers him to come back. Then the phone rings, cutting him off.

I look over. 'You want me to get that?'

He waves it away. 'Probably Stanley calling again. Hankering for his money.'

Doreen sighs and makes a tut-tut sound with her tongue. When Beverly asks, the three of us explain about Stanley trying to nose in on Roger's job when he retires.

'If you want to retire anyway,' she says, 'then what's the difference?'

Roger just stares at his hands for a minute. 'It's the principle of it,' he says. 'What I'd like is somebody I can trust, who I can train up to take the old girl over when I'm gone.'

Doreen is nodding and smiling. Looking right at me. And I know I should tell them. I've got to bring myself to tell them. But I just can't, in front of their granddaughter, with all of us sitting here like this. And while I'm trying to figure it out, to figure it all out, my gaze wanders over to the window. I catch a glimpse of movement out there, on the water.

'Roger,' I say, not quite believing it. 'Look.'

Roger springs up from his chair, followed by me and Doreen and Beverly, still cradling little Josh in her arms. We all gather at the window. About twenty yards away, a mother Mallard is paddling along near shore, trailing half a dozen ducklings behind her. Through the glass I can hear their muted quacking.

'Well I'll be damned,' Roger says. 'Who would have thought?'

'Shhh,' Doreen says.

She reaches for his hand. Beverly shifts Josh to her other hip, and I feel her shoulder brush mine. Then there is a settling, a stillness. The four of us gaze out together, framed by the windowsill like a family in a portrait, as the ducks drift slowly past.

Fishhook

My lure hit the water with a satisfying plop.
I locked the reel and waited until the tip of my rod bent
from the weight. Then I pulled back on the rod, eased up,
and reeled in. You have to pull gently and not yank because
yanking makes the lure look all wrong, and the fish can sense
something fake in how it moves. To attract them the bacon fat
should sort of flap in the water, fluttering along like a moth
with busted wings, because that's what bullheads want. Dale
explained it to me one time. He said, 'Bullies like to bite stuff
that looks maimed and hurt. That's the trick.' I've never really
understood why, but it works. I guess it's instinct.

'Nice cast,' Dale said.

We were fishing where we always fish: on this old wharf
near Port Moody, way the hell out at the end of Burrard Inlet.
The water was still choppy, slopping at the pontoons, and the
pilings of the dock creaked and groaned like an old man's
bones. Evening was coming on and a few crows shrieked from
among the sycamores that lined the shore. The dock isn't too
far from the city, but it's far enough that you still feel like

you're getting back to nature when you're down there. No people, no cars, no bullshit. Just this primal sort of feeling. I figure that's part of what makes fishing such a thrill.

On my first cast I didn't catch anything, and neither did Dale. That was typical. The bullheads aren't usually interested right away. You got to get their attention first. I reared back and leaned into the next cast. The lure sailed out a long way before I heard the slap of lead and bacon on water.

'Beer up,' Dale said.

I took the can of Lucky he offered me and began reeling in.

I got the first bite. I don't know what it's like to catch a big fish, but with bullheads sometimes you can't tell they're on the line. You feel the resistance and your rod bends like a bow. Maybe you're hooked in weeds, or snagged on a rock – it's hard to say. Then, when you give it a tug, the rod starts trembling and nipping up and down like a needle on one of those lie detectors.

'Got one.'

I said it like it didn't matter but it did.

When you're reeling in, you got to keep the tension on the line or you'll lose the fish. I never use a barbed hook on account it hurts them – gets stuck in their mouths too easy, and tears when you pull it out. I use plain hooks, but without a barb you need that tension or the fish can slip off if he's cagey enough. Bullies aren't very cagey, but once in a while you get one with some savvy. Dale doesn't have to worry about that, because he uses barbed hooks.

'Ain't a goer,' I said. 'Fight's gone out of him.'

I could see a white shaft sliding up through the water to meet me. Sometimes the littler ones do that – they go all limp and passive so it isn't any fun. It's like playing with yourself or something. Fishing is supposed to be a two-sided sort of exercise.

The fish cleared the water and got lighter without the drag.

'Aww, man,' I said. 'Just a baby.'

'Still a catch.'

'It's barely bigger than the bacon.'

Dale snickered. 'Bit off more'n he can chew.'

We never keep the fish we catch, but even so I don't like hooking the babies. I think it's kind of unfair, seeing as how they're so young and all. I mean, where's the sport in that? Dale doesn't care one way or the other. He always says, 'Thrill's just the same to me.'

Dale's funny like that.

I scooped the fish up with my left hand. I hate that part most of all and wanted to get it done quick. The fish thrashed about and I had to tighten my grip so as not to lose him. I was working the hook out of the mouth when Dale's rod dipped sharp towards the water.

'Got one,' he said.

After that things picked up. Usually we nab about half a dozen bullheads each by the time night drops her skirt and they stop biting. But the fish were acting crazy that day and we hooked at least that many in the first hour.

'This is really weird,' I kept saying. 'Man, this is weird.'

And Dale would reply, 'These fish are going loco, man.'

I think loco is Spanish for crazy. I took it up on my tongue, because it's one of those words you like to roll around inside your mouth. 'Yeah,' I'd say, 'these fish are loco, man.'

But mostly we didn't have time to say anything except, 'Got

another.' After the first one it was always, 'Got another.' We kept saying that until we didn't even have to do much more than grunt and the other would understand.

At one point I started thinking about how many bullheads were in the water. I always figured that after you hooked one and let it go, it would shoot off and go hide someplace. But we'd caught at least twenty, maybe thirty bullies so far that night. It seemed like too many.

'You think these fish are all new ones?'

I could tell Dale hadn't considered it because he didn't answer straight away.

'Reckon so. Wouldn't make sense to come back for more, would it? Even bullies ain't that stupid.'

'Yeah. Reckon so.'

'Seems like an awful lot of fish, though.'

'That's what I thought.'

We were both poised with our weight on one foot, ready to cast. But we didn't.

Dale said, 'Maybe we could find out.'

I looked at him. Even before he told me, I'd cottoned on to what he had in mind. It made a kind of sense. We'd been stapling posters all day – my uncle had paid us to put them up on notice boards and telephone poles around town, advertising his landscaping company. The big industrial stapler he'd lent us was still in my car, back at the parking lot.

I was the one who went to get it.

I would hold the fish and Dale would staple them. We figured the best place to do it was between the spines of the dorsal fin. There's this thin skin between the spines, like the webbing on a frog's feet, and when we clipped a staple there the bullies didn't even seem to notice. Dale said it would be like the tags you see those scientists using to track whales or dolphins or whatever. This way, we'd be able to tell if we'd caught a fish before. It worked, too. We'd only tagged eight or nine fish before I caught one that already had a staple. I held my rod upright, so the fish dangled at eye level. He was as thick as a fist, and about ten or twelve inches long. That's pretty sizeable for a bully.

'I remember him,' Dale said. 'It's that big mother I caught first.'

'Looks like it.'

'What a dimwit.' Dale flicked its belly with his finger. 'You stupid dimwit.'

'Let's double him up,' I said.

Dale wrested the dimwit off the hook and turned him sideways so I could clip a second staple behind the first. Then Dale hucked him. He grabbed him by the tail and just threw him, high and far in the air. He splashed into the water on his back.

'Last can of Lucky says he comes back for more.'

'I don't know, man,' I said.

'Come on.'

I didn't care about the bet, or the beer. I would've given it to Dale if he'd asked. I just didn't like how Dale said it – as if it meant something. But I knew how he could get.

'Okay,' I said.

We plunked our lures back into the water. Then we both stood silent, thinking.

'Maybe they don't have such hot memories,' I said.

'Why would that matter?'

'My uncle told me goldfish only remember things for seven

seconds. That's why they never get bored swimming around in circles. Maybe bullies are the same.'

'Maybe.'

Dale didn't sound convinced.

'What, then?'

He didn't answer. His line jerked once and he had another. I stopped jigging and let my own rod go limp to watch him reel in. The fish came out, trembling and flicking its tail, and Dale waited for it to settle. This one was smaller, but its fin was already stapled, too.

'Got me another gobbler,' Dale said.

I tried to make some joke about these fish being *really* loco, but Dale wasn't having any of it. He didn't say much after that first big one came back, and even less after it came back a second time. There must have only been about twenty fish out there, all taking turns to chomp down on our lures. We stapled a dozen of them twice, and then a few others three or four times. Most of all we stapled the big one – the one Dale called Dimwit. With Dimwit we had to stop using the stapler after seven times, because there was no more room on his fin.

Dale always put the staple in. He wanted to. He said he liked it. I was the opposite, but I didn't say anything as I held the fish for him. I just cupped them cold and slick in my hands and wondered what they wanted, these fish that kept coming back for more.

'I know – these fish ain't so dumb, after all. They're pretty smart, right Dale? I mean, they know we throw them back, so they figure it's okay to keep on being caught since they get a bit of bacon for all the trouble. Man, these fish ain't loco. They're real savvy, right?'

Dale wasn't listening. He was crouched down, fiddling with his hook. The sun had slid behind the mountains, and the waves had settled, and the inlet had gone all dark and lonesome and still. Most of the fish had stopped biting. That wasn't why I'd given up casting awhile back, though. I'd caught so many bullies I'd had a bellyful by then. I was beginning to feel as if I was the one who'd eaten all that bait, not them.

'Gonna try it without any bacon,' Dale said.

It took me a second to figure out what he meant.

'That won't work,' I said. 'Even a bullhead isn't as stupid as that.'

Dale just shrugged. I started packing up our stuff. I put the lures in the tackle box, flipped shut the lid, and snapped the clasps in place. Then I squatted down on it and waited with my rod lying limp across my lap. Dale lifted his own rod high, stiff and straight, before whipping it forward. Line whizzed from the reel, and the hook traced a long, loping arc that disappeared into the murk. A second later the splunk of the weight on water came back to us.

'I want to go, Dale. They're not biting any more.'

'He'll bite.'

We waited. All the crows had gone quiet. A breeze rustled the sycamores and stirred the surface of the water. In the distance you could hear a siren whining, but that was the only sign of the city. We peered into the water and the dark. You couldn't tell which was which by then, since they seemed to blend together out there. Dale's lips were half-parted and he was breathing through his mouth. Every time he inhaled there was this sucking noise, eager and hungry, like somebody sipping hot soup. That happens sometimes, when Dale gets excited, on account of the asthma he had as a kid.

'No fish is gonna bite a bare hook,' I said. It didn't make any sense. I mean, you snag them sometimes – in a gill or under a fin – but that's different. 'Even if they got no memory, and can't remember, why in the hell would they bite a hook without any bait?'

'Maybe they do remember. Maybe it ain't the bait they like.'

I had a think about that. I was hugging myself, even though it wasn't really cold.

'Course it's the bait. It has to be the bait.'

Then Dale grunted, in the way we did when we'd got a bite, but this time it was different. It was closer to a groan – as if he'd tasted something sweet, or seen a pretty girl.

He began reeling in. The tip of his rod bent low towards the water, but there was no tugging or fight in the line. I figured it was just a snag. Something that big had to be a snag, or else it wouldn't have been so willing. Then the white shape rose up from the depths like a torpedo and breached the surface.

'It's him,' Dale said. 'It's Dimwit.'

Dale hoisted him up, and held the line steady as he stroked the belly-flesh with his forefinger. He cooed at it like a lover. The fish blinked and puckered its mouth repeatedly, sucking at the air. Between its soft, rubbery lips, I could see the gleaming barb of the hook.

Carving Through Woods on a Snowy Evening

'**Imagine that. You're up the mountain, having a blast,** and then – bam.'

'I know. It doesn't seem real.'

The exchange was greeted by nods and murmurs of solemn agreement. Half a dozen of them sat around the basement, nursing cocktails, nibbling on rum balls, and gnawing over the same subject matter. Some of them were Mark's friends; others he'd only met in passing.

'I don't even like to think about it,' the girl to his left said. She'd told him her name but he'd forgotten it. Crossing her legs, she took several seconds to adjust her dress, which was sleek and black and hugged her knees, and they all watched her doing this. 'I mean, it's the kind of freak accident we always assume could never happen to somebody we know.'

She glanced at Mark for confirmation, and he took a sip of his rum.

'Tell me the whole story,' Rob said. He'd had a few highballs, and since it was his party he was talking with a certain authority. He leaned forward and rested one hand on his knee, looking around the circle. 'Does anybody know exactly what happened to this guy?'

Everybody did, apparently. Or they claimed to.

'It was some kid called Damian, from Windsor.'

'Half the mountain just fell away.'

'Harsh.'

'I heard he was sponsored, or semi-pro, or something.'

'Did you know him, Mark?' Rob asked.

'I'd met him a couple of times, up the mountain.'

There was a respectful silence. They were all looking at him, now, as if expecting him to elaborate, so Mark said, 'He rode for Endeavour, I think. He was good. A decent guy.' He stopped, made a circular gesture with his glass, slinging the ice around the base. 'But what you gonna do, right? When your number's up, it's up.'

The girl in the dress made an affirmative sound. Somebody mentioned their friend from school, who'd died in a car crash up Indian River Road, and they started talking about that. Mark didn't listen; he was thinking about what he had just said, and how stupid it had sounded: when your number's up, it's up. He tossed back the rest of his drink and excused himself, saying that he was going to get a top-up. Nobody paid him much attention; his exit didn't even disrupt the flow of conversation. He could still hear them as he headed upstairs.

'Did your grade ever see that drinking and driving slideshow?'

'Yeah – the one with all the photos of crash sites and bodies.'

'That was sick!'

'This one guy was even decapitated.'

The voices faded as he entered the kitchen.

*

The fridge was loaded with cases of beer and twixers of hardbar. He stood in front of it and held the door open, letting the chilly air wash over him, feeling numb. He wasn't supposed to be drinking when he was on call, but he needed another; he dumped some rum in his glass, added a splash of orange juice, and wandered around the main floor, looking for different people, different conversations. In the hall two guys were leaning against the wall, shrouded in a cloud of haze, smoking a bowl. One of them he didn't know. The other was Brian, who worked as a liftee and dealt a bit of weed and had been a half-decent skier at one time.

They were talking about it, too.

'You heard about Damian, eh?' Brian asked him.

Mark nodded. 'Shitty luck.'

The other guy said, 'Fuck luck. He shouldn't have been riding up there.'

'Mark's ridden up there.'

Mark said, 'A lot of people ride that valley.'

Brian held the pipe out to him. 'Hit this, man. We're burning one for Dee.'

Mark took a few token hoots, not really inhaling, faking it a little. When he handed it back, Brian sucked on it anxiously. He thumped his chest with a fist, fighting a coughing fit.

'He was a fucking bro, man. You know?'

Mark agreed and listened to them talk about it awhile longer – saying the same kinds of things that were being said downstairs, but in a different way. When he got the chance, he asked them if they knew where he could find some grub, and Brian told him to try the living room. He went that way, assuring them he'd come back later to burn another one.

The living room was empty. Christmas lights lined the

window, flashing on and off like a department store display, and in the far corner a plastic tree stood planted on a metal stand. Atop the tree was an angel with a gold halo and rice-paper wings. She was tilted too far forward, and seemed to be leering down at him, looking slightly drunk or deranged. Next to the tree, laid out on the sideboard, were various snacks: bags of cheese puffs and pretzels, a plate of Nanaimo bars, a carton of eggnog. Somebody had also assembled a nativity scene made up of chocolate figurines. The manger was in disarray: baby Jesus overturned, Mary lying on her side, animals all over the place. Mark picked up one of the three wise men and bit off his head. The chocolate tasted dry and bland as plaster. He put the figure back and stood gazing out the bay window that overlooked Rob's yard. A few inches of crusted snow covered the ground. The sun was still up, but its light was watery and yellow, fading. The evening sky remained clear, just as the forecast had predicted. He pressed his palm to the glass, feeling the cold through it. The conditions would be perfect up the mountain tonight.

He heard footsteps and looked back. The girl in the black dress came into the room; when she saw him she changed directions, veering towards him. She was tall and wearing heels and walking slightly off-kilter, like a horse that had been tranquilized but was still stumbling around. She came and stood too close to him, so that he had to look up at her.

'Rob wondered where you'd gone,' she said.

'Just needed a drink.'

'I don't blame you.' Something about her expression – the leering smile, the look of drunken concern – reminded him of the tree-top angel. 'It must be even harder for you, since you knew him.'

'Only in passing.'

'But you're a snowboarder, too, right?'

'I've been in a few competitions.'

'That's what I mean. It's that much more real for you.' She lowered her voice, as if confiding something. 'You know what's weird? My friend was supposed to go up with him that day but he got sick. Isn't that creepy? It reminds me of *La Bamba* – when they do that coin toss to see who'll ride in the plane, and then it crashes. Have you seen that movie?'

He said that he had. He liked it, too.

She said, 'Lou Diamond Phillips was the best.'

'The Eighties was the best.'

'*Young Guns*, anyone?'

She kept talking about that, as they drank. The rum was warming him, but he found it hard to hear what she was actually saying. That happened to him, sometimes. It was as if the words didn't register. They were just consonant and vowel sounds. Like listening to another language. He was looking at her, and nodding, but what he was seeing was the view through the window behind her: the snow smothering the lawn, the hedges, the boulevard opposite.

'You sure you're okay?' she asked.

'Just tired.'

'Yeah, me too.' She sighed and took a swig of her cocktail. 'This kind of thing just takes it out of you. It seems wrong, somehow, to be having a party after somebody's died.'

Down the hall, one of the stoners laughed and said, 'Totally, man. Totally.'

In the back pocket of his jeans, Mark's pager started vibrating. He slipped it out and checked the display: it showed 888, the code for a search. Apparently they'd gotten some action. The girl leaned forward, peering incredulously at the device in his hand.

'Is that a pager?' she said. 'Oh my God. I haven't seen a pager in years.'

He told her that it was, and that he had to make a phone call. He ducked into the front hall and used his cell to call in. It rang a few times, and clicked.

'Mark? Hello? Are you hearing this?'

The line was faint and crackling – at the edge of reception – but he could tell it was Minette, their team leader: she spoke in slightly broken English, with a Québécois accent.

'What's up, Min?'

'Where are you, superstar?'

'Christmas party.'

'You are not drinking?'

He looked at the glass in his hand. It was half-full. 'No,' he said.

'Good. I am so sorry, Mark. But we've got one up on Seymour. This snowboarder – he has gone missing. We think he was riding out of bounds. He was meant to be back for Christmas dinner, and his family, they are totally freaking out.'

'What's the plan?'

'We'll get a big ground crew together for a night operation. But I want to sweep the slopes with the helicopter, first – and drop a few people in the back country. You up for it?'

'For sure.'

'Wicked. Jamie's coming too. But we do not have long until civil. You must hurry.'

They weren't allowed to fly past civil twilight, which occurred about half an hour after the sun went down. Beyond that, all rescues were supposed to be ground based. He checked his watch: it was coming up on five. He said, 'I can be there in fifteen minutes.'

'You are that close?'

'I'm right in the Cove.'

'Perfect. We will pick you up in the upper parking lot.'

After ending the call, he ducked into the front bedroom to get his jacket. He didn't go back downstairs to say goodbye to Rob, or anybody else. He didn't have time, and doubted they'd notice his absence anyway. On his way out, he glanced down the hall. The girl in the black dress had joined Brian and his friend. In the haze of smoke they looked like a mirage.

'You knew him, too?' she was saying to Brian.

'We used to ride together. We were pretty tight.'

'Oh my God. What was he like?'

'He was golden. A cool fucking guy.'

'His poor parents.'

They hadn't noticed him. Mark slipped out and eased the door shut behind him.

He had all his gear in his Jeep, so he was able to go straight to Seymour from the party. It only took a few minutes to reach the base of the mountain. The woman working the gate recognised him, and waved him through without any questions. Only rescue crew would be allowed up. The resort shut at four on Christmas Eve. Whoever they were looking for would have been riding during the day, and must have stayed on after the lifts closed down.

The radio in his Jeep was broken and he drove in silence, with his board wedged sideways between the front seats. Pine and Fir trees formed walls on either side of the road. The asphalt had been ploughed that afternoon, and salt kicked up by his tires rattled and spat off the undercarriage. On the shoulder jagged snow banks – stained brown by dirt and grit – rose and fell like miniature mountain ranges. He opened his window to let in a blast of alpine air, which tasted crisp and sharp and painfully cold. He suspected that it was going to snow, regardless of what the forecasts had indicated, and if it did they'd lose any chance of finding tracks. There was also the fading light, and the fact that they didn't know where to look. Each of those things would make their job more difficult, but of course that was part of it. Already he felt the prickle of anticipation on his forearms, his neck – like static electricity. It was the same feeling he got while waiting in the starting gates, before a boardercross race.

As he considered that he thought he glimpsed something moving out the window to his right, but it was only the reflection of his snowboard. He was sponsored by Osiris and the design on the tail of the board depicted an Egyptian figure: a man standing in profile, holding a flail and a crook, with feathers arching on either side of him. In the window-glass, the man's image seemed to be floating past the tree trunks and branches, keeping pace with the Jeep.

Mark stepped on the clutch and downshifted.

The parking lot – normally so crowded by day – was empty except for a small cluster of cars, all coated with frost. At the far end crouched the Talon rescue helicopter, its rotor blurred like the blades of a fan. Mark pulled up about twenty yards away. When he opened the door he felt the wind whipped up by the blades, and shivered at the surge of cold. While he sorted his gear Minette hurried over from the helicopter to meet him. She had a stocky build and long arms and walked with a gangling gait, like an orangutan. She gripped his bicep in greeting and thanked him again for coming. As he pulled on his gear – helmet, gloves, jacket and goggles – she explained a little about what was going on. The majority of the crew was assembling at the search and rescue hut in preparation for the larger ground operation. But before they lost the light, and the helicopter, she wanted to drop him and Jamie off higher up the mountain, in the hope that they could find some sign of where the missing rider might have gone.

'It'll mean rappelling,' she said, raising her voice to be heard.

'Safer than the long-line, in the dark.'

They approached the chopper together and Minette climbed up front with the pilot. Mark slid his board in first, through the open side door, and clambered over the landing skid into the back. The helicopter was already rigged for the rappel, and Jamie was already there, slouching in one of the seats that faced the tail. He was a muscular guy, part Hispanic, with a day's growth of stubble on his chin. He looked at Mark and yawned languidly, like a bear that had been prodded out of hibernation.

'What's up?' Mark shouted.

He extended a hand and Jamie slapped at it in greeting.

'I was balling my girl when these jerk-offs called me.'

'The old withdrawal method, huh?'

Mark shut the side door, sat down across from Jamie, and strapped in. Eddie was flying for them tonight. Minette gave him the signal, and the helicopter tilted forward before lifting off into darkness. Mark stuffed his First Aid pack beneath his seat and leaned back, resting his board upside down across his knees. The base showed a gray wing stretched from tip to tail, a larger version of the pair in the design on the other side. Mark didn't know what type of bird it was supposed to belong to. A heron, maybe. He studied it as he considered what lay ahead. Minette had told him about the operation, but not much about this rider.

He leaned forward and tapped Minette on the shoulder and asked her who it was they were looking for. She half-turned in her seat, and they conversed like that, yelling into each other's faces. She said that the kid's name was Patrick. He was seventeen, and he'd come up that day to ride the park with his friends. When they left, he didn't. But he was experienced: a local who'd been riding for years.

'So he knows the mountain,' Mark said.

Next to him, Jamie yelled, 'Him and every other joker who gets lost on it.'

'Gives us something to do,' Mark said.

'I got better things to do on Christmas Eve.'

'I'd rather be up here.'

'Maybe you two can get lost together, like soul mates.'

Mark flipped him the finger without looking at him. He was still thinking about the kid, trying to get a feel for the situation. He asked Minette, 'Do you have anybody in Suicide?'

Suicide Gulley was where they found most of the skiers, boarders, and hikers who got lost in the backcountry. It acted as a funnel: it started out wide and made for good riding, but got steep and narrow quickly, and after a certain point was nearly impossible to climb out of.

Minette nodded vigorously, signalling that she had, and shouted, 'Christy and Les – they have been searching there since four, but no luck so far. Others are checking the main runs. We just have time to drop you off and do a couple of final sweeps before it gets dark.'

'It's dark now,' Jamie yelled.

There was still a grey smear of light on the horizon to the west, but that wouldn't last.

Minette said, 'We have a few more minutes.'

'What does Talon think of that?'

Talon was the company they rented the chopper from, and the pilot. Minette said something to him they couldn't hear. Eddie was ex-military, and accustomed to Minette's style. He looked back at them and mimed drawing a line across his lips.

'You see?' Minette yelled. 'Eddie is cool with it. I want to find some sign of this kid – to know where to look. Then we can go in by ground. Otherwise, it's just the needle in the haystack. We won't find him tonight. And by morning...' She waved a hand dismissively.

'You'll take shit for this,' Jamie said.

'*Pas de probléme.*' She grinned. One of her upper front teeth was missing, from where she'd cracked it jibbing a rail. 'I think we will put you two down above Brockton, where the kids hike in to build kickers.'

'Split us up,' Mark said. 'We can cover more ground.'

'It is against regs, and risky.'

'We're big boys. Jamie can handle Brockton. I'll check the cliffs east of First Peak.'

She asked Jamie if that was okay with him.

'*Pas de probléme*, right?' he said.

The helicopter banked east. Mark leaned over to look out the window, gazing down at the white mounds passing beneath them. The ridges looked like waves in a frozen sea. A fat gibbous moon was rising in the east; beneath it the snow seemed to glow, luminous, and the shadow of the helicopter was clearly visible as it flitted across the ground. At the top of Mystery they passed over the ski lift, its chairs hanging still, the cables coated with crystals of frost. During the day the mountain was filled with skiers and boarders, colour and motion. Now it felt more like an abandoned playground, a twilight realm. There was no movement and no signs of life. Further west, towards Grouse and Cyprus mountains, a haze of clouds had formed.

'We're coming up to Brockton,' Minette shouted back.

Jamie held up a fist, and Mark punched it in farewell.

'Watch it out there,' Mark told him. 'Snow's coming.'

'Not according to the weatherman.'

'According to me.'

Jamie grinned, then twisted around to converse with Eddie. The chopper dipped and slowed to a standstill, about thirty-five feet above the snow. Jamie clipped himself onto the rappel line – which was hooked to a donut ring bolted to the fuselage – before unstrapping from his seat and getting into a crouch. He fastened the chinstrap on his helmet and lashed his telemark skis to the back of his First Aid pack, then shrugged it on and buckled it across his chest. Opening the door, he took a look at the terrain below, and casually tossed out his deployment bag; it plummeted towards the ground, the rappel line ribboning out after it. He checked his safety belt and the anchor point, tugging on it with the full weight of his body to ensure it was solid. It was. He got in position on the landing skids: facing inwards, braced against the fuselage, brake hand reaching behind him to grip the rope. He did all this with the precise confidence that comes with experience. At the last, he looked up at them, his face focused and serious, waiting for Minette to give him the signal. When she did, he leaned back against the landing skids, angling away from the helicopter until his body was nearly horizontal. Then he shoulder-checked, pushed off, and dropped down out of sight.

Mark stood up, still strapped in by a safety line, and leaned out to watch the descent. When Jamie reached the ground, he unclipped from the rappel line and waved them off.

'He's good,' Mark shouted, and gave Minette the thumbs up.

Mark gathered in the rope as they floated away. Up front, he could see Minette talking to Eddie, but none of the words reached him over the furious drone of the rotor. While they cruised higher up the mountain, well into the backcountry, Mark gazed ahead to First Peak. He wasn't sure about searching beyond it. He considered what he would have done, had he been alone up here on a night like this.

'Min,' he yelled, leaning forward. 'Forget First. If this kid knows the terrain he wouldn't be stupid enough to fall off the cliffs. Take me past Second Peak and drop me on the far side, towards the glades.'

Minette considered. 'Why?'

'There's good riding there. I can cover that ground then join Jamie if it duds out.'

'Fine.'

Minette relayed his message to Eddie, who banked westward. Mark unzipped his pack and did a quick equipment check – radio, GPS, First Aid kit, avalanche beacon – and then zipped it up again and strapped it on. He was fastening the buckles when Minette called back to him, and signalled that they were closing in on Second Peak. Mark leaned forward between the seats, surveying the terrain through the convex windshield. Second was a white dome of snow surrounded by glades, gulleys, and forests. Above it lay the summit, and below it First Peak and the rest of the mountain dropped away towards the city. From that distance you could see the shimmering spires of downtown and the strands of streetlights, strung out in grid-like patterns. But it all looked faint and far off and part of another world, separated from the North Shore by Burrard Inlet, which was now just a vast stretch of black.

'Put me down on that slope,' he shouted, pointing.

Eddie nodded and angled that way. Mark removed his snowboard from the equipment rack. Minette wasn't watching him, so he laid the board flat on the floor of the helicopter and squatted down to strap in: fastening the right binding first, then the left. He flexed his feet. There was still a bit of give, so he cranked the ratchets on both bindings to tighten them. Last he tugged on his gloves and cinched the drawstrings around his wrists, taking real pleasure in these small details, and the ritual of preparation. As Eddie swung the helicopter around and slowed to a hover, Mark shifted into a sitting position with his legs hanging out the door, the board resting on the landing skids. He unclipped from the safety line and held onto it, one-handed. Twenty feet below his board lay a smooth slope, glowing white in the twilight.

That was when Minette turned to look back at him.

'What are you doing?' she shouted. 'Use the rappel line, idiot!'

Mark pretended not to hear and heaved forward with both hands, springing clear of the door. He fell through darkness and roaring wind and landed in an explosion of powder; his knees buckled and snow splashed up into his face and his momentum carried him forward and down, half-submerged in snow that was thick and tangible as water. To keep himself afloat he leaned back hard, riding the tail of his board, and the slope swept beneath him as he swerved back and forth, fighting for control, executing quick turns that sheared swathes off the face and created a small slide, a tumbling crystal-cloud that cascaded down around him.

When the terrain leveled out he eased onto his heels

and stopped to get his bearings. He experimented with his headlamp, but the bright beam only lit up the ground in front of him, leaving everything else shrouded in darkness. He switched it off and let his eyes adjust to the moonlight instead. He was on the west side of Second Peak, which overlooked an open glade lined by dense bunches of pine. At its base, the glade folded into a gully – the sides steep and smooth as an average half-pipe, but four times as wide. Snowboarders loved it, despite the avalanche danger. Any snow sliding off the peak got channelled straight down the gully. That night, though, there was no real risk of a slide. There were no tracks, either.

He dropped into the gully, sweeping back and forth across its base, hunting for any sign of the missing rider. He was not being methodical about it but instead simply trusting his intuition and following the route that seemed to present itself, in the hopes something would come of it. He thought it was the best chance that they had, and maybe the only chance, under the circumstances. If it started snowing, even that would be lost.

For the moment, visibility was still good. The moonlight made the snow sparkle, as if the slope was covered in shards of glass. Over the past three days fifty centimetres of fresh snow had fallen, and beneath his board the powder felt soft and dry as icing sugar. He lost himself in the gentle, metronome rhythm of the turns, cruising like a low-flying bird across the frozen landscape. Further down, the gulley forked into two natural runs: a steep, straight slope that ran past First Peak towards Brockton, from where you could get back to the ski resort if you knew the way, and a more challenging trail that zigzagged through the woods and had been an old logging road at one time. Mark turned that way without hesitation, dropped over a series of rollers, and aired off a nice hip near the left-hand side, landing so deftly that it felt as if his board was barely brushing the surface of the snow.

Just below, off to the right, he noticed what could have been markings or tracks of some kind. He pulled up sharply, sinking into the knee-deep powder as soon as he lost his momentum. He stepped out of his bindings and trudged across the hill to examine the spot. A set of footprints, climbing up, receded down along the logging road. About a mile below, the road connected with one of the resort's snowshoe trails, which in turn led back to the parking lot. That was where whoever it was must have come up from.

Mark reached for his radio and hailed Minette. She answered immediately, as if she'd been waiting for a chance to chastise him.

'Mark – you gave me some kind of heart attack with that stunt.'

'It was just like heli-skiing.'

'Bullshit. It is unnecessary. It is dangerous.'

'Listen – I've got something. Looks like a hiker below Second.'

There was a pause as she digested this, and maybe debated whether to drop the issue of the helicopter jump.

'Going where?' she asked.

'I don't know yet. I'll follow.'

'You should not be riding. You know this.'

'I can cover more ground this way.'

'I do not want to be rescuing you, too.'

'I'll take it easy.'

'Keep us posted.'

He said that he would, and signed off. Cradling his board under one arm, he followed the tracks, which ran upslope for a few hundred yards before veering to the west. At the edge of the logging trail, where the tree-line thickened, it looked like the kid – if that's who it was – had strapped in. Mark knelt down in the same spot. He was breathing hard, and sweating, and had that distinct, copper-taste of cold in his throat. Slogging around in all that powder was about as easy as wading through knee-deep water.

'Where are you going, buddy?'

His voice sounded odd in the quiet, and he felt foolish for talking aloud.

From there, it looked like the kid had ridden further west, into the trees. It didn't make much sense because in that direction the woods became too dense for riding. Within ten or twenty yards the kid would have been forced to turn back towards the trail.

Once his breathing steadied, Mark brushed the snow from his bindings and strapped in. He twisted around and angled his board downhill and slipped into the other track. It was a familiar game and one Mark played well. Following the kid's line, he wove in and out of ice-encrusted pines, heading west, always west. Branches slapped across his thighs and torso, showering him in snow. He pulled his goggles down to protect his eyes. He'd never ridden this route before, and as he went deeper into the woods the trees thickened and the riding became more of a challenge.

The treetops created a canopy, blotting out the moonlight. The turns grew tighter, with less time between them. Huge rooster tails showed in the powder where the kid had made cutbacks to avoid obstacles: stumps and rocks and fallen logs. He was thinking that this kid had to be good, to be able to carve like that, and then he didn't have time to think anymore because the darkness made it dangerous and he had to almost feel his way through the trees, focusing on his own turns and not losing the line. He bent low and his mind emptied and he dissolved into an awareness of his body in which everything became attuned to right, left, right – that rapid weaving rhythm as he slipped through the dark with tree trunks flashing past and branches whipping at his body and snow whispering beneath his board.

Then the trees broke and the ground dropped away and he was floating, airborne. He instinctively grabbed the front side of his board with his left hand, like he would have during a jump, and extended his right arm to keep balanced in midair. White ground rushed up from below. On impact his knees buckled and he fell backwards against the slope, sinking into a pillow of snow, but managed to spring upright without losing his momentum and without losing control. He was covered in powder and as he surged forward downhill he pumped his fist and yelped like a coyote into the night because it felt as if he'd pulled off the impossible – landing that cliff blind and in the dark – something nobody else could have done, except maybe the kid he was following.

He'd come out in a wide and empty bowl that went on and on and on. The only marking in the snow was a single track of sweeping arcs nearly perfect in their symmetry. He knew then that this was why the kid had come here, and why he'd come here tonight, and why he'd come here alone. And it was only through following him that Mark had found a part of the mountain that he'd never known about. He felt as if he'd come across hallowed ground, and he leaned into each turn with special reverence, stretching his body out parallel to the slope, trailing one glove through the soft powder. With the wind pulling at him, and the cold burning his cheeks, he mirrored the turns across the bowl, so that where the kid had cut left he cut right, and vice versa, weaving figure eights into the pristine snow. As he did this Mark glimpsed something flickering at the edge of his vision, but when he glanced over he saw that it was nothing – just his own moon-shadow skirting the snow, keeping pace.

Further on the bowl became a glade dotted with pines, ten or fifteen yards apart. The snow-heavy trees were bowed towards the ground, and the white, gnarled shapes looked like shepherd's crooks, planted on the slope to mark the way. Each curve of the figure-eight turns now encircled one of the trees. Mark carved around a trunk, the branches brushing against his shoulder like a slalom gate, and cut back across the kid's line and flew past another, and back again around another, and another, and another.

And then he stopped.

He hadn't crossed any track on the cutback. He reached down to undo his bindings. They were encrusted with snow from the ride, and he had to brush them off before he could pop the clasps. He suspected what had happened but couldn't be sure. There was the chance that the kid had hurt or injured himself – clipping a tree branch, maybe – and had managed to hold on. But it was a small chance, and by the time Mark had stepped out of his bindings, a coldness had settled in his stomach, leeching the exhileration out of him. Grabbing his board, he dragged it behind him as he trudged upslope, and that was how he found the body.

He could see the heel-side edge of a snowboard jutting out of the snow, and the kid's feet, still strapped into it. The rest of him was buried. He must have been doing a frontside turn when the loose snow at the base of the tree had given way. He would have sunk into it like quicksand. His head looked to be five or six feet below the surface. More snow had probably fallen from the tree as he struggled.

Mark radioed Minette.

'Mark here.'

'Minette, over. Any luck?'

'I found him. He's dead. Tree-well. Just shitty luck.'

Silence.

'I'm south-west of Second Peak, east of Suicide Gully. Below that old logging road.'

'We've put the Talon to bed, and the ground crew – it will take time to get up there.'

'I'll wait with him.'

'You don't have to.'

'I don't mind.'

She asked him for his GPS coordinates, which he gave her before signing off.

Mark wedged his board upright in the snow, shrugged off his pack, and assembled his three-piece shovel. He began to dig. The snow was loose and treacherous and he sank in up to his waist several times, and each time had to crawl and wriggle out. He cleared as much snow as he could with the shovel, and when it became awkward working around the body he dug with his hands. He worked too hard and too fast, and by the end he was gasping at the thin air, the clouds of his breath surrounding him like smoke. Manoeuvring the body was made more difficult by the kid's board, and so Mark unstrapped it and brushed it off. When he saw the design on the base he had a feeling not of startlement or surprise but of recognition: it showed a single gray wing against a black background. He wedged the board upright in the snow next to his own. By chance he'd arranged the boards tip to tail, so that the two wings mirrored each other, forming a haphazard set.

Then he hauled the kid up. There was a marble-hardness

to his flesh, and his limbs would no longer bend or move. Chunks of snow filled his mouth. Mark scooped it out with a finger, mostly because he didn't like looking at that, and laid the kid down below his board before removing his goggles. His eyes were open and cloudy, opaque. Icicles clung to his hair, giving it a spiky, cartoon-like appearance. The cold had kept rigor mortis at bay, and his face had not set in the rigid expression that Mark had seen on other corpses; it was instead still peaceful. He had probably been lying there for a couple of hours, cooling and freezing and going solid. All the heat and life had drained out of him and was possibly still around him, spreading slowly through the snow and dissipating.

Something cold touched Mark's cheek. He looked up. Across the sky a cloud front was spreading like an incoming tide, on the verge of washing out the moon. Fat white flakes spiralled down in the darkness. In some places islands of stars remained visible. Letting his knees bend, he sank back into the snow beside the kid. He lay like that and stared at the wide black sky and the softly falling snow, which seemed to emerge from a fixed point overhead and spiral out as it got closer to him. The hypnotic motion made it feel as if he were floating upwards through a vortex, rather than watching as the flakes drifted down to him. Those that landed on his face melted into beads of water, and every so often one caught in his eyelashes, making him blink.

As he waited, the sweat cooling beneath his jacket, he tried not to think about what would come next, and the aftermath: the newspaper headlines and the official inquiries and the six o'clock sound bites. They would present it as a minor tragedy, all the more poignant for its timing. He tried not to think about what people would say over dinner, and at parties: that it was such a shame, such a waste, a young man who'd had so much potential. They would shake their heads and click their tongues and point their fingers and find somebody to blame, and if there was nobody else to blame they would blame the kid himself; they would castigate him for riding out of bounds, for being irresponsible, for taking unnecessary risks.

To block all that out, at least for a while, Mark thought about the ride on which he had been led. He went over each turn and cutback, each crescent curve, replaying the nuances in his mind as he had been trained to do before a race. He closed his eyes and visualised it – the trees, the cliff, the last graceful turns – and then he imagined how it must have felt, to slip so freely and easily into the snow and have it close around you like a blanket or a shroud. The brief flare of panic, the struggle, and then a settling, a stillness, when you relaxed and let go and allowed yourself to dissolve into the cold. And as he lay there imagining these things, still the snow came swirling down, and as he lay there he imagined, too, what might come next, what might come after: the darkness and the nothingness and the endless peace.

'Mark.' The crackling voice sounded very far away. 'Mark!'

His hand must have already been on the radio; otherwise he wouldn't have known where to find it. He raised it to his mouth.

'Here,' he said, but it came out oddly. His lips felt fat and awkward.

'Why have you not answered?' It was Minette. 'We're at your location, but there are no tracks and we can't see anything in this snow!'

He worked his mouth, testing his jaw, then said, 'I'm right here.'

'Are you okay?'

'I'm okay.' He paused for breath. 'I'm right here.'

'Right *where*? We don't see you. Can you use a flare?'

'Okay,' he said. Mark tried to open his eyes. It was harder than he expected, and that was when he fully understood what he had done. 'Okay,' he said again, as if repeating the word could make it true. 'Okay, I think I can do that.'

'What is with you?'

He shut off the radio. He didn't need it. Eventually he got his eyes open and sat up. His jacket was slathered in snow. A cyclone of white whirled around him. He had to blink repeatedly to clear his vision, which was foggy and blurry, as if he'd awaked from days of slumber. He squinted into the dark, trying to get his bearings. Falling snow had completely covered the kid's body; it was now a long white mound, at the head of which the board stuck up like a tombstone. He heard voices nearby, shouting and calling. About fifty yards away, he thought he could see faint shapes moving about in the white-out, insubstantial as ghosts.

He reached into his bag for a flare.

Tokes From The Wild

The bus ride to Kurt's hometown costs fifty bucks and lasts about eight hours. For the first ninety minutes or so, we're giddy as kids heading off to day camp: we drink cans of no-name cola and play poker with loose change and talk about how awesome it's going to be once we get there. But eventually Kurt runs out of coins and we run out of things to say, and we both end up staring out the windows. Even the landscape is boring – an endless panorama of flat, burnt-out fields and barren hillsides. And we've still got six hours of driving ahead of us.

I pull out the hunting knife my parents got me, showing off for Kurt.

'Sweet, man,' he says. 'What are you gonna do with that?'

'Stab some bears.'

Kurt grins. He has shoulder-length hair and a full beard, a rarity in our grade. Except for his tie-dyed shirts and tattered cords, he looks a bit like Jesus. We're not exactly best friends – he's lived in Prince George most of his life and only came down to Vancouver to finish high school. I was a little surprised when he invited me to go tree planting and stay with his family. I think he was a little surprised when I accepted.

Halfway there the bus stops at a greasy spoon diner for a food break. We pour out onto the hot pavement, a mixed group of people too old or too young or too poor to drive themselves. While the others file inside, Kurt asks me if I want to smoke some weed. I've always been a bit of a chicken about pot but I tell him I'll go with him. We sneak behind the diner; he magically produces his pipe and sparks it. The smoke hangs sweetly in the heat.

'This is going to be great,' Kurt assures me, casually exhaling. 'I've never done it before, either – but my dad says tree planting rules. We'll make wicked money.'

'Sure,' I say.

I'm still too chicken to smoke any.

At the bus depot we're picked up by Kurt's mom, Miranda: a middle-aged, frizzy-haired woman driving a station wagon. She gives me a tour of Prince George on the way to their house, which is a few miles out of town. Kurt keeps rolling his eyes, obviously embarrassed, but I like her. She seems cheerful, weary, and completely unassuming.

She tells me, 'The town might not look like much, but it's home.'

Everything is flat in Prince George – a collection of strip malls and bungalows and squat apartment buildings. On the edge of town we pass through an area of run-down stucco houses with untended yards. I catch glimpses of illegible graffiti, broken windows, a snarl of old wire fencing. Miranda shakes her head, clucking sadly.

'This is the Indian Reserve,' she tells me.

'Oh,' I say, as if that explains everything.

At the next corner two children are playing hopscotch, grinning madly, their sun-browned skin gleaming in the sun.

Over pasta and meat sauce that night I meet the rest of Kurt's family. His dad, Fred, is a big, balding bushman who burps and farts at the table. Fred is a broker for the forestry companies. He's the one who sold our boss, Clayton, the tree-planting contracts that Kurt and I will be working on. Then there's Neil, the brother, who looks like a younger version of Kurt. He dresses the same, but can't quite grow a full beard.

Kurt also has a kid sister, called Sorrel. She's about five or six years old, and seems out of place among the rest of the clan: she's the only one with blonde hair and doesn't take after her mother or father. When introduced she smiles secretively and says nothing, but throughout the meal I catch her sneaking discreet glances at me, sizing me up.

'This sure is tasty,' I say.

Everybody nods politely.

After dinner Neil takes me outside to show me his dirt bike: a two-stroke, 150cc Yamaha that he bought second-hand and fixed up himself. He hops on, twisting the throttle until my ears ache and a cloud of smoke surrounds us like noxious gas.

'Ain't it great?' he shouts.

I give him the thumbs up. He peels out of the drive, not quite in control, and tears off down the road. I stand and listen to the whine of the engine in the distance, wondering if he expects me to wait until he gets back.

*

Their house is a renovated cabin with no room for new bodies. Kurt and I will be sleeping in a canvas tent pitched on the front lawn, with square sides and a peaked roof. Inside, there's a pot-bellied stove, a dirty rug, an old sofa, and two cots. I feel like I'm on safari. Kurt's parents are charging me ten bucks a day and fifteen for the weekends. I'm not used to paying to stay at a friend's house, but Kurt's not quite my friend and the fee includes food, so I guess that makes it fair.

I pick my cot, arrange my things, and get out my dad's old Walkman. He gave it to me as a going-away present, along with his collection of battered tapes, instead of the MP3 player I asked for. I crank up the volume, sprawling out on the sofa, wishing I had something to read. The springs creak and groan as I shift around, trying to get comfortable. I'm on the second side of *Harvest* when Kurt comes in and asks me if I want to smoke some pot.

'I don't really feel like it,' I tell him, without knowing why.

I listen to him sucking on his pipe outside the tent.

'Jesus Christ,' Kurt moans, stamping his feet.

We're standing at the roadside in front of Kurt's house, shivering, dressed in army pants, heavy plaid shirts, gardening gloves and hiking boots. It doesn't feel like summer; the morning murk is cold, the sky a slagheap of cloud. Drowsy from lack of sleep, we wait in miserable silence for the sun to rise or for Clayton to arrive – whichever comes first.

Headlights appear at the end of the road. A Ford pick-up with missing hubcaps and a rusty undercarriage rattles to a stop in front of us. We toss our gear in the back and hop in the cab to meet our boss. Clayton's wearing an Oilers hat and has a can of Molson in his hand. When he grins it looks like a sneer because of an obvious harelip. As soon as we're settled he puts the truck in gear and starts giving us the third degree: calling us rookies and city slickers and bed-wetters.

'I've lived up here most of my life,' Kurt protests.

'The city's made you soft. What a couple of bitch-tits.'

He only lets up to swill from his morning beer. When the beer's finished, he starts fishing around in the glove box. He pulls out a glass pipe and a sack of weed and packs the pipe while he drives, alternating between glancing down at his lap and up at the road.

'Hope you rookies are ready to work. Us three are the only crew today.'

He sparks, inhales, and thrusts the smoldering bowl at me.

Kurt says, 'He doesn't smoke.'

'What the fuck?'

'Sure I do.' I take the pipe before Kurt can argue. 'Once in awhile.'

As I puff on the mouthpiece, I can see Kurt staring at me in the rear-view. I want to tell him that I'm not inhaling, but I guess it wouldn't make much difference. For him, I didn't even bother to pretend.

Tree planting is simple.

At the worksite, you're given a shovel and a belt with two sacks that dangle from your hips like giant gun holsters. You load the sacks with yearlings – baby trees – and head out to your allotted portion of forest. You stick the shovel in the ground, open a hole, drop in the tree – making sure the roots are good and deep – and stamp the hole closed with your boot.

Depending on the terrain and what type of tree you're planting, you've just made anywhere from five to thirty-five cents. Then you do it again. And again. And again.

By the end of the first day my hands are raw with blisters that have popped and oozed, the arch of my right foot throbs from stomping on the shovel, and I'm so covered in bug bites that I look like I'm suffering from some strange disease. I've made about thirty bucks. Once I deduct my camp costs and the price of Clayton's equipment rental, I'm breaking just about even.

Tree planting is simple, but not easy.

Clayton drops us off, already on his third beer, and tells us we did okay for a couple of rookies. He says it sarcastically, but I'm still grateful for the small scrap of respect.

'Be ready on time tomorrow because we gotta pick up the rest of the crew.'

Neither of us points out that we were the ones waiting for him this morning.

Kurt and I doze our way through dinner, staring at our plates, slumping in our chairs. His folks ask us questions about our day and we answer vaguely, not really hearing. Fred ribs Kurt for planting less trees than me, but Kurt barely cracks a smile. After we wash up Kurt tells me he's going to buy some beers from the local store. He doesn't invite me along but by that point I'm too tired to care. I collapse on my cot. I never want to move again. The thought of getting up tomorrow morning makes me feel nauseous. I want to phone my parents, tell them I'm through. Nobody will really care if I do, but I'll always know that my first big adventure was a failure. I turn my face into the seat cushions, feeling the sting of tears in my sinuses, wishing I could just dissolve into the air, into nothing.

'Are you okay?'

I look up, rubbing hurriedly at my eyes. Sorrel's at the entrance to the tent, one hand pulling back the canvas flap. I smile, both embarrassed and relieved that it's her who's caught me acting like a baby.

'I hurt my hands today, that's all.'

I hold them out so she can see the open sores.

'I'll get you my cartoon band-aids,' she says. 'That's what I use.'

She goes to get them for me and helps put them on. They're decorated with Looney Tunes characters: Bugs Bunny and Daffy Duck and Wile E. Coyote. She concentrates very hard on placing the brightly coloured strips carefully over my blisters, getting the angle just right. Her head is bent over my hands, and her hair is a tangle of twigs, grass, and whirlpool snarls. At that moment I'm certain she's a changeling.

'When I grow up,' she says, 'I'm going to be a doctor.'

Five of us squeeze into the truck the next morning.

The two new crew members are Annie and Walter. Annie's got dreadlocks and the well-muscled arms of a seasoned planter. On the front of her shirt is a picture of Bob Marley, grinning and smoking a huge reefer. Walter is Clayton's friend from way back. He's fidgety and soft-spoken with a pinched, rodent's face. When he does speak it's difficult to understand him because he's missing five teeth from the upper front row. Just before we arrive on site he lights a joint, which gets passed around. I puff at it tentatively, still faking my inhales, hoping I don't look like the amateur I am. The cab becomes a giant hot box. When we open the doors to get out clouds of smoke follow us like ghosts.

I shove trees in my sacks and head for the woods, hoping the second day won't be as bad as the first. It's not. It's worse. Sorrel's bandages peel off in minutes and my hands start to bleed. I can barely hold my shovel. I know I'm not going to plant enough to cover camp costs. It's raining today, a penetrating drizzle that slithers off my slicker and works its way into my boots, until my socks squelch at each step. By lunch, I'm so miserable that I forget not to inhale when the half-time joint comes my way. After two or three tokes I feel better. Much better. I stand up. The sun has come out and the trees are very green and the air smells very fresh. Clayton's looking at me. They're all looking at me. Annie asks me how I feel.

Great. I feel great.

They snicker at my virgin-high, but I don't care.

The rest of the day is much easier, and the rest of the week.

On Friday Clayton takes Kurt and I out to a bar in Prince George. There are about a dozen TV screens mounted from the ceiling, displaying NHL highlights or Keno results, and the walls are decorated with ice hockey sticks, signed jerseys, old team photos, and other sports memorabilia. Clayton's warming to us, finally. He buys me my first beer, telling me I've earned the rookie of the week award by planting more trees than Kurt. I clock Kurt's expression and try to make a joke out of it, saying I got lucky with a good patch of ground. For awhile we talk hockey, debating whether the Canucks will make the play-offs this year, and then we talk movies. Apparently Clayton used to run a video store, which delivered the tapes to your house, but it went out of business.

By that point Clayton's getting pretty hammered.

'I cheat on my wife,' he tells us.

'You're married?'

'Yeah. But I go pig-fucking sometimes.'

He explains that pig-fucking involves picking the biggest, ugliest girl in a bar and taking her home for the night. I can't get a line on his tone. It's part boast, part confession – he's proud and ashamed at the same time.

'Got one chick pregnant. Still paying alimony on that little piglet.'

I wash it all down with another beer.

I learn more about Clayton from Kurt's mom while we're doing the dishes one night. She tells me he wasn't always a drunk, didn't always act like he does. In school he wrote plays and got all the other kids to perform them. He even won an essay-writing contest.

'Clayton?' I ask. 'Are you kidding?'

'I used to volunteer at the school. Everybody adored him.'

'What happened?'

She shakes her head, places the last cup gently on the draining board.

Sorrel's teaching herself to ride a bike – this rickety low-rider with spoke beads and a banana seat. She doesn't have training wheels and nobody wants to help her so on the weekend I'm recruited to be her trainer. The idea is for me to jog along behind her, balancing the bike by the back of its seat. She wears Neil's dirtbike helmet for protection. It's too big and keeps slipping over her eyes, but she doesn't seem to mind.

'Ready, cowgirl?'

'Let's roll.'

Once she gets up a head of steam, handlebar streamers snapping in the wind, she signals for me to let go. I do, and she immediately wipes out in the gravel. She hops up and starts kicking the bike, the helmet bobbing crazily on her head. Her knees are skinned and bloody, and there are tears on her cheeks but she's not actually crying – she's more furious than hurt. Once she wears herself out she picks up the bike and gets back on.

'Well?' she demands, looking back at me. 'Ready to go again?'

I wonder if I could convince my parents to adopt her.

Our next contract is for a plot of land an hour from Prince George. Clayton has arranged to have us all stay at a nearby campground. Walter drives his own car so we can pick up a new crew member along the way: Brady. He's our age, with a smooth, feminine face and eyes so blue that they look somehow feral, wolf-like. The first thing he says to me is, 'You're a city-sucker, huh? From Vancouver? I can tell by your skin. It's gone all yellow from hanging out so many chinks.'

Clayton finds that hilarious. With Brady around it's worse than day one; I become the source of all their amusement, the target of all their mockery. They make fun of my clothing, my hair, the way I talk. And when they're not ridiculing me, they're telling jokes about the chinks and the chugs and the ragheads and the nippers.

I keep my mouth shut and my head down.

The only good thing about the new place is where we sleep. Instead of tents Clayton has rented a battered aluminium trailer for the crew to share. Kurt and I take the double room, isolating Brady in a single. This pisses him off even more, makes him like me even less. Before dinner on the first night, the rest of the crew go off to smoke up and hackey-sack; Annie invites me along, but by then I'm sick of it all and say I'm going to stay behind.

'He wants to jerk off,' Brady says, and mimes tugging at his crotch.

Everybody laughs, including Kurt.

Clayton and his wife stay in a separate trailer, which doubles as our mess hall. Over dinner Clayton tells us about the girl on his crew who got mauled by a grizzly the previous summer. She was listening to her Walkman and didn't hear the bear until it was right on top of her.

'Stupid,' Annie says.

'Practically tore her head off. All those fuckers who want to ban bear hunting should have seen what it did to that girl.' Clayton glances at his wife. 'Right, babe?'

His wife nods in demure agreement, serving up another helping of sloppy Joes. The meat is chewy and smells strange. She's not as good a cook as Kurt's mom but she's prettier. In her polka-dot apron, with her permed hair, she looks like the housewife from one of those old appliance ads. Watching her, I find Clayton and his pig-fucking even more bewildering.

Later, as we're getting ready for bed, I ask Kurt about Clayton.

'Your mom said he used to be different. He wrote things.'

'I remember that. He could have got a bursary to go to UNBC, if he wanted.'

'What happened?'

'I don't know.' Kurt unzips his sleeping bag – one of those mummy bags that tapers around the feet – and wriggles inside. 'He never went. I don't think he even finished high school. Not as many guys do, up here. That's why my folks sent me down to the city.'

He tells me it's easy to get work, in the forestry towns. There's the lumber mills, the tree planting, the logging companies. You can make good money doing any of those jobs.

'Probably more than he could have with an English degree.' Kurt yawns, rolling away from me and curling in on himself. 'And Clayton's always liked to party. You've seen him.'

It's not much of an explanation, but it's as much as I'm going to get. I reach over and click out the bedside lamp. I lay in the darkness and listen to Kurt snoring as I wonder about Clayton's other life, and all the things he could have done.

Brady and Clayton are convinced that the Chinese are taking over Canada. They explain their elaborate theories to me in the pick-up on the way to and from the planting ground.

'It's a chink conspiracy,' Clayton says.

'Sure,' Brady says. 'They come to Vancouver, get their immigration status, then fly all their relatives in. Pretty soon there'll be more of them than us.'

'Amen, brother. A-fucking-men.' Clayton's features twist as he struggles to hold in his lungful of smoke. 'And next they bring in their drugs, set up their gangs. We wouldn't have half the drug problems if it wasn't for the chinks. Those Yakuza motherfuckers.'

I say, 'Yakuza are Japanese.'

'They're all in it together.'

Brady's never been to the city, and Clayton's only been once. All he remembers is the tall buildings and the junkies on Hastings Street. He and his wife saw some guy, dressed in a burlap sack, standing in traffic and staring at the sun. After that they stayed in their hotel bar.

I try to think of some defence that will make sense to them.

'There's some pretty cool Chinese people, too.'

'Chink-lover,' Brady says, blowing smoke in my face.

My only refuge is the forest.

Nobody can touch me there. I just plant and plant and I do it better and better each day. My blisters have hardened into calluses and my body has hardened, too. I've become a machine, running on a steady supply of weed and billowing smoke as exhaust. My totals are climbing. The only one who plants more than me is Clayton, and he's a veteran, a highballer. Kurt has been trying to keep up, and getting more and more frustrated. I've considered lying to him about my totals, but it's no good because Clayton gets us to announce them in front of everybody at the end of each day.

I'm in the woods, thinking about that, when I hear a snorting and pawing and grunting coming from a cluster of trees. I put a hand to the knife strapped to my belt and start singing at the top of my lungs. Clayton's told me to make noise if I come across a bear. The snorting gets louder. The bushes are shaking. I turn, getting ready to run. There's a wild roar and the snapping of branches and Brady appears, arms outstretched as he charges towards me.

'Oh, Jesus,' he says, laughing so hard he can't breathe. 'Your face was priceless.'

I'm still gripping my knife. I feel like I could stab him.

'I knew it was you,' I say.

'My ass.'

Back at our stockpile, over lunch, he tells the others about the prank. They all love it, and there's a lot of laughter at my expense.

'So the rookie fell for it!' Clayton says.

'Poor kid,' Annie says.

'Once a city-sucker,' Kurt says, 'always a city-sucker.'

I look at him. He's got the decency to look away, at least.

Around the others Kurt and I have kept up pretences. But back at the trailer, in our room, we no longer really act like friends. We're quiet most of the time and move around each other, as if we're both living there alone. I listen to my music and read dog-eared paperbacks that I've found in the trailer: Stephen King and Clive Cussler and Tom Clancy. Kurt smokes roll-ups or hacky-sacks by himself or lies on his cot, staring at the ceiling. Sometimes I try to pinpoint when and how things changed between us, but it all seems childish and petty and strange.

Usually, Kurt's the last to quit each day – frantically trying to top up his total – so when I go to reload my sacks on Wednesday afternoon I'm surprised to find him lounging by the boxes of yearlings, his equipment strewn about him. It's only two o'clock.

'How you doing?' he asks me.

'All right. You?'

He yawns dramatically, and waves a hand as if shooing away a mosquito. His gesture takes in the equipment, the baby trees, and the surrounding forest.

'I'm all through with this.'

The next day, Fred picks him up in their family van, an old Chevy Astro. The rest of the crew, except for Clayton, come out of the trailers to say goodbye. We shake hands and wish Kurt luck and nobody mocks him for bailing on us. He climbs up front into the passenger seat; Fred gives us a nod, and then they're pulling away. Kurt doesn't look back or wave.

'I don't get it,' Annie says.

'Fucking couldn't take it, could he?' Brady says, and spits.

'Just seems weird. Especially when your dad's the contractor.'

I try to imagine explaining it to my own dad. It wouldn't go down so well.

'Shitty for you, man,' Clayton tells me later, when I'm helping him unload firewood from his truck. 'Come all the way up here, then have your buddy sell out on you like that. That's tough.'

It's not, though. It changes things for the better. Clayton eases off on me, I suspect mostly because he can't afford to lose another crew member. Brady seems to be less hostile, too. In part this is Annie's influence; it's obvious he's got a crush on her. Instead of bullying me, he flirts with her. He's always trying to tickle her or wrestle with her or chat her up, and he likes having me there for their mating rituals. It takes the pressure off, I guess.

As a result, camp life becomes less of a torment. During our downtime, the three of us just hang around, smoking and drinking and badmouthing Kurt. Sometimes Walter joins us, sometimes there are other crew members; if we ever fall behind schedule, Clayton calls in a few of his friends, casual highballers, to help us catch up. Annie sells me my own bag of weed, and at the end of each night, I lock myself in my room, light a joint, and crank the volume on my dad's Walkman, listening to Neil Young's high, rasping keen.

The hours pass, and the days, in a hazy, almost hallucinatory fog.

On weekends we abandon camp.

Everybody else gets to go home, but I'm forced to stay at Kurt's. He's sleeping in his old room, now – the charade of his independence having fallen apart. Fred and Miranda treat me politely, if a little coldly. Nobody ever mentions Kurt quitting, and I wonder what he's told them. Whenever I go inside, Kurt finds an excuse to keep himself occupied. I ask him to come have beers with me, to smoke a joint, to toss the football around. He'd rather play on his computer, shooting monsters or building alien cities.

The one person happy to have me back is Sorrel.

She doesn't seem to have many friends from school, and spends most of her time with me. I help her ride her bike and toss horseshoes with her. She's only six but she can read and write and likes me to read her books in the yard. Her favorite is one about a vampire bunny that sucks the juice out of vegetables. I read that to her a dozen times, both of us laughing at the good parts like we've never heard them before. While she listens, she has a habit of twisting her hair in a knot around her forefinger, tight enough to turn her fingertip white.

When Clayton picks me up on Monday mornings, I always see her pale face peeking through the curtains, watching me go.

Apparently, we'd have a lot more tree-planting work if it wasn't for the Indians. Just like the Chinese are responsible for all of Vancouver's problems, according to Clayton everything from bad weather to petty crime can be attributed to the local Native Americans.

'All they do is huff gas and rip people off and steal our work.'

He goes on to tell me that the Natives are given a certain amount of tree-planting contracts by law, and other companies are encouraged through tax breaks and bonuses to support the Native community, because of its unemployment problem.

'So they get all our fucking cream just because they're Indians.'

Brady says, 'If that's not racist I don't know what the fuck is.'

Walter just nods along, like always, even though he's part Native himself.

I take the morning joint that we're sharing, toke long and hard – scalding my throat with smoke – and point it at Clayton. 'Maybe they're getting something back for all the times our government screwed them over.'

But my voice is squeaky from holding my breath, and Clayton just snorts.

'Chug-lover,' Brady says, and elbows me.

'Leave him be,' Annie says. 'You sound like a bunch of fucking rednecks.'

There's a pause. Then Brady sniggers.

'We are rednecks!' Clayton shouts.

Even I have to laugh at that.

Campfires become our nightly ritual.

Clayton and his wife carry over the stereo from their trailer. If we're blitzed enough we make our own music. Walter brings a rusty harmonica that he blasts on. Annie has a five-string guitar and a voice like an old bullfrog. Everybody sings along.

'That's great,' Brady says, slapping his thigh. 'Listen to that, huh?'

We're always drunk, always stoned, always happy.

I'm flying, now – earning one-thirty, one-forty a day. Then the ground gets gnarly: rocky and rugged and hard as concrete. You can feel every shovel stroke from your tailbone up to your skull. We're being paid a little more per tree but our totals have been cut in half.

'Don't worry,' Clayton assures us, one night at the firepit. 'We got some cream lined up for Monday.'

He's been hyping the cream all week, and I finally get the guts to ask him what he's talking about. He looks at me like I've got a dick growing out of my forehead. He explains that cream is the holy grail of tree planting: soft, open ground that melts under your shovel like cheesecake. Usually, since it's so easy, the price per tree is dropped, sometimes to as little as a nickel. But Fred's hooked up a deal for us – ten cents a tree. Clayton slaps me on the back, tells me I'll plant my thousand.

'First rookie to hit a thousand always gets a case.'

I laugh. 'I'm the only rookie now that Kurt's bailed.'

'Yeah,' Clayton says, 'but the dog-fucker wants in on this.'

We fall silent. Clayton picks up a rock, throws it skittering into the bush.

'Don't worry – I've told Fred what I think of that.'

I wonder if that was such a good idea.

The thought of that cream gets us through the rest of a gruelling week. Come Thursday, we're ahead of schedule and Clayton lets us take the day off. He goes shopping for food supplies with his wife; the rest of us fuck around all morning and spend the afternoon smoking up, bragging about how sweet the cream's going to be. Brady attempts to punch a hole in the trailer wall, doesn't, and nearly breaks his wrist instead. Annie wraps it up in a tensor bandage from the First Aid kit, treating him with more sympathy than he deserves.

Maybe he's doing something right.

Before dinner, we decide to make a beer run into town. On the way back from camp, Walter tears up the dirt road, fishtailing Clayton's truck around every corner. We're singing 'Buffalo Soldier' together, shouting the chorus out the windows. I'm riding shotgun and for the first time since I came up here, I feel like I'm part of something. Then I see the caravan lumbering around the next bend. The road isn't wide enough for two vehicles.

'Shit!' I shout. 'Watch out!'

Walter's already seen, and pumps the brakes. The truck goes into a skid, twisting left, right, left, and he works the wheel to compensate. Walter's good – he holds the road – and as the caravan approaches I'm convinced we're going to squeeze past until our front wheels bite and lurch to the left. There's a crunch and the shriek of metal on metal as we grind along the side of the caravan. Then we're sitting in silence and a cloud of dust.

One by one we pile out to assess the damage.

Clayton takes the news of our accident surprisingly well, considering we were wasted and mangled the front of his truck, and that most of the liability will be with him.

'Insurance will cover it,' he says.

But his face is hard. There's something else on his mind. We're standing around the table, in the dining room of the trailer he shares with his wife. He clears his throat and looks out the window; it's almost dusk and I can hear the cicadas whirring in the underbrush.

'Just spoke to Fred.' He pauses, picking at a callus on his palm. 'He's decided to go ahead and plant the cream himself. Him, Neil, and Kurt.'

The crew deflates. We slump down at the mess table. I feel

like the projector of my life has sputtered and died just before the big finish.

Brady brings his fist down on the tabletop, and winces. It's his bad wrist.

'That motherfucker.'

Clayton hands out beers. There's nothing else to say or do. We skip dinner and drink without enjoying it, smoke joint after joint like we're on a mission to get as fucked up as possible. Time evaporates; the evening hazes over. After several hours, Annie and Brady walk back to our trailer, holding hands. Walter starts weeping, telling Clayton over and over again how sorry he is about the truck, and passes out on the table. Clayton's wife has already gone to bed, and at the end it's just me and him. We shift to Alberta Premium. Between each shot, he stares moodily into his glass, harelip twitching in the way it does when he's wasted.

'You know,' he says, looking up, 'they offered to take you on. Fred and Kurt. You can still plant the cream. I just didn't want to bring it up in front of the others.'

The strange part is, it's obvious he expects me to do it.

'Fuck that,' I say.

With the cream taken from us, the relationship with Fred broken, and no other contracts on the horizon, Clayton disbands the crew. Walter offers to drive Brady and Annie home in his car. Since Clayton has to go into town to see his insurance company, he says he can drop me off at the bus station. His truck is still roadworthy, though the wheels dog-track now, and the steering alignment is shot. We all pile into our vehicles, and it only occurs to me then that I won't see them again. I roll down my window and they do the same. Walter waves.

'See you later, city-sucker!' Brady shouts.

Annie hits him, and he grins like a kid. I have time to flip him the finger and then Clayton hits the gas and we're heading off in different directions. On the way into town, we pass Kurt's place, and I ask Clayton to pull over. I've forgotten something. Fortunately, I don't have to deal with seeing Kurt or the rest of the family. Sorrel is sitting by herself in the front yard, reading. I walk over and crouch next to her. She doesn't look up from her book.

'You're going, aren't you?'

'Looks like it,' I say.

'Well, you might as well have this. I made it for you.'

She hands me a crayon drawing of a long-limbed stickman standing in a field of baby trees. He looks enormous, like a modern-day Paul Bunyon – except with a shovel instead of an axe. I smile, thank her, and give her a hug goodbye. Over her shoulder I can see a dark head peering through the living room window. I don't acknowledge it.

Sorrel walks with me to the truck, holding my hand. When I let go to get inside she doesn't cry. She just stands at the end of the drive, growing smaller with distance.

At the station, the Greyhound bus is already out front, and a line of people is waiting to get on, tickets in hand. I hop out of the truck with my bag and walk around to the driver's side. Clayton reaches through the window and we shake. He smiles at me, but it still looks like a sneer.

'It's been an experience, man,' I say.

'Sure,' he says, starting the truck. 'Take care in the city.'

I'm still thinking about Clayton when I get off the bus in Vancouver. The station is right downtown, close to False Creek and the inlet, and the air is rich and thick with the salt smell of the sea. I stretch out in the park at Main and Terminal among the rest of the drug addicts that so terrified Clayton, and roll up the last of Annie's weed. But it's not the same – the buds have gone stale. I only smoke half the joint, and flick the roach into the grass, where it sits and smoulders. I should probably call my parents but don't think I'm ready for that, yet. Instead I just lay there with my eyes closed, feeling the sun on my face. A sky train rushes overhead, shaking the tracks. Across the street a busker is plucking at his guitar. I listen to that, and the traffic humming in the street, and the tap-tap of passing feet, and all the other sounds of my city, my home.

Mangleface

She had been beautiful once. I could tell by the way
she walked: straight-backed, long strides, confident. She walked
like a beautiful person. The first time I saw her I was putting
rentals back on the shelves. I noticed her studying our foreign-
film section. I couldn't see her face but I had a good view of her
body. That was enough to make me put down my armload of
movies and saunter over.

'Can I give you a hand with anything?'

She turned towards me. She had her hair styled so that it
partially obscured her features, but it didn't really hide much.

'Yeah, I'm looking for—

She saw my expression. I couldn't help it. The skin of her
face was cross-hatched with scars, dry and leathery. Her nose
seemed to melt into her mouth, which twisted down on one side.

'Never mind,' she said.

I stood beside her for a minute, couldn't think of anything to
say, and slunk back to my till in a daze. As she moved around
the store I watched her out of the corner of my eye, like I usually
did with potential shoplifters. I wasn't satisfied with how I'd left

things. After several minutes I tried again.

'Hey, I'm sorry about that.'

She picked up a display box, avoiding my gaze.

'Don't worry about it.'

'You like foreign films?'

A shrug. 'I'm getting bored of the normal stuff.'

I figured if I was in her place I'd watch a lot of movies, too.

'That one's all right.' I tapped the case in her hand. It was a Brazilian film about this lady who falls in love with a dolphin man, and has his kid. 'Weird, but kind of cool. I dug it.'

She smiled at me. It was hideous enough to shatter all the mirrors in the world.

'Thanks,' she said.

I wouldn't say she came in frequently after that, but she came in regularly. She stopped by in the mornings, when I was the only cashier and the store was empty. On Fridays, she always rented two or three movies. She never came in on weekends.

She walked in one day when I was training a new kid on the till, this kid from West Van. He served her politely – giving her our usual sales spiel – but after she left he turned to me and asked, 'Did you see good old mangleface there?'

I told him to shut his mouth.

'Sorry,' he said, 'I didn't know you had a thing for her.'

He was a lippy little shit. She probably got that kind of comment a lot, from assholes like him. At the end of the week, I told my manager I'd seen the kid taking pop and pretzels from the confectionary without paying for it, which was something I usually did. He was still on his two-week trial period. That was enough to ensure he didn't get the job.

The nickname stuck, though. I started thinking of her as Mangleface. I never learned her real name. She rented movies on her father's account. I only knew that her last name was Rice. Mangleface Rice. It seemed to fit.

Mangleface had a boyfriend. I only saw them together once, but that was enough. They made the mistake of coming in just after five. The pre-dinner rush is our busiest time of day. I didn't notice them until they got in the checkout line, which snaked halfway to the back of the store. Between customers I kept an eye on them as they waited. He was dressed in black jeans and a silk shirt – a real cold lampino. They stood a little apart, muttering to each other occasionally. Everybody was staring, of course, while pretending not to. It was almost as if they were celebrities of some sort.

When they reached my till, the guy asked, 'Is this flick any good?'

He thrust the tape into my hands. I glanced at the title on the spine. It was a documentary about this crazy Italian guy, driving around on his scooter, looking for Jennifer Beals.

'Sure, it's kind of all right.'

'Kind of all right,' he said to her. 'You hear that?'

'I want it,' she said.

He lowered his head and shrugged his shoulders, then slapped ten bucks down on the counter. I took it and asked him if they wanted any popcorn or candy. I didn't address her, or look at her much, because we were both pretending we didn't know each other, in that way you do.

'Why would we?' he said.

'I have to ask.'

'We don't need any of that crap.'

I scanned the movie, fed the ten into my till, and gave him his change. The store had gone quiet. He took the movie and walked out without waiting for her. As she left she glanced at me. It was hard to read her expression, because her face didn't work like a normal face. It always looked sad, clownish, the mouth drooping down on one side as if she'd had a stroke. But just then there was something resigned about it, as if she knew what was coming, and soon.

The more accustomed I grew to her disfigurement, the more I was able to ignore it. It was as if her face was changing. For me, anyway. And as it did, over time, we got to know each other. If there was anybody else in the store, she was anxious, shy. When we were alone, though, she wasn't afraid to talk to me. I learned that she liked pecan ice cream and skiing. Her favourite movie was *Night of the Living Dead* – the original black and white version.

I never asked about her face.

Sometimes, though, when she wasn't looking, I'd check her out. If her back was turned to you she was hot. She had a great body: tanned and lithe and toned. Then you'd see her face, and that would be it. It could be pretty unsettling. I wondered if her boyfriend felt similarly. Did they ever have sex? Maybe every so often – but only with the lights out. In the dark it could be anybody's face. He wouldn't kiss her. He'd just grab her tits and squeeze her ass and imagine she was somebody else. That asshole didn't deserve her. He really didn't.

Chatting with Mangleface became part of my routine, like unlocking the store and emptying the returns bin. I opened at nine, and she usually came in just after ten. She would linger at my till, telling me what she thought of the movies I'd suggested. I started keeping a copies of the new releases behind the counter, which we weren't supposed to do, in case she wanted to rent one. Sometimes she did, other times she didn't. But the choice was always there.

If she didn't turn up, I got worried. What had happened to her? Maybe she'd had a fight with her boyfriend. I would wait for her to come running to me. She would be in tears. She would need a shoulder to cry on. Who else could she turn to? Me, of course. I was the only one who could see past the horror of her face.

Other times I imagined she was in trouble. She would rush in, distraught. She was sick, injured. She had an enormous debt. Loan sharks were after her, or some lunatic. A lunatic who only stalked chicks with disfigured faces. Or maybe it was something simpler, like her car had broken down. Whatever the scenario, I would help her. I'd take care of her.

I had a lot of time on my hands at that video store.

I was talking to her one day when this guy came in. He wore a pinstripe suit with burgundy leather shoes, and his hair was crusted with mousse. He looked like the kind of guy who managed a bunch of other people for a living. He was drunk, too. Vodka. I could smell it. Drunks think you can't smell vodka, but you can.

Mangleface was at my till. When he saw her he did a double-take.

'Holy shit – what happened to your face!'

Silence. Nobody else was in the store.

'I'm sorry – I don't mean to pry – but Jesus Christ.'

He turned to me. He wasn't trying to be cruel. He was just another asshole.

'You seen this poor girl's face?'

'I seen it, man. Settle down.'

'I'm sorry. I just couldn't help it. What happened?'

Mangleface had a hard time controlling herself. She was looking down at the movie she'd just rented. She didn't cry. I never saw her cry, not even once. I sometimes thought her tear ducts might have been damaged, somehow. But her eyes were fine, so I don't know if that makes any sense.

'Car accident,' she whispered.

'Jesus. That's tough.'

I gave Mangleface her change. She left without saying anything. Even after she was gone he couldn't let it go. He went to the window to peer after her. He was really unsettled by it.

'Did you see that, man? I never seen anything like it.'

He kept saying that. I kept telling him I'd seen it. Eventually he left. Afterwards, I accessed his account and ran a pre-authorisation on his credit card for three hundred bucks. We do that for renting games consoles, occasionally. It wouldn't take the money out, but it would freeze the funds for a month, or until he caught on. It wasn't much, considering how he'd behaved, but hopefully it would screw things up for him a little.

I started thinking of Mangleface outside of work. It was weird. My friends and I would be shooting hoops, or down at the beach, and she would be there, in my head. It worried me because that usually only happens with girls I like. Somehow, without my realising it, Mangleface had become one of those girls. That was okay, I told myself. Nobody has to know. You've got a secret crush on Mangleface – so what? It's not like you're going to do anything about it.

A date with Mangleface would be agonising. Everybody would stop and stare and wonder what the hell you were doing with a chick whose face looked like that. And those were just strangers. What would happen if my friends found out? I'd never hear the end of it. My friends could be merciless like that.

Some days I wished everybody were blind.

At night, I began to think of doing things with her. I focused on her body. That was safe. Her body was beautiful. I wouldn't admit what I really wanted. Her body eased me into it.

I imagined running my hands over that body. I was always very tender with her. She was timid. It had been a long time since she'd been appreciated. I took my time, kissing her legs, her belly, her breasts. I didn't look at her face, not at first. I approached it indirectly. I kissed her throat, her earlobes, the nape of her neck.

A few weeks went by before I imagined kissing her face.

It was a frightening experience. Her lips were dry. All the skin on her face was withered like a scorched prune. But I liked kissing her. It drove me crazy kissing those twisted lips. Soon enough we were making love.

I fantasised about that every night for months.

Though in my head we had gone all the way, during the day our relationship remained chaste. She would come in, wander for a bit, then ask my advice on picking a film. I'd walk with her up and down the aisles. Sometimes she wanted a horror movie, sometimes a love story, sometimes an arthouse flick. With Mangleface it was never the same. I would take my time helping her. I knew that she appreciated my company as much as my advice. She liked hearing me summarise the plots of films.

'What about this one?'

'It's awesome. There's this guy who goes around killing people with his electric guitar.'

'His guitar?'

'Yeah. It's got a drill attached to the end. Whenever he hits the strings the drill starts spinning, and he drills people.'

'That sounds hilarious.'

'It is. You'd love it.'

We had pretty similar taste in films. That was part of why we got on so well. Any movie I liked she usually liked. Or maybe she was just being nice to me because I was being nice to her. Maybe she secretly hated all those movies but kept renting them just so she wouldn't hurt my feelings.

I'd never thought of that.

I knew it was finished between her and her boyfriend when he came in with another girl. She was wearing heels and a miniskirt and no tights. She had these legs. Bare and smooth as a mannequin's. In the kids section, where we keep all our cartoons, I saw him snort something off the back of his knuckle, like a total Carlito. As they stumbled about the store he kept slipping his hand up her skirt. Whenever he did this, she giggled and swatted it away.

They grabbed the latest blockbuster – this movie about an asteroid hitting earth – and came to my till.

'You got your membership card?' I asked.

'I forgot it. I can give you my phone number.'

'Can't rent to you without a card. It's policy.'

I rent to tonnes of people without a card. Not him, though.

'I've done it before,' he said.

'It's a new policy.'

She leaned over the counter so I could see her cleavage, and put her hand on my wrist. 'Can't you make an exception, just this once?' she said, making a pouty-face. 'Just for me?'

I wondered if Mangleface had been like that, before the accident.

'Sorry,' I said. 'I can hold the film for you, if you want to come back.'

'Forget it,' he said. 'Come on – let's go someplace else.'

'Have a good night.'

'Fuck you, pal.'

He flipped me the finger on the way out.

In the parking lot, car doors slammed. An engine roared to life. I looked out the window and watched his Jetta fishtail around the corner, the engine whining, the wheels screaming.

I thought about things for a few minutes, and then went to get three pornos from our adult section. It's a family store but we have this backroom. I got real dirty ones – the dirtiest. I scanned the tapes onto his account, carried them outside, and tossed them in our dumpster.

In a week or so, after the films hadn't been returned, they'd be added to our late list. Our manager would start calling up his house, asking after them. And the next time he came in, the enormous late charges would show up on his account, along with the titles.

Everybody would know what kind of guy he was.

*

I was happy about the break-up. My fantasy was coming true. Mangleface would need me more than ever now that the asshole was out of the way, and she was alone.

I was surprised when she didn't show up that week, or the week after.

I started to worry. What if being dumped had made her do something crazy? What if she'd killed herself? It had to be something like that. Poor Mangleface. I concocted all kinds of scenarios. She had cut her wrists. She had hung herself. She had overdosed on Tylenol, or sleeping pills. She had thrown herself off the Lions Gate Bridge. Mangleface was no more. She would be laid to rest. Ashes to ashes, dust to dust.

Nobody would think to invite me to the funeral.

She came back.

I hadn't seen her for a month. I heard the chime over the door and turned, and there she was. She looked terrible. She'd really let herself go. She was wearing sweatpants and a dirty blouse and her hair looked as if it had gotten caught in a fan.

I pretended not to notice.

'Hey – haven't seen you for awhile.'

Her mouth twisted into a smile.

'No,' she said.

'Are you okay?'

'No.'

Then she started sobbing. I had imagined this. I went around to the other side of the counter and held her. She smelled of sweat and felt fragile as a bird in my arms.

'It's okay,' I said. 'It's okay.'

It was just what I'd wanted. I was her great protector.

After a few minutes she stopped sobbing. I held on until it passed, rubbing her back, then let go of her. She still hadn't really cried at all. I mean, there were no tears on her face.

'You know what's strange?' she said, staring at my chest. 'I've gotten so used to seeing this face in the mirror that I can't tell how hideous it is anymore. I only remember when I see other people's reactions to it.'

'It's not that bad.'

She sniffed. 'You don't react to it like other people.'

'It doesn't bother me.'

She looked up at me. She had such nice eyes. They hadn't been damaged at all. They were clear, and blue, and wide open. A baby's eyes.

'But would you ever be able to kiss it?'

I thought of countless lonely nights, of all the times I'd kissed her in my mind, but for a few seconds I couldn't bring myself to act.

The chime above the door rang out like an alarm. Two teenagers sauntered in. They were laughing and shoving each other, horsing around a bit. That all stopped as soon as they noticed her. One of them whispered something. They lingered nearby, watching.

Her question still hung unanswered between us.

'I don't know,' I said, stepping back.

I barely whispered the words, but she flinched as if I'd shouted. She didn't say anything else. She just turned and walked out. The door eased shut behind her, sighing on its hydraulics. I gazed at the space where she'd been, still stuck in the scene. I wanted to press pause, and rewind, and play it out all over again, with a different ending.

Those two kids were still standing there, gawking.

'Get the hell out of here.'

They looked at each other uncertainly. One of them tried a smile, as if he thought I might be joking. I wasn't. I started towards them.

'I said get the hell out of here!'

They did. I followed them to the door and slammed it behind them and flipped the lock. Further down the street I could see her, walking away, getting smaller. I pressed my forehead against the glass and watched her go, feeling as if I'd crushed a butterfly in my fist.

Edges

Ben had just started his morning shift when the guy came in. He walked with a wrestler's swagger: puffing out his chest, holding his arms away from his sides, turning his whole upper body at each step. His head was shaved into a crew-cut, bristling grey, and he had that look about him. But he also had a paunch that spilled over the waistband of his snow pants, and jowls that shivered under his chin. There was a kid with him – a boy of about ten – who gazed around the rental shop as if he'd never seen skis or snowboards or any of it before.

Big Jane, Ben's coworker, was already busy serving two schoolgirls so the guy led his kid up to Ben's counter and smiled. Ben knew that smile – the kind of fake plastic smile customers use when dealing with a sales rep or employee, somebody who has to serve them. He saw it every day.

'We want to rent some ski equipment.'

'Sure,' Ben said. 'What size boots?'

'Size eight for me. Michael – what size are your shoes?'

The boy held up one hand, spreading the fingers wide.

'You can talk, can't you?'

Michael lowered his arm and said, 'Five.'

His father nodded, satisfied.

'All right,' Ben said. 'Sizes five and ten. You skiing or riding?'

'We're going skiing for Michael's birthday, right Michael?'

'Maybe we could snowboard, Dad?'

His father stared at him. Michael started to fidget; he grabbed the side of his pant leg with his right hand and tugged on it.

'We came up here to go skiing, Michael.'

Michael looked at his feet. 'Okay.'

Ben said, 'Maybe you could ski and he could snowboard.'

The guy's head came around in a quick, jerking motion, like a turkey. 'No,' he said. 'We'll ski because I can teach him to ski so we'll ski.' He finished with another fake smile. 'Okay?'

Ben said that it was okay.

He walked back among the racks of gear, where they kept the helmets and ski and snowboard boots. As he was taking the two sets of boots down Big Jane wandered up to get some ski poles for the other customers. She was a forty-year-old hippy with a wild mane of dreadlocks. She had worked up Seymour since dropping out of high school, and smoked even more weed than Ben. He'd heard Jane had a little grow-op in her cabin up Indian Arm. Wherever she got her stuff it was good.

'Man,' Jane whispered. 'That guy you're serving has a mad-gruesome vibe.'

'I just feel bad for his kid.'

Ben took the boots to the front and handed them over. In front of his counter was a circular bench where people could sit to try on boots, and Ben left the man and his son there while he handled another group of customers – a Japanese family who were pleasant and smiled constantly and spoke no English at all. They were going snowshoeing.

When Ben finished with them and returned to the father and son, the guy was walking around, testing his boots.

'How are those?' Ben asked.

'They'll do.'

Michael was still sitting on the bench. He said, 'Mine feel too tight, Dad.'

'Ski boots are *supposed* to be tight, Michael. That's the whole point.'

'But they hurt.'

'I can get another size,' Ben said.

The guy held up his hand to him, palm out, like a traffic cop. 'Look,' he said to Ben, 'I'm paying nearly a hundred bucks for this and we're wasting time. Where are the skis?'

Ben went to get the skis.

At the till, when the guy paid up, he put the rentals and lift tickets on his credit card. The name on the card said Mr Schroeder. The name seemed appropriate, for a guy like him. Ben rang up eighty-six dollars on Schroeder's credit card and sent him on his way.

He figured that would be the end of it.

It was a lazy weekday, a Thursday, and after the early rush of customers there was the usual mid-morning lull. Ben went out back with Big Jane to smoke up; they lounged on the snowbanks by the groomer and burned a bowl of her organic grass, passing the pipe back and forth and taking huge, chest-scorching hoots. It was a warm spring day; the sky glowed neon blue and the snowpack glittered in the glare of the sun. You could see for miles: the inlet and the city and the sea beyond, shining like sheet metal. Between tokes Ben told Jane about Schroeder. Jane listened and shook her head, releasing smoke slowly from her nostrils like some kind of ancient sage.

'You be careful,' she told Ben. 'The last thing we need is for you to get involved in an altercation with a guy like that.'

Ben nodded. Management knew about his record and had already tried to get rid of him twice: once when some cash had gone missing from the till and once when he'd lipped off Ed, their supervisor. Both times, Jane had gone to bat for him. Jane was good like that.

'I'll watch myself,' he told her.

The rest of the morning passed in a smoky daze. Ben worked through lunch because he'd had a late breakfast, and if he waited until the end of his shift he could score some free cafeteria grub. After the midday rush, he gave his board a hot wax. It didn't really need one, but he enjoyed the process, especially when he was stoned. The way the block of wax liquified against the iron, turning clear, and drizzled onto the base of the board. The smoothness of it, and the smell of it: pleasant and pungent. And then the satisfaction of scraping the wax off, once it had cooled, and seeing it fall to the floor in flakes, like snow.

He'd just begun buffing the base when the doors opened and Schroeder came back in with his son. The kid's face was scarlet-red and sticky with tears and he was crying silently.

'Come on, Michael,' Schroeder said. 'Quit dawdling.'

He was holding Michael by the arm and dragging him along behind him like a doll. Michael's ski boots scraped and clattered across the floor; he couldn't walk quickly enough to keep up and kept faltering and tripping. Schroeder hauled him over to Ben's counter and let go and Michael collapsed on the ground in a tangled, cross-legged position.

'He thinks his boots are too small.'

'My feet,' Michael said, between sobs. 'My feet.'

Schroeder smiled at Ben, then bent to one knee and gripped

Michael by the face with one hand, squashing his cheeks. 'You're acting like a baby girl right now. Do you hear me? You have got to stop whining about every little thing. This is not appropriate behaviour on your birthday...' It went on and on like that, in a terse, restrained monotone that was hard to make out: a kind of low-fidelity virulence. As Schroeder spoke Ben could see the tendons in his neck and jaw flexing – as if every word, every syllable, was an effort to articulate.

Eventually Michael's sobbing faded.

'That's better.' Schroeder used his sleeve to wipe the tears and snot off his son's face. 'Good boy. We'll get you a bigger pair, okay?'

Then he stood up and smiled his plastic smile and asked Ben if he could please get his son a new pair of boots.

Ben had to consciously relax his grip on the counter. He nodded and retreated to the back of the shop; from there he could still hear Michael whimpering – these faint sounds like an injured dog. Ben stood and listened to it and studied the boots on the boot racks. He was still feeling pretty stoned and didn't know what to do, exactly. What was there to do? There was nothing to do, except his job. He would just do his job. Big Jane must have noticed him standing like that, because she came over and touched his shoulder and asked if he was okay.

'Sure,' Ben said. 'It's just that Schroeder guy.'

Jane glanced towards the counter. 'You want me to deal with him?'

'It's all right,' Ben said.

He got down some kids' size six boots and took them back to the front. Michael was sitting on the bench with his knees tucked against his chest and his arms wrapped around his shins. He looked up hopefully as Ben approached. Schroeder reached to take the boots but Ben pretended not to notice and instead knelt down in front of Michael.

'Here, buddy – let's see if these ones fit.'

Schroeder hovered at Ben's shoulder as he eased the first boot onto Michael's foot.

'How's that feel? Better?'

Michael nodded. But when Ben went to put on the other boot Michael winced and a made a small, startled sound. He said that it hurt. Ben stopped and placed the boot to one side. He guessed what had happened and tentatively touched the bridge of Michael's foot.

'There?'

Michael nodded again. The boot had been pinching him, bruising the bones.

'This might not work, then,' Ben said.

'Of course it'll work,' Schroeder said. He'd already picked up the boot. He moved in, shouldering Ben aside. 'He's just being a big baby. Sit still Michael, for God's sake.'

He took hold of Michael's foot and worked it into the boot. As he did Michael's face seemed to wilt and shrivel up: his mouth pinching to a pinhole, his eyes squinting into slits.

'Look, man,' Ben said, 'I don't know if he should go back out there.'

Schroeder did not answer immediately; instead he very carefully and very deliberately finished fastening the bindings on the boot. When he was done he let Michael's foot drop to the floor and stood up and turned on Ben.

'You telling me how to treat my kid?'

'I'm just saying.'

'Don't say, okay? Don't say anything.'

'Whatever.'

'That's right.' Schroeder stepped in closer. Too close. He had something wrong with his left eye – there were tiny flecks of red in the white, like the blood dots in an egg yolk. 'I spent good money on those tickets and your shitty gear and he's going to ski so maybe you should keep your parenting tips to yourself unless you want me to talk to your supervisor.'

Ben didn't say anything. He couldn't say anything. The muscles in his upper arms and across his shoulders had gone tense and taut and he could hear a faint buzzing noise that seemed to be all around him and also in his head, right inside his skull. Insistent as a hornet.

'Is everything all right here?'

It was Jane. She put a hand on Ben's forearm, and her touch acted like a grounding wire, draining that tension out of him.

'Fine, fine.' Schroeder smiled and jerked a thumb towards Ben. 'Your employee here is just telling me how I should treat my boy. I guess that's included with the rental package?'

Jane looked at Ben, and Ben shook his head. 'Kid says his foot hurts.'

It took a lot of effort to shape the words.

'How you feeling, little guy?' Jane asked Michael.

Michael stood there blinking. For a second he looked as if he might say something, but the words never formed and he just gaped up at her with his mouth half-open. Schroeder didn't give Jane the chance to ask again. He took Michael by the wrist and lifted him back to his feet. Michael hung there like a puppet.

'Thanks for all your help,' Schroeder said, and glanced deliberately at the nametag pinned to Ben's fleece. 'I'll be sure to remember it, Benjamin.'

As he said that, Ben felt a fleck of spittle hit his cheek. He didn't wipe it away. He didn't move at all. He just stood there. The guy was a son of a bitch but that was okay and Ben wasn't going to do anything. The fat son of a bitch. Schroeder was walking away, now, dragging his son towards the door. Michael plodded along behind him, head down, resigned and obedient. That was the worst part – the kid was so used to it that he didn't even know he had a fat son of a bitch for a father.

'Somebody should report that guy to social services,' Jane said.

'Somebody should kick that guy's fucking ass.'

'Hey,' Jane said, and patted him on the back. 'Forget it, okay?'

She asked him if he wanted to take a break from the sales desk for the afternoon; he could stick to sharpening and repairs instead. Ben told her he thought that was a good idea.

Before doing anything else he ducked out back to burn a quick joint, the smoke warm and mellow and comforting in his lungs. Then he grabbed a Pepsi and some pretzels from the snack machines and took them with him into the work room, which was off to one side of the rentals shop. In it they kept their tools, belt sander, sharpening machine, and a workbench for making equipment adjustments and doing repairs. Their rental boards tended to get battered and there was always a lot of sharpening to do. He picked up the first board from the stack to inspect it; the edges were riddled with nicks and gouges.

He switched on the sharpening machine and while it warmed up he used a gummy stone to remove the worst burrs. Then he configured the machine to grind side edges, set the angle for 90 degrees – standard for rentals – and laid the board flat on the loading tray. He held the board steady and pressed down on the foot pedal, which started the grinding disc and feed rollers. He could feel the vibrations through his forearms. He wasn't wearing earplugs and in the confined space the noise was deafening. It overwhelmed all other sounds, all other thoughts. He didn't have to think about that son of a bitch or the stuff he'd said or anything except the edge of the board, and holding it steady as he ran it through the machine, which he did several times, on both sides, before adjusting the set-up to do the base edges. When that board was finished he put it aside and started on another.

He must have done half a dozen boards before he glanced up and saw Ed. He was out in the rentals shop, talking to Jane; Ben had a good view of them both through the door, which he'd left ajar in case Jane needed him. He turned off the grinding disc to listen. He caught his name and the word 'complaint' and that was enough. He switched the machine back on to drown out the rest of the conversation. He knew Jane would come tell him as soon as Ed had left, and she did.

She poked her head in and said, 'That guy lodged a complaint.'

'I heard. What's the verdict?'

'I backed you up. You're clear.'

Ben could only stare at her. He was just so relieved.

'Go grab some chow why don't you? Don't worry about that guy.'

'Thanks, Jane,' he said. 'Thanks, eh?'

The cafeteria was packed with the usual end of day rush. People sat shoulder to shoulder at the long tables. There were families and older couples and packs of teenagers and larger groups of schoolkids. Jackets hung dripping on benches and off the backs of chairs. The laminate floor was slick with slush and melted snow, and a haze of grease hung over the grill at the back. Ben got in line behind two boys in ski suits who were swatting and poking each other. They couldn't stop giggling.

'You bailed so huge!' one said.

'Whatever,' his friend answered. 'I'd rather bail than wuss out.'

The food was sitting in steel serving trays under heat lamps. Ben loaded up his plate with fries and peas and chicken nuggets, then waited in another line to flash his staff pass at the cashier, who waved him through. He found a spare seat and sat down next to some girls about his age. One of them glanced at him and said something and the others giggled, but he ignored them. He was burning out and had a bad case of the munchies and didn't want to do anything except eat, which he did quickly and mechanically – raising and lowering his fork, shovelling back mouthful after mouthful. The food was old but still good and greasy. As he was eating like that, behind him he heard two voices emerging from the background noise.

'Can I have some fries, Dad?'

'Eat your sandwich.'

'I ate my sandwich.'

'What's that, then?'

Ben didn't have to turn around to know who it was. He put down his fork and glanced towards the door. People were passing in and out. He could see the glare of the sun on the snow, white and pure as icing sugar. He pushed his plate to one side and pressed his palms onto the tabletop, ready to stand up and go. Then he just stayed like that. Not moving.

'Can I have some for my birthday?'

'Be quiet now, Michael.'

'But Dad—'

'What did I say?'

There was scuffling, followed by a muted whine.

'Dad – that hurts.'

Ben turned around in his seat to look. Schroeder had Michael by the back of the neck – gripping it with one hand. As he spoke he shook his son to drive the points home. In the din and chaos of the cafeteria nobody else had noticed and if they had Ben doubted it would have mattered. It was the kind of shit that went on every day, everywhere.

'You have been misbehaving ever since we got here, haven't you?'

'I'm sorry...'

Ben stood and picked up his tray. He was going to walk back to the rentals shop and lock himself in the workroom and turn on the sharpening machine and spend the rest of the day holed up in there, grinding edges, drowning out everything else with the sound. That was what he intended to do. But when he moved instead of heading towards the door he was walking over to them, up to their table. He dropped his tray, with its half-finished plate of food, down in front of Michael.

'Here, buddy – I'm done. You can have mine.'

It wasn't much. Just this pile of tangled fries, smeared with ketchup. Schroeder stared at it, then up at Ben as if he couldn't quite understand what was happening. He still had his hand on Michael's neck. He seemed to remember that, and released it. Pushing back his chair, he slowly stood up, so that he and Ben were facing each other across the table.

'What is this?' he said.

'I just heard him say he wanted some fries.'

'Take your goddamn plate away.'

'Or what? You'll lodge another complaint?'

Schroeder swept the plate off the table with his forearm. The plate shattered and nuggets went skittering across the floor. Up until then the confrontation had gone unnoticed, but the crash cut through the cafeteria racket: conversations tapered off, and people stopped eating to watch. Amid the silence Ben heard a familiar buzzing sound, soft and persistant.

'I don't know what you're doing,' Schroeder said, 'or think you're doing, but now's the time for you to walk away.' He leaned across the table, his whole face quivering. Ben stared at those spots of blood in Schroeder's bad eye. They looked even bigger now – as if they were spreading. 'Do you hear me? Just go away.'

Ben didn't go away and he didn't say anything; the noise in his head had crescendoed to a drone, as loud as the grinding disc, so loud he couldn't even hear what Schroeder was saying. His mouth was still moving, flapping on the hinge of his jaw, but all that came out were these faint murmuring noises. Ben stood there without hearing until Schroeder shouted something that reached him mutedly, as if from underwater.

'What are you, some kind of retard?'

As he said 'retard' he poked Ben hard in the chest. That was when the roaring in his head broke like a wave and the tension inside him uncoiled and he reached for Schroeder and grabbed him by the shirt and tried to pull him forward, but the table between them got in the way, and Schroeder was squirming and struggling and all Ben could do was sort of shove Schroeder's face down against the tabletop and hit him like that, the punches glancing off the back of his scalp.

Then Ben was being dragged back by somebody: two cooks from the cafeteria had him by the arms and he strained against them, struggling to break free and go again, and he didn't stop straining until he heard a plaintive voice, from just behind him, saying, 'Leave my dad alone. Please don't hurt my dad.'

Ben let up and went limp. The two guys guided him to a chair and eased him down, and the crowd pressed in around them. A handful of people went to help Schroeder. He was up, now, and bleeding from his nose. He started yelling about getting Ben fired and pressing charges and suing the whole fucking mountain. As this went on Ben sat with his head down and his elbows resting on his knees and his hands cupped in front of him. He was quivering and the front two knuckles on his right hand were purplish and split and already starting to swell. He knew that Michael was standing off to his left but he didn't look that way for a long time. When he finally did, Michael flinched and stepped back, towards his father.

Scrap Iron

Me and Wilbur are crouched in a pit the size of a shallow grave, dug into the sand and gravel beside the boathouse. There's no boat in the boathouse. It's more of a shack, really. The company rents it to a fisherman we call Chinese Henry who keeps his crab traps and lobster pots in there. The shack's crooked and rickety and looks ready to collapse, teetering above us on rotten pilings. Beyond them, the reflection of our ice barge, the *Arctic King*, wavers in the shallows. The air around us is filled with gnats and flies, engaged in an endless dogfight, and every so often one detaches from the fray to dive-bomb me or Wilbur. The stench down here is something terrible. It must be all those crab traps, baking in the heat of the shack.

'What a shitshow,' Wilbur says. 'What a total shitshow.'

He picks up his magnet and shoves it into the sand. They gave us both magnets – these big red horseshoe-shaped magnets, like the kind you see in cartoons. We're using them to poke and comb through the sand, picking up old bolts and screws and washers and ingots. We shake the scrap metal into a bucket, banging our magnets against the side to clear them off. It's like being a beachcomber – except without the hope of finding anything valuable.

'Of all the jobs they ever saddled me with,' Wilbur says, 'this tops it.'

Wilbur's the deckhand from our sister barge, the *Icecap Rider*. For about a week near the end of season they moor up alongside us, at an old dock near the Westco shipyards. The two crews work together, cleaning the barges and offloading supplies, before a tug comes to tow the *Icecap* further up Burrard Inlet.

'Yeah,' I say. 'They sure stuck it to us this time.'

'They stuck it *in* us this time, more like it. Fucked us royally.'

Back in the day, the fishing company we work for dumped all this scrap iron along the shore, right next to our dock. It was their land and I guess they figured nobody would complain. They didn't, either. Except, twenty years on, that iron is starting to rust, and some guy from Environment Canada has detected the run-off – traces of iron oxide, leeching into the water. It didn't take him long to find the source, and contact the company. Roger woke me up early this morning, to break the bad news. At least he had the decency to call it that. He said, 'Seems like they want somebody to clean it up. All that iron.' By 'somebody' he meant me and Wilbur.

'The thing that gets me,' Wilbur says, shaking off his magnet, 'is that I know they're sitting up in the barge, drinking coffee and watching TV. Sitting on their asses.'

'Roger's oiling the chains in the ice bin.'

'Shit – I know that,' Wilbur says. 'I wasn't talking about Roger. I meant Bob and Mabel. It would take a cattle prod to get them off their asses these days.'

Bob is Wilbur's boss, the skipper of the other barge. He runs it with his wife Mabel – just like Roger and Doreen run ours. All four of them are well into their sixties.

I say, 'Guess they're getting older.'

'They should fucking retire, then.'

Wilbur tosses his magnet down in disgust. He's a lanky guy with thick-rimmed glasses, held together by a piece of white tape on the nose-bridge. His hair is thinning and stringy, like the silken tufts on the tips of corncobs, and he always wears the same plaid shirt and tattered pair of jeans, whatever the weather or temperature. Today it's about twenty-five degrees and climbing. His face is already shiny with sweat, which the dust sticks to like make-up powder.

'Hell – I'll retire myself if they keep giving me jobs like this.'

He says it like he means it, but I can't really imagine him quitting. He's worked on the *Icecap* for years. I get the impression that he's vaguely related to Bob and Mabel in some way – a nephew or a cousin or something. It's hard to tell. Maybe it just seems like that because the three of them have been stuck with each other for so long.

'Hopefully we'll get it licked this afternoon,' I say.

'You kidding? We'll be here for days. Look at all this.'

I don't need to look. Our little sand pit seems to just keep getting bigger and bigger, the sides crumbling like a shale slope – each layer revealing more scrap iron to be removed. I don't know how we're supposed to clear it all out. It could go on forever.

'What would you do?' I ask him. 'If you quit, I mean.'

He pokes at the sand with his magnet, looking for answers there.

'Get a cabin up north. Could maybe grow some weed or something.'

That's all he says, and for awhile we work in silence. I can hear a helicopter circling overhead. Probably a traffic chopper eyeing up the Lions Gate Bridge. In the shadow of the boathouse our family of ducks – seven in all – are squawking away. Roger will be happy to know they're doing well, especially since we had to wait so long for them to arrive this year.

'Jesus,' Wilbur says, stretching his back. 'I'm dying, here.'

By that point, our bucket is almost half-full. It takes both of us to lift it up and carry it to the parking lot in front of Chinese Henry's shack. Our rental truck is parked up there, the flatbed already covered with a rusty mound of scrap metal. We empty our latest load onto the pile – the bolts and nuts rasping out of the bucket and clanking atop the rest. For a minute or so we take a breather. Just slump against the tailgate and stare out at the dock. Next to it, the two barges are nestled side by side like bloated geese, resting in the shelter of the harbour.

'I'm thinking of quitting, too,' I tell him.

'Yeah?'

'Might go see a girl I know, in Wales. On a working-break kind of thing.'

'Can't be any worse than this.' He yawns and checks his watch, rubbing grime off the face so he can read the digital display. 'Speaking of breaks, reckon it's time for ours.'

He goes to fetch two cans of Coke from the fridge on the back deck of the *Arctic King*. I stay up by the truck, walking in circles and stretching my legs, wondering if I'll manage to do it – if I'll actually get my shit together and go to Wales. When Wilbur comes back, we crack open our cans and hunker down in the shade of the boathouse. A breeze is wafting in off the water, fanning my face, and with my eyes half-closed I sit listening to the tinny noise of Henry's radio. He's hard at work up there, mumbling to himself in Cantonese. Or Mandarin. I think it might be Mandarin, but I've never asked where he's from. I should. I should ask him what it's like to leave home. He'd probably just smile and nod. That's all he ever does, really. He doesn't speak much English.

While we're resting like that, Bob happens to waddle up from the dock to the parking lot. In passing, all he sees is the two of us drinking pop, slacking off in the shade.

'Hey!' he calls. 'Looks like you guys got it pretty good, eh?'

He's this big guy with an enormous potbelly, one of those potbellies that balloons out, pregnant with lard, right above the waist. I sort of grin and wave him off. He doesn't really mean anything by it – he knows we got a raw deal – but of course Wilbur is raging.

'Plenty of room for you over here, Bob!' he yells back.

Bob doesn't hear, or pretends not to. He's getting in his car, an old Pontiac saloon, and shutting the door. As he drives off, Wilbur slams down his can of Coke. It bounces once and lays there, fizzing brown froth. Then he grabs his magnet and stabs it into the dirt, over and over, as if he's trying to kill something underneath.

'That fat bastard,' he mutters. 'Show him. Get off his fat ass.'

I sip my Coke, watching, waiting for it to blow over.

'You know what?' Wilbur says, and jabs at his can. It's not magnetic and won't pick up, so he starts poking it around, leaving a slug-trail of pop. 'I'm through taking his shit.'

'You gonna grow your weed?'

'To hell with growing weed. I don't need another job. I'll go on E.I. for awhile. Rake in a fat pay check for sitting on my ass. See what that's like for a change.'

He flips the can up, chipping it towards me. It lands between us in the sand.

'I got a friend who done that,' I say. 'Good money.'

'Damn right. I would have left already, if it weren't for Jane.'

Jane is Don and Mabel's daughter. This farm girl who works on their barge as a deckhand every season. Lean and tough and tanned. The only woman we see for months at a time. The only one that counts as a woman, anyways. I catch glimpses of her whenever our barges cross paths, but Wilbur gets to work with her throughout the season.

'I mean, without me who would help her? They'd make her do everything.' He shakes his head, as if it's a bona fide tragedy. 'They'd drive her like a mule.'

'If you left they'd probably hire somebody else.'

'No,' Wilbur says. 'They couldn't do that. No way.'

He's resting his elbows on his knees, now, staring at that can. And as he stares he starts telling me about this time, during herring season, when he took Jane out in the skiff.

'It was during a lull – one of those long lulls that bores you to hell.'

I know exactly what he's talking about. There's always a rush to get our barges out to sea. Tugs tow them hundreds of miles up Georgia Straight. We drop anchor near the tip of Vancouver Island, and start making the ice. Everything's got to be ready. A few skippers might stop by for a smattering of ice, to chill their holds. But after that, it can take days – weeks even – before the herring season opens, before the boats come back for water and ice and temperature readings. Hurry up and wait, Roger calls it. He and I kill that time doing woodwork: cutting patterns with his scroll saw, carving salad spoons and forks, making fruit bowls and candle lanterns and napkin holders. Roger likes to have a project.

'Took some crab traps with us,' Wilbur says. 'Just as an

excuse, you know. Drove Jane way out into the middle of the bay, away from the barge and all the boats, away from everything. Then I cut the engine and let us drift. "Hear that?" I asked her. So she goes, "Hear what?" And I just look at her and say, "Exactly." How do you like that? Exactly!'

Wilbur's told me this story before, and I know that's the whole point – the punchline. So I grin like he expects me to, and tell him that it's really something. Wilbur just nods and gazes past the pilings to the flickering water, as if he's spotted something important out there.

'I bet Jane likes me,' he says. 'You think maybe she'd go out with me?'

I've seen the guys Jane dates. They pick her up some nights during the pre-season, when we're moored here in Vancouver. They're all big men who wear big boots and drive big trucks. The last one worked on the rigs, I think – the kind of guy who wouldn't so much as glance at Wilbur, let alone see him as a threat. I don't know how to answer him, so I make this sound in my throat and stare at the ground, like I'm still considering his question. Next to his can I notice this slender piece of metal, exposed by our digging. I bend down to pick it up, and find that it's a loop of cable, half-buried in the ground.

'Hey,' I say, 'what the hell?'

I tug on the cable. It's maybe an inch thick, with fine strands woven together like a rope. I stand up, grab it with both hands, and give it a good yank. The loop comes free, and now we can see that it's connected to a longer line. A section rises up like a snake emerging from the sand, shaking off dust. I tug loose about two or three feet before it gets stuck again. The rest is buried deep. Wilbur, who's on his feet now, comes around to join me.

'Let's see what we got,' he says.

Together, the two of us take hold of the loop and really haul on it, throwing all our weight against it, leaning way back on our heels. The cable slithers out a little more, but it looks as if the length we've freed is just the beginning. There's more to come – except it's not coming. We reef and yank for a good five minutes, like two guys playing tug-of-war with themselves. By the end our hands are raw and we're both panting, sweating, fuming.

'This sucker's huge,' Wilbur says.

'It's the mother load, all right.'

'Worth all the ingots and bolts combined.' He pauses, wiping his brow. 'It's got to be the real culprit, here. If we get it out, we're done. The rest of this crap can probably stay.'

'Shit,' I say. 'I hadn't thought of that.'

He grabs at the cable again and gives it a quick jerk, like he's hoping to catch it off-guard, take it by surprise. But it doesn't budge. For awhile we pace around, eyeing it up.

'We could dig it out,' Wilbur says, 'with shovels.'

We get the shovels from the barge – the same shovels we use to clear ice from the ice bins at the end of the season. On the way back, we pass Chinese Henry working in front of his shack. Half a dozen crab traps are strewn around him, in need of mending. He's scrawny as a scarecrow, draped in baggy blue coveralls, and to shade his face from the sun he wears a straw cowboy hat, tatty and riddled with holes, as if rats have been chewing at it.

'Hot enough for you?' Wilbur calls to him.

Henry just smiles and nods, like always. I can't tell if he gets the joke.

Back in the pit, before we take on the cable, we stand over it and eye it up. I like the feel of the shovel in my hand, the weight of it. Wilbur uses his to prod at the cable – as if he expects it to react in some way.

'We'll get her out of there,' he says. 'No problem.'

Together we set to work, digging a trench on either side of the cable. We take turns ramming our shovels into the gravel. Each impact jars my wrist, rattles in my skull. We strike at the ground again and again – setting off sparks whenever our shovel blades hit a larger stone. Every so often one of us puts down our shovel to tug on the cable, and each time a bit more slides free. For a while it feels as if we're making progress – real progress – until my shovel comes down with a hard 'thock' that I feel right through to my jaw.

'Damn,' I say, dropping it and shaking out my hand.

We poke around a bit. Testing. Under the ground there's something big and solid. Wilbur shears more dirt away with his shovel, and I get down to dig with my hands. It takes us a few minutes of delicate work to reveal the stump. It's about five feet across, lying on its side, with a snarl of roots sprouting out one end. The remains of an old oak or sycamore tree, maybe. Leftover from when they cleared the shoreline. The cable's all wrapped and tangled around it – almost as if somebody was trying to use it to drag the stump loose, and gave up.

'Well,' Wilbur says. 'Now we're really screwed.'

We squat down in the sand, panting. I've taken off my shirt and can feel the sun searing my back, my neck, my scalp. A fly settles on my forearm, drawn by the sweat, and I swat it away. We stare at the stump. It's huge and greyish-white and looks like a fossil that we've partially unearthed. Maybe the bone of a dinosaur that died a million years ago.

'Shovels aren't gonna do it.'

Wilbur snorts. 'That's the truth.'

'What about the forklift?' I say. Roger keeps a forklift in the company shed, next to Chinese Henry's shack. 'We could use it to haul this sucker out.'

We look at each other, and Wilbur punches me in the shoulder.

'Damn straight. Use it like a tractor. Think Roger will let us?'

'Probably. If I explain it to him.'

I go looking for Roger alone, since he's not so keen on Wilbur. I check the ice bin first, but Roger's finished his work in there. So I clamber up to the galley to ask Doreen. She tells me he's down in the aft hold, adjusting the pump that was acting up all through herring season. Back there the hatch is open, and the air rising out stinks of stale oil. I squat down above it and peer in. I can see Roger lying on his side. In the dark he's just a shadow, silhouetted by a work lamp. Instead of calling down to him, I crouch and watch him work. He's struggling with something – turning a valve with a pipe wrench, by the looks of it – and grunting every so often. He's having a time of it, and for a second, seeing that, I'm convinced that I'll stay. Stick it out on the barge, to help Roger. At least until he retires. Even if we end up like Rob and Wilbur, snarling and spitting at one another. A pair of polecats trapped in the same cage.

'You need a hand, Roger?' I say, raising my voice.

'I got it, greenhorn,' he yells, and rolls over. A shaft of light from the open hatch catches his face, which is smudged with grime. He squints up at me. 'How you getting on?'

'We're a bit stuck out here, Roger.'

He stops what he's doing and lies there listening as I explain the situation to him. He gives me permission to use the forklift, but I can't tell if he thinks it's a good idea. He's been hard to read, lately – ever since I finally mentioned that I might not be back next season.

'Just stay out of the bite,' he tells me.

Roger always worries about the bite – the area where a snapped cable is most likely to recoil. He lost a crewmember one year, in the days when he worked on the seine boats. A tie line broke in a storm, and whipped right back at the guy standing beside Roger. Broke his neck. Nearly tore his head off. Ever since then Roger's had this paranoia of the bite – a paranoia he's passed on to me.

When I trudge back up the gangplank, Wilbur's waiting for me at the edge of the parking lot. 'And?' he asks.

'We got it.'

He whoops and punches the air. Neither of us has a forklift license, but we've both driven it before. During pre-season, we use it to lift palettes of supplies off the delivery trucks. Together, we head over to the shed and throw open the doors. The forklift is waiting in the middle of the floor. The grill is black with oil, and in places the yellow paint is peeling and flaking away like sunburnt skin. I hop up into the driver's cage and start the engine. It coughs diesel fumes and the whole frame starts shuddering, raring to go. As I back her out, Henry stands up to watch. I salute him, pivot the forklift around, then rumble past his crab traps. Beneath the wheels, bits of gravel pop and crackle and spit out backwards. I ease the forklift into place at the edge of the parking lot, as close to the sand pit as I can get.

Wilbur meets me there with a chain and some tie lines – sturdy lengths of three-core nylon rope. I hop down, putting the brake on and leaving the forklift running, and we discuss our various options. We could use the tie lines as tow ropes, but the stump is stuck so fast the lines would probably snap before it came free. It makes more sense to use the chain. The only problem is attaching it to the cable. We decide to use the tie lines as links – lashing one end of the chain to the loop in the cable, and the other end to the back of the forklift. There's no hitch, since forklifts aren't supposed to be used for towing. So instead we tie the rope to the bars of the carriage guard, weaving it between them five or six times for added strength.

'She looks solid,' I say, reefing on the chain.

Wilbur's already climbing into the driver's seat. I stand to one side, making sure I'm out of the bite. He pulls on a lever to lower the forks. Then he puts her in gear. The forklift inches ahead until the slack goes out of the chain and the cable stretches taut, quivering like an elastic. Wilbur half-turns around in his seat and leans out the window to get a better view.

'Keep your head inside,' I shout. 'You're right in the bite.'

He looks at me blankly.

'If something snaps, the chain is going to whip back at the forklift.'

He holds up a hand and withdraws, turtle-like. I don't see him give it more gas, but the forklift lurches forward, straining. I watch the cable. A section slips free, then another. Each time, the forklift gains a bit more ground: lurching and stopping, lurching and stopping. Then it just stops. I can see the whole line – rope and chain and cable – quivering with the reverberations of the engine. But that stump is holding fast. Wilbur gives her a bit more juice, and the forklift wheels start to spin – slipping on the dirt and gravel in the parking lot.

'Hold up, Wilbur,' I call to him, raising a hand. 'It's not working.'

He lets the engine idle for a second, and when he does the

cable actually retracts from the tension, drawing the forklift backwards a foot. I stand with my hands on my hips, looking at the stump, the cable, the chain, the forklift. I've still got my shirt off and I can feel the slap of the sun on my shoulders. In my work boots my socks are squishy with sweat. Henry has come to this side of his boathouse to watch us. There's a wooden railing up there and he's leaning on it, his face shadowed by his big straw hat. I can tell he's still smiling, though.

'What if I hit it harder?' Wilbur says.

'Like with a burst of gas?'

'Uh-huh – just give her.'

'I don't know, man. Seems sketchy.'

'It's all good. Watch.'

He stands up and guns the engine. The forklift pitches forward, like a horse throwing itself into the harness. The line goes taut and the stump seems to tremble.

'I think that did something,' I yell at him.

He eases up on the throttle, letting the line slacken, and then hits it again, and again – yanking on the cable, jarring the stump. It's working, too. The stump shifts and shivers in the dirt and looks ready to rear up, roaring, like a prehistoric beast. Seeing that, Wilbur starts hitting the gas even harder, and each time the forklift lunges ahead I swear I can feel the force of the impact trembling through the ground. I can see it, too. Not just in the stump, but in the dirt, the gravel, the pilings. The whole area is quivering with aftershocks.

'Hold up there, Wilbur,' I call.

He pretends not to hear. He's working the forklift like a rocking horse, forward and back, stuck in a rhythmic trance. His glasses are all fogged up, so I can't even see his eyes. I wave my arms above my head, trying to get his attention. On the other side, Henry is doing the same thing and shouting at him in Mandarin. I think I know what he's trying to tell us.

'It's stuck in the pilings, Wilbur!' I shout. 'The boathouse pilings!'

He seems to hear, but he still doesn't look at me, still doesn't stop.

'Fuck it,' he yells. 'Something's gotta give!'

And he hits it one more time, full throttle. The engine roars as the forklift hurdles forward, belching black smoke. The cable line goes taut and the stump actually moves and for a split second I think he's done it – he's torn that sucker free. Then I hear the distinctive crack of splitting wood, and this deafening moan, like the wail of a dying elephant. I don't see the recoil of the chain as one of the tie lines breaks – it's too fast – but I see the rear piling on the boathouse topple over gently, slumping into the mud along the shore. The floor it was supporting comes down next, bringing the back wall with it. That whole section tears away with surprising neatness, as if the shack has been cut in half by a giant axe. The wall and floor collapse into our gravel pit, splintering and breaking apart. The impact kicks up a mushroom cloud of dust.

Then everything goes quiet.

The forklift is lying on its side. The sudden release of tension, combined with the recoil of the chain, must have knocked it over. I walk up to the cab. I have this vision in my head – this vision of opening the door and finding Wilbur lying there, headless, a victim of the bite. Blood still spurting from his stump neck. And when I peer inside, I do see blood – but only on his forehead. Other than that he's fine, curled up in the overturned cab, looking as stunned as me. The door won't open so I help him out through the window.

'Oh, shit,' he whispers, when he sees what we've done. 'Oh, shit.'

Neither of us says anything else. We trudge back to the gravel pit, moving like the survivors of a plane crash, to examine the wreckage left behind. The floor and wall of the boathouse has formed a perfect pyramid – almost temple-like – over our stump, which looks as stuck as ever. We squat down outside it, huddled together like penitents. I hear a whoop from above us. Henry is up there, standing at the hole we've torn in his boathouse. Behind him are crab traps and lobster pots, stacked as neat as Lego blocks, and a light bulb dangles from the ceiling on bare wires, knocked loose in the accident. He doesn't look as pissed as I expect. He's laughing, actually – laughing so hard he can barely breathe. Every so often he stops and points at us and shouts something in Mandarin, which makes him roar even louder.

I don't understand any of it.

There's a War Coming

It was past midnight on a Friday and there were only six customers left in the restaurant: an elderly English couple, three Korean businessmen, and the American actor who had been causing problems all night. He had broken a champagne flute and sent back his bison steak and gotten in an argument with his female companion. After an extended bout of yelling and swearing, she'd dumped a glass of Perrier over his head and walked out; now he was sitting alone on the patio, smoking a cigar. He was being observed from inside by Seb and Hamed. They were both standing at the rear busser station, leaning against the bar as they watched the actor through one of the windows that looked out on the patio, and the harbour beyond.

'He's our real worry,' Hamed said. 'He'll be here all night.'

'He better not be.'

'Two o'clock, easy.'

'I'm beat, man.'

It had been a manic night; the restaurant had been packed and they'd turned over three hundred tables. Now everything had settled into that certain stillness that came at the end of a shift: the kitchen cool and cleanly metallic, the tables stripped and reset in preparation for the morning. All the servers had been sent home, and all the kitchen staff, too. Only he and Hamed were left, and their manager, César, who was in the back counting the cash.

'We should have kicked him out,' Hamed said.

'César knows where his bread's buttered.'

A few of the other customers had complained about the actor's antics. One couple had even left without finishing their meal.

'Those people were regulars. And good tippers.'

'They don't rack up six hundred dollar tabs, though.'

'True that.' Hamed had a toothpick in the corner of his mouth. He was gnawing on one end, grinding it between his molars. 'I bet you he pays in cash. Yankee dollars.'

'He was bragging about staying in the penthouse at the Metropolitan.'

'He must have dropped a few bills on that prostie, too.'

It took Seb a moment to realize Hamed was talking about the actor's date. She had been wearing a strapless blue dress, and she'd been very pleasant to him when he'd brought the bread and water and tabernad to their table. She had told him that it all looked delightful.

Seb said, 'She was pretty nice.'

'Well, she sure wasn't his wife.'

'Didn't something happen with his wife?'

'She reported him for beating her up.'

'That's it.'

'But they dropped the charges.'

'Because he's famous, probably.'

'Or he paid her off.'

They were talking without looking at each other; they were both still looking at the actor. His head and torso were framed perfectly by the window, and it was as if they were watching him through a television screen.

'Have you seen his new show?' Seb asked.

'I saw the first episode.'

'What's it like?'

'The same as the other one.' Hamed turned the toothpick over with his tongue. 'He plays an old, washed-up cop.'

From behind them came the sound of the kitchen service door swinging open and shut on its springs and they both looked back. César had appeared. He was a small man – as short as Hamed, but not as muscular – and he had a goatee and a smoothly shaved scalp that shone like mahogany under the restaurant lights. He spotted them standing there and started towards them. They straightened up. Seb clipped his bowtie back on and Hamed took the toothpick out of his mouth.

'Hands and feet,' César said. 'What have I told you about your hands and feet?'

Seb had begun wiping down the bar top. 'To keep them moving.'

Hamed said, 'We've done everything. We're just waiting for people to clear out.'

César glanced around. Seb knew he was looking for something amiss, something to catch them out on, but there was nothing; all the tables were set, all the chairs in place. The bar had been bleached and wiped down, the wine glasses polished to the point of gleaming.

'The customers aren't paying to see you stand around. Go ask if they want anything.'

'They don't want anything.'

'How do you know, Hamed? Are you telepathic, now?'

'The oldies and the suits have already had their bills.'

César jerked his chin towards the actor. 'What about Mr Hollywood?'

Seb said, 'I'll go see.'

He folded his napkin and adjusted his apron and went out to the patio. It was on a balcony that overlooked Coal Harbour. From that side you could see across to Stanley Park, and the marina, which was full of yachts, sailboats, and pleasure cruisers, all sitting still in their births. Some of the cabin lights were on, and the reflections wavered blurrily in the black water of the harbour. It was late August, tourist season, and the air was heavy with humidity and the rich stink of the sea. There was no sign yet that autumn was on its way.

The actor was sitting at one of the central tables. Seb knew César was watching through the window, so he did everything as they'd been trained: he strode over with the napkin draped on his left forearm, which was braced against his abdomen, and asked the actor if they could get him anything else. The actor gazed at him dopily. His eyes were bloodshot, his hair tousled, his collar crumpled.

'Another drink, perhaps?'

The actor looked down into his highball glass, as if considering it, then back up.

'Are you a socialist?' the actor asked.

'I don't think so.'

'You either are or you aren't.'

'I guess I'm not, then.'

'I'm thinking of moving up here. Too many damn socialists in America, these days. Socialists and communists and liberal queers. Pretty soon they'll be painting the place red.'

'Canada's pretty liberal, too.'

'Is that so?'

'Yes sir.'

'Get me another goddamned drink, then.'

'Do you have a particular preference, sir?'

'Do you have a particular preference, sir?' the actor repeated, mimicking his tone. Then he made a face and laughed. 'You'll never get anywhere acting so diplomatic, kid.'

'I'm just doing my job.'

'Well, do your job.'

'Whatever you say.'

'I'm just messing with you, kid. Get me a bourbon. And nothing cheap.'

Seb nodded and turned and went back inside, still holding his arm across his stomach like a marching soldier. César had waited to hear the outcome. When Seb told them that the actor wanted a bourbon, something expensive, César snapped his fingers and pointed at Hamed. 'There you go,' he said. 'The man wants a drink.'

'He'll drink in here till dawn, if we let him.'

'And if that's the case, you'll serve him till dawn.' César pinched all the fingers of his right hand together, holding them up as if displaying a gem. 'That's what you do. You serve. You're servants. *Comprenez-vous*?'

Hamed didn't answer. He didn't look away, either.

'Now get him some bourbon.'

César stood and glared until Hamed took down a bottle of Pappy Van Winkle's and measured out two ounces in one of the stainless steel shot glasses. He dumped it neat into a tumbler, the amber liquid sloshing smoothly, and placed the glass on a tray for Seb to carry out. César grunted, satisfied, and turned to go. As he walked off, he called back, 'And bring one to me while you're at it.'

Hamed got down another tumbler. 'Goddamn César.'

'He's too sober tonight. Stiffen that up.'

'Don't tell me what to do.'

'I just meant he's more likely to make nice when he's got his drink on.'

'Take that out to Hollywood, why don't you?'

Seb shrugged and palmed the tray and returned to the patio. The actor was leaning back in his chair, smoking another cigar. Seeing Seb, the actor grinned and blew a smoke-ring towards him. To Seb it smelled rich and foreign and exotic, something that he didn't have access to and probably never would.

'It's the diplomat.'

'I've got a diploma, all right.'

The actor guffawed. 'You bring my drink, diplomat?'

Seb put the whiskey on the table.

'What is it?'

'Pappy Van Winkle's. It's good stuff.'

'I know what Pappy is. Tell me something, kid – whose side are you on?'

Seb said that he didn't know. He didn't know what the actor was talking about.

'There's a war coming, sooner or later. And everyone will have to pick sides. You're either with us or against us. America's got a lot of enemies out there.' The actor held up his glass, considering it. It was a very rehearsed gesture, and Seb felt as if he had stepped onto the set of one of the actor's movies, as an extra or walk-on part. 'And enemies inside, too. They're the worst. But when it all goes down, you'll have to choose, kid. Think about it.'

'I will, sir.'

'You do that. I want an answer.'

On the actor's table were a few empty glasses, a cup and saucer, and a coffee press, down to the dregs. Seb cleared those away and carried them back inside. Behind the bar was a glass washer, which he placed the glassware in and then turned on. The conveyor belt slid into motion and the heat and steam started up, smelling faintly of bleach. As he was waiting for the cycle to finish, Hamed came out from the back. He stood beside Seb and said nothing and they both gazed down at the machine. When the cycle finished Seb took out a wine glass and began polishing it with his napkin. Hamed took the other. While the two of them worked, the English couple gathered their things and left, leaving their bill holder folded shut on the table. Seb went to clear it, flipped it open to check the tip, and wandered back with it.

'How'd we do?' Hamed asked.

'Ten bucks and shrapnel.'

'Typical.' Hamed took the bill holder from him, and asked, 'You want a drink?'

'Did César say we could?'

'Forget César. I'm the bartender.'

'I'll have a beer, then.'

Hamed pulled two sleeves of Cream Ale and handed one to Seb. The glasses were kept in a freezer below the bar, so they were coated in a glaze of frost. Seb took a sip and made a satisfied sound and pressed the glass to his forehead. It felt like an icepack. They carried their drinks down to the busser station, and stood with their backs to the kitchen, in case César came out again. As they sipped their beers, it seemed natural to gaze at the actor.

'What was Hollywood saying?' Hamed asked.

'He kept talking about socialists. He thinks they're taking over America.'

'They should.'

'He says he's immigrating to Canada.'

'With his record? Yeah, right.'

'I thought they dropped the charges.'

'There was a bunch of other stuff. Drunk and disorderly, resisting arrest.' Hamed took a swig of beer, smacked his lips, and peered into the froth as if he could taste something a bit off. 'And didn't he get busted for shouting racist slurs at some cops?'

'I don't know about that.'

'The guy's lost it.'

'He's a good actor, though.'

'He used to be.'

What Seb didn't admit to Hamed was that he had admired the actor at one time, and watched all of his films. It hadn't been all that long ago – when Seb was in his early teens – but back then the actor had been at his peak. He'd made a career out of playing good, honest men: all-American heroes. He had foiled bomb plots and fought terrorists on home soil and flown fighter jets in top-secret operations. Now he was sitting in their restaurant acting like a jackass, and Seb was embarrassed for both the actor and himself, for ever having been a fan.

'What a poor bastard,' he said.

'Poor nothing. He's rolling in it.'

'The poor rich bastard, then.'

'Look at that.'

The actor had reached over to ash out his cigar, and nearly fallen out of his chair. He managed to catch himself, but in doing so dropped his cigar. It lay on the floor, smouldering.

'I wish he *had* fallen,' Hamed said.

'And knocked himself out.'

'Then we could go home.'

'Who'd cover his tab?'

'We'd charge his credit card, and throw him in a cab.'

The actor seemed to sense their scrutiny. He twisted in his chair and peered at them through the window – as if he was looking out of the screen-world in which he lived. Then he held up his empty glass and waggled it from side to side, demanding service.

'Look at this prick,' Hamed said.

He reached for the bottle of Pappy, and splashed some in a fresh tumbler. As Seb slid it onto his tray, Hamed said, 'Tell him it's the last one. We're closing up shop.'

'César will flip.'

'César's the one who told me.'

'When did he tell you that?'

'When I took him his drink.'

'If you say so.'

Seb carried the bourbon out. When he put the drink down on the table the actor didn't even look at it; he was watching Seb's face.

'We're going to be closing up soon, sir,' Seb said.

'Don't worry about me.'

'It's last call.'

The actor picked up his bourbon and sipped at it. From the nearby tables Seb began gathering the tealights, which sat in bulb-shaped candle holders. He took each one, blew it out – the wick smouldering with that fragrant, waxy smell – and placed it on his tray.

'Have you decided?' the actor said.

Seb looked up, holding a tealight in his hand, still glowing.
'Decided what?'

'What side you're on.' When Seb didn't answer, he went on, 'When it all goes down, and the socialists attack, are you going to be with the good guys, or the bad guys?'

'The good guys, I guess.'

'You don't sound very sure.'

'I'm not sure who the good guys are.'

'Who do you think?'

'America?'

'We're always the good guys.'

Seb blew out the tealight, and added it to his tray. 'Maybe I won't be on any side. Maybe I'll just be in the middle, or neutral, or whatever you call it.'

'There's no middle ground, here. You're either with us, or against us.'

'But I'm neutral.'

'You goddamned Canadians. Grow some balls, why don't you? Being neutral is the same as being neutered. It's no better than being a socialist. Or worse – a communist. Are you a communist? You talk like a little commie. A little commie lefty. A pinko queer.'

'That's me. I'm pink as a baby blanket.'

The actor laughed. 'Pink as a baby blanket. That's good.' He patted his palm on the table, as if applauding. 'I'll have to remember that. Pink as a baby blanket. Hah! You know something, kid? You're all right. Now get the hell out of here and let me finish my drink.'

Seb continued gathering the tealights. 'We're closing up.'

'I said screw off!'

Seb left the last three tealights where they were and went

inside. Hamed watched him come up. Seb put his tray down on the marble bar. The candle holders rattled together and made a tinkling, wind chime sound.

'What did he say?'

Seb tried to laugh it off. 'He called me a pinko queer.'

'He said that?'

'He doesn't know what he's saying.'

'He better not say anything like that to me. Goddamn Yank.'

'It's just talk.'

'That's how it starts.'

Hamed plucked the toothpick from his mouth and studied the end. He'd gnawed it to shreds. He turned it around and started on the other side.

Seb said, 'I don't think he'll leave.'

'We'll see.'

They stood and watched the actor through his television-window. The three Korean businessmen got up and gathered their things and left. Then it was just the two of them and the actor and this stand-off. The actor seemed to know it, too. He raised his glass and put it to his lips and tipped it back, slowly and deliberately, draining the bourbon. Afterwards, he held up the empty glass and made that same waggling gesture, without bothering to look at them.

'There you go,' Seb said.

'I got it.'

Hamed took his toothpick and flicked it towards the sink. Then he walked around the bar and out to the patio. He was a short-legged man, and when he was incensed, like now, he moved with a certain waddling swagger, like a wrestler approaching the ring.

Seb stayed at the busser station and watched. Hamed went up to the actor's table, and stood with his arms crossed and said something. The actor said something back. Seb could hear the muted sound of their voices but not the words. He saw Hamed make a spreading motion with his hands, passing them one across the other, palms down – signalling that it was all done, finished. Then some more words were exchanged, louder this time, and angrier. The actor began shouting, and pointed repeatedly at Hamed with his index finger. Hamed's expression was fixed and brittle. After a moment, he turned away and came back inside. He was smiling the oddest smile: thin-lipped, compressed, and meaningful.

'What's up?' Seb asked.

'Wait'll César hears this.'

'What?'

'He just called me a raghead.'

Seb glanced at the actor, who was watching them, and waiting.

'I guess that does it.'

'I'll say.'

Hamed was already headed for the back. Seb hustled after him: past the outer kitchen, with its wood-fired kiln, now dark and silent, and through the swinging metal service door to the inner kitchen, where the bread ovens, sinks, and dishwashing station were all situated, and around the corner to the changing rooms and the manager's office. The door was ajar. Hamed knocked and pushed it open further and stepped right in. Seb lingered on the threshold.

'We've got a little problem,' Hamed said.

César looked up. He was sitting at his desk, which was covered in piles of money and till receipts. At his elbow was a tumbler of bourbon, nearly empty, and in his hands he held a stack of twenties that he was in the process of counting – the topmost bill pinched between his thumb and forefinger. He looked like some kind of criminal kingpin.

'What?' César said.

'That Yank just called me a raghead and a sand nigger.'

Seb couldn't see Hamed's face – he was looking over his shoulder – but he could see César's and the way it changed. He pivoted halfway towards them in his swivel chair, and looked at Seb inquisitively. Seb nodded to confirm it, even though he couldn't be sure. At that point César reached for his bourbon. There were still two cubes of ice in the bottom of the glass. He made a circular motion with his hand, so the cubes spun around inside. César watched their movement, as if trying to read tea leaves. When they came to a stop he put the tumbler down and said, 'Get that *connard* out of my restaurant.'

'He won't go.'

'Make him go.' César swivelled back to his money, and receipts. 'We're closed.'

Hamed was smiling even wider, now. He inclined his upper body in a half-bow and back-stepped out of the office, pulling the door shut behind him. Then he snapped for Seb to follow him, which he did. They headed out to the busser station. The actor had lit another cigar and was oblivious to their return. Hamed reached around behind his back to untie his apron, and Seb did the same. They both laid their aprons down on the bar top, carefully folded. Then they undid the cuffs of their shirts and rolled up the sleeves to the elbow. This sort of preparation was all new to Seb. Hamed also undid the top button of his collar, but Seb left his alone.

'What are we going to do?' he asked.

'Just get him by the arms – one of us on each side – and guide him out.'

Seb nodded. He'd seen that kind of thing on TV. 'What if he puts up a fight?'

'He won't. He's drunk and old.'

Hamed led the way onto the patio, with Seb trailing a little behind. The actor heard their footsteps and looked over as they approached. He grinned at them, the cigar clenched between his teeth. He said, 'Here comes the cavalry.'

Hamed said, 'I'm afraid we're going to have to ask you to leave now, sir.'

'You can ask me whatever you like, Muzzie.'

Hamed grabbed him by the collar and yanked him out of his chair. The actor made a surprised sound and the cigar fell from his mouth, bounced once on the table, and landed on the floor in a sprinkling of sparks. Hamed got hold of one of the actor's arms and locked it in the crook of his elbow. The actor began to flail and windmill with his other hand.

'What the fuck is this shit? You can't touch me. You can't touch me.'

'Help me, here,' Hamed said.

Seb jumped in and caught the other arm, pinning it against his own chest. The actor was helpless, now. As they hauled him through the restaurant, towards the staircase that led down to the entrance, he went limp as a cat, dragging his feet against the stone tiles. He was yelling, too – asking if they knew who the hell he was, and threatening to call the cops. 'This is assault,' he kept saying, over and over. 'This is a felony!'

'We don't have felonies in Canada,' Hamed told him.

At the top of the stairs was a glass door, and Seb had to release the actor to hold it open before they could guide him through. But as soon as Hamed had him at the threshold, the actor went berserk. He began to claw and swing with his free hand, then grabbed at Hamed's face and pulled it, making the skin stretch like putty, and in return Hamed drew back and punched at him – a quick jab to the side of his jaw. Seb tried to intervene, saying something about taking it easy, but they were scuffling by then, toe-to-toe, the actor's face focused with real fury, and it actually did look like a fight scene from one of his movies, a climactic struggle, with Hamed cast as the villain, except in this case the actor was all run-down and worn-out and didn't have it in him to win. And as they tussled the actor threw a haymaker, missed, and lost his footing on the top step; he seemed to teeter there theatrically, the space around him going vertigo. Seb was standing close enough to reach out, to grab him, but didn't, and then the actor was toppling backwards, falling, tumbling down the staircase in a series of messy somersaults, and eventually coming to rest at the landing, where his head hit the hardwood and made a hollow sound, a very real sound. Not like in a film at all.

'Oh, man,' Hamed said.

The actor was lying still, one arm folded under him. From somewhere outside a horn sounded – just a little comic toot to punctuate the end of the performance. The two of them hurried down there, and crouched next to him, moving as guiltily and furtively as footpads.

'Don't move him,' Seb said.

'What are you talking about?'

'His neck might be broken.'

Seb checked for a pulse, pressing his middle finger and forefinger against the actor's throat, on the jugular. He had never done this before, and didn't know how to do it, but it was what they always did in movies, didn't they? You checked for a pulse. He couldn't feel much of anything, but at his touch the actor groaned and turned his head.

'Thank fuck,' Seb said.

He and Hamed looked at each other, with the actor sprawled between them.

Hamed said, 'We've got to get him out of here.'

'We can't just dump him outside.'

'The Metropolitan, right? You said he's staying at the Metropolitan.'

'Call a cab.'

While Hamed hustled back upstairs to get his cellphone, Seb hoisted the actor by his armpits, like they did with bodies, and dragged him through the front doors. A wide wooden walkway connected the restaurant to shore, and on it were some Yucca plants in big ceramic pots. Seb propped the actor up against one, and squatted down beside him. The movement and fresh air seemed to be reviving him: he was moaning now, and muttering incoherencies.

'Repercussions,' he said. 'There'll be repercussions.'

Hamed came back, breathing hard, and announced a cab was on its way. While they waited they worked out their story, in tense and conspiratorial tones: the actor had drunk a bit too much, and tripped coming down the stairs, and bumped his head a little. That was all.

'We were helping him out.'

'That's right. We were just helping.'

The actor mumbled belligerently, as if to contradict them, and they both went quiet, the lie hanging uneasily between them.

'Anyways,' Hamed said, scuffing his shoe on the deck, 'he deserved it.'

'He could have died, man.'

'He didn't deserve to die, but he deserved something.'

Seb shrugged and didn't argue. He was thinking back to

when it happened, and how there'd been that moment, just before, that he maybe could have done something to prevent the actor from falling. But he'd stood there, watching. Knowing what was coming.

'What's up?' Hamed asked.

'Nothing.'

'You worried he'll remember?'

'I don't know.'

There was no way he could explain it, that sense of foresight and anticipation. So they waited for the cab in silence, while the actor muttered something about the communists, and the Muslims, and them all being in it together. And in the bay the waters churned, and in the city a siren droned, and above the inlet Seb noticed a plane coming in to land, flying low, so close that he could see not only the running lights but the landing lights and some of the cabin lights, too. He watched as it slid towards the skyscrapers downtown, moving in slow-motion, and seemed to collide with an office tower, before emerging, miraculously, on the other side.

The Art of Shipbuilding

I ease forward on the throttle and spin the wheel, steering one-handed. Real lazy. My bow swings from port to starboard and back again, like a wayward weathervane trying to suss the wind. I'm chugging around the Westco marina in my garbage tug, going from boat to boat in the hope that the union guys will have a job for me – some junk or scrap to clear. There's not much. A couple of dead batteries on the *Western Tomahawk*, some cabinets from the galley in the *Cape Breton*. That's not even a full load. But there's nothing else to do today so I keep making my slow circuit of the shipyard, sometimes actually going in circles, pretending I'm in search of something. And maybe I am.

I drift on over to the east side of the marina, where Frank's working. He's the contractor who's been hired to fix up the *Chief Seattle*, one of Westco's fishing boats, before the start of salmon season in August. In the lunchroom there's always a lot of talk about Frank. The union guys, they say he lives up near Grand Forks, in a cabin he built by hand. It's totally off the grid. Powered by a generator, with a gray water system and septic tank. He's got a cabinet full of hunting rifles, a shed packed with snares and leg-traps. He kills and grows his own food, up there. He claims the Russians are still a threat and thinks the internet is alive. The guys, they make jokes about all this stuff. They say Frank's gonna go postal one day. They say he murdered his wife. They say he's crazy as a shithouse rat. But they don't say any of it to his face, and so far me and Frank have gotten along just fine. Just fine.

As I approach, I see him working on the dock next to the *Seattle*. He's a lean, limber guy who can't weigh more than one-fifty or one-sixty, soaking wet. His grey coveralls hang off him in these big baggy folds, like some kind of smock. He's hunched over a couple of sawhorses. I putt to within twenty feet and holler to him across the water.

'You got anything needs doing, Frank?'

The way I ask, it sounds a bit desperate. Pathetic, even.

Frank looks up. 'What do you know? It's Liam, the scholar. Got more dead strakes. That's a job, if you want it, scholar.'

'I want it, all right.'

I steer closer and Frank shuffles down the dock to meet me. His coveralls are all spattered with pitch and glue and tar and paint. He's even got gobs of the stuff in his hair. He looks like Pollock or Picasso, some kind of eccentric artist.

I loop my tie line into a lasso and toss it to him, letting it uncoil in the air. He snags it deftly and lashes it to a cleat. As I step on dock he nods at me, but he doesn't say anything, and I don't either. We just walk back towards the *Seattle*, where he's working. She's an eighty-six-foot seine boat, over a hundred years old, with a timber frame and carvel hull. She's really something. I don't know a thing about boats and even I can see that. But lack of upkeep in recent years means she's all shot through with dryrot. Frank's already rebuilt the bridge and cabin, and over the past few days he's started work on the hull. Today, from the starboard side, he's pulled out half a dozen rotten strakes – the wooden planks that make-up the shell of the hull, keeping the vessel afloat. The gaps stand out starkly: narrow strips of shadow running horizontally along the hull, revealing the frame beneath. They're an odd sight, those gaps. Something that should be there, but isn't. Like missing teeth.

I say, 'You been busy.'

'One of my favourite jobs, replacing strakes.'

'Easy work?'

'Hard. Real skill involved.'

The three strakes he's removed this morning are piled up on one side of the dock. They're huge pieces of timber – each one at least twenty feet long.

'Well,' I say, 'guess I'll get started on this mess.'

'Should give you a load, at least.'

With a handsaw I cut the strakes into manageable pieces, which I carry down to my tug and transfer onto the deck. Then I start sweeping up the rest of the refuse: mostly old caulking cotton and oakum and lead putty, raked out from the seams between the strakes. It's mindless work. My kind of work. As a temp without a trade, I don't do much except clean up the messes left by the union guys or the contractors like Frank.

While I sweep, I'm also watching him. I try to do this real subtle-like, without staring or looking directly at him. He's preparing the first of the replacement strakes. He has it laid across the two sawhorses as he scallops out the back and fairs up the sides, using both hands to push the planer along the wood. He's got to do this because the planks on an old carvel boat like the *Seattle* aren't straight; they're all curved to hug the frame, and each one can be bent at a different angle, and in different places, depending on its location in the hull.

I say, 'Can I ask you something?'

He takes his time in answering. He doesn't like to be disturbed, Frank.

'Go ahead.'

'How do you know how much to plane off?'

'You mark it out, some,' he says, without looking up. 'And work by feel, too. It's less like carpentry, more like dressmaking. Nothing's flush or square. You got to take into account the shape of the old girl's body, the way she'll move in the water.'

I nod, as if this makes sense to me, as if we're on the same wavelength, me and Frank. Then I go back to my cleaning. When I'm finished I stand and watch, holding my garbage bag in one hand and my dustpan in the other. As he shapes the plank, shavings of wood – wide and delicate as ribbons – curl up before the blade of the planer. Every so often Frank gently brushes one of these aside, letting it drop to the dock. His movements are confident and certain, like a sculptor carving soapstone. Eventually he notices me gawking at him.

'After lunch,' he says, 'you want to help me fit this?'

'If you don't think I'll get in the way.'

'You'll be fine. Long as you're ready to work.'

'I can handle it.'

By this point it's closing in on noon, and the union guys are already plodding up the dock, all dressed in the same blue coveralls. They always punch in and out on the dot, and count the seconds of their breaks like misers counting money. Not Frank. As a contractor, he's free to do what he wants. He doesn't take coffee breaks, and he eats his lunch on the boat. Some nights he even sleeps on the damned boat, in the cabin he's rebuilt. Says it saves him money on the costs of a hotel, and that he gets a better sleep on the water, anyways.

Today, instead of going in, I stay out on the *Seattle* to eat with Frank. I don't ask him if it's okay, but he doesn't seem to mind. We just clamber up on deck and sit perched on the starboard gunnel. For a while we chew our sandwiches in silence, the only sound the slurp of water beneath the docks and the barking croak of seagulls.

Then I ask, 'You got another job lined up after this?'

'A few. Gonna head up to my cabin, first. City's making me squirrelly.'

Frank takes a long swig of water, and I figure that's the end of our conversation. But after he swallows he adds, 'Got work out in Steveston. Doing the bridge on this old trawler. Then an engine repair on some rich prick's yacht. A few other commercial jobs, too.'

'Lots of work, eh?'

'Too much.'

Frank stands up, taking his sandwich with him. He can never sit still for long, Frank. He's noticed something on the gunnel – a bit of bubble in the paint job. He picks up a steel spatula and scrapes the paint away, revealing the crayola-orange primer beneath.

'Partly why I became a contractor in the first place. I make a killing because there's not enough hands to go around. Not enough good hands, anyway.'

'How's that?'

He hasn't sat back down. He's padding around the deck, now, restless as a hound, the sandwich hanging forgotten in one hand as he sniffs out unseen deficiencies in his girl. 'Unions are being strangled, for one. So all that work's being contracted out.'

'That why the union guys don't like you?'

'They don't like me for a lot of reasons,' he says, as if it's not important. 'On top of that, though, there's no new blood coming up. Nobody learning trades. All these young fellows your age want to be suits or desk-jockeys or pencil pushers.'

I smile. 'Or starving artists.'

'But none wanting to take the time to study a craft.'

'I hear you.' I look down at my hands, resting palm-up across my knees, like I'm wearing shackles. The palms are all sore and peeling with blisters, but in places the blisters have started to turn into calluses. 'We all got big ideas for ourselves, I guess.'

'You going back to school in the fall?' Frank asks.

'Guess so. Don't know what else I'm gonna do.'

'Well, if you need some money give me a call. I could use the help.'

He tosses the rest of his sandwich overboard and it lands with a plop in the water. As the seagulls descend to squawk and bicker over it, Frank vaults the gunnel and drops down to the dock. Lunch is finished, apparently. For him, at least. It's like the guy doesn't need to eat. I'm still famished. I shove the rest of my own sandwich in my mouth and twist open a bottle of Sprite, swigging from it to help me swallow.

By the time I clamber down to join Frank, he's already gotten started on the next job: applying a layer of varnish – or what looks like varnish – to the inside of the strake. It's still laid out there on the sawhorses, like an offering on an altar, and it's really something to see: this huge length of butter-pale wood, sawn into a bow-shaped bend, the edges bevelled and the sides sanded. I just want to reach out and touch it, stroke it, so I do. Under my palm the surface feels smooth and polished as a piece of ivory.

'Is this pine?'

'Oak. They wanted me to use pine, and I said no-way, no-how. Not in the *Seattle*.'

He shakes his head, as if the very idea of using pine is crazy, unthinkable, and dips his brush into the pot of varnish. I stand back and watch, with my hands clasped before me, like an attendant at some religious ceremony. He applies the varnish in gentle strokes, tender as a lover. I ask him about the stuff, and he explains that it's penta-phenol – a wood preservative.

'Keeps that rot from creeping back in.'

'I get you.'

'Some cowboys will tell you to use creosote – but it's toxic as hell.'

When he's finished with the preservative, he adds a layer of linseed oil to the edges of the strake, to act as lubricant. Then we're ready. Frank takes the front end of the strake, I take the back, and we lift it off the sawhorses and carry it over to the hull. The gap we're fitting it into sits at about head height, so I cradle the strake on my shoulder while Frank aligns his end with the stem-post at the bow. He explains that it's best to start with the end of the strake that has the most bend. Something to do with the plank acting as a lever.

'Raise it up, there.'

His tone is terse, impatient. I adjust my position, standing taller.

'Sorry,' I say.

'That's better.' After checking the angle, he adds, 'Normally I'd lash it to the gunnel with a length of rope, but you'll do fine.'

He uses shores and wedges to fit his end in place, and then drills a series of pilot holes through the strake and into the frame beneath. Next he changes his drill bit to countersink the holes. I'm still standing at attention, watching all this from about twenty feet away. He's got himself a carriage bolt, now. He lines it up with his left hand, hefts a mallet with his right, and swings it to strike the bolt once, twice, three times – driving it into the pilot hole. The sound of the impact – metal on metal – is rich and dolourous as a church bell, ringing out across the shipyard.

'Just hold her steady, scholar,' he calls.

He begins to work his way towards me, repeating the ritual every few feet: lining up the strake, positioning it with shores and wedges, drilling his holes, countersinking them, and then pounding the carriage bolts home. He develops a steady rhythm, doing this. It's tough work, physical work, and every so often he pauses to take a breather and backhand the sweat from his forehead. During one of these breaks he looks my way and, as if we've already been talking about it, asks me, 'Can you believe they wanted me to short-plank this old girl?'

I don't know what that means, and I guess he sees it in my face. He tells me short-planking is a cheap way to replace a strake. Instead of using one long piece of wood, you use two shorter ones and scarf them together. It saves money on timber since you don't need so much width to accommodate the bend. He tells me it's also called a Dutchman. I don't know if this is because the Dutch invented it, or because they're known for their frugality, or what.

'I told them to go to hell. No way I'm doing a Dutchman on this job.'

'Why not?'

He peers at me suspiciously. As if he thinks I'm asking on behalf of the company. As if he thinks I'm some kind of spy, advocating the use of short-planking. He's got that mallet in one hand and he looks about ready to take a swing at me with it.

'I mean, what's wrong with short-planking?'

'What's wrong with it?' he says. 'Christ, what's wrong with it?'

He leaves those words hanging there, and turns back to the strake, shoring up the next section and reaching for his drill. As he pushes in the pilot holes, coils of wood wind their way up the drill bit and fall off, spiralling to the dock like exotic leaves. He raises his voice over the whine of the drill.

'Weakens the hull, for one. And increases the chance you'll spring a butt. But it's more than that. You don't short-plank a boat like the *Seattle*.' He drops the drill, and reaches for his mallet and bolts. He keep talking as he hammers the bolts home, emphasising his points with each stroke. 'You don't do no goddamn Dutchman. Not on a boat that's older than this damn city. I thought you were doing some schooling. You ought to know that. A thing was built a certain way. You don't change that just to save a few bucks. If you change the way it's built, then you change its form, and it ain't the same thing, no more.' He stops and turns to stare at me. He's panting and sweating and one of his eyes is twitching. It's the most worked up I've ever seen him. 'It's about the essence of the thing. Do you know what that is? The essence?'

I tell him that I do. I think I do, anyway. And that seems to calm him. He hammers in the next bolt and takes another step down the hull, getting closer to me. About half of the strake is in place, now, and I don't really have to hold up my end, but I still am – just to have something to do. As he starts on the next section, Frank keeps talking, but I can tell he's not really talking to me anymore.

'It's like out there, somewhere,' he waves his mallet up towards the sky, 'is the essence of what this boat is meant to be. The form of it, if it was built perfectly. You'll never get it there entirely. You'll never make it perfect. But if you want to be a shipwright your job is to get as close as you can. Or keep it close as you can. Not many people know that. Not many people understand it. They think it's crazy talk.'

He looks at me, then. As if I'm gonna call it crazy talk.

'I know what you mean,' I say. 'It's about getting it right.'

'That's it. That's just it. Getting it right.'

He's about to swing the mallet, then seems to change his mind. He flips the mallet around, takes a few steps towards me, and holds it out, handle first. I just stare at it.

'Your turn, scholar,' he says. 'Give it a go.'

I reach for the handle. The wooden grip is worn and stained from years of use. I can feel the slickness of Frank's sweat, and the warmth of his palm, as if the wood has soaked it up, absorbed it. I stoop to take one of the bolts from the box on the ground at our feet. Then I step up to the hull. He's already drilled the pilot holes. I just have to fit the bolt to the hole and hammer it on in. I brace it against the strake. Then I hesitate. I've got this image in my head of my first blow knocking the whole boat apart – the kind of thing you see in those old cartoons: the bolts shooting out like shotgun slugs, the planks peeling off in huge strips, the frame crumpling and the cabin collapsing. The entire skeleton going down in a slow-burbling scuttle. And me left standing there with the tools in my hands, a Looney-Tunes expression on my face. I glance back at Frank.

'Go on,' he says.

I swing away. The mallet connects sweetly with the bolt, and I can feel the repercussions resonate through my hand, my elbow, right up into my shoulder and chest. It's as if my whole body is resounding. I'm so startled that I miss my next swing, denting the strake, but the third and fourth are on the mark, driving it home.

'Not bad, scholar,' Franks says. 'Now do it again – after me.'

He shores up the next section of strake, drills the pilot holes, and steps aside to let me drive in the carriage bolts. We keep on going like that, swapping positions and taking turns, adopting a tag-team routine. I'm so slow that the job probably takes longer than if Frank were doing it alone. But if that bothers Frank, he doesn't show it none. Eventually we're nearing the end of the strake, which Frank has left long to ensure an exact fit. He takes a measurement and sheers it off, and we pound the butt into place, cushioning the mallet blows with a block of wood. Then we step back to survey our work.

'Job done, eh?' I say.

'Still got to caulk the seams.' Frank's squinting a little, as if he's already envisioning the work to come. 'But I'll fit the other strakes first. You around to help some, tomorrow?'

'Boss has got me clearing out the gear locker.'

'Too bad.'

But he says it as if it doesn't really matter, and I guess it doesn't.

Somewhere along the way, the day has evaporated. The sun is sitting lower in the sky and the gulls have all settled on the roof of the cannery. We've worked right through our afternoon break. My shoulder is smouldering from the constant swinging and my throat is parched something fierce. I hold out the mallet, offering it to Frank. He takes it back and begins packing his tools away. For the last quarter hour, I putter around, gathering up any remaining junk and loading it onto the tug. When the five-thirty buzzer sounds, all the union guys appear like clockwork men and start marching up the docks. I feel it, too: that reflex relief. All I want to do is crawl into my car, cruise home, and crack open a cold Kokanee.

I sidle over to Frank, and offer to ferry him back on the tug.

'Save you the walk through the marina,' I say.

He's gazing at the next strake, laid out on the sawhorses.

'Reckon I might get one more ready for tomorrow,' he says.

He reaches for his planer, and begins to shape and scrub the plank. I stand there for a few minutes, resigned to watching again. I reckon he'd probably let me stay, and teach me, if I asked him. I don't, though. I just turn and shuffle away towards the end of the dock, where my tug is tied up. Hopping aboard, I start the engine and cast off. Frank, already engrossed with his sculpting, doesn't notice or acknowledge my departure.

I make my way back alone. There's a late-afternoon wind blowing up the inlet. The water coming into the marina is choppy, and my tug, she doesn't want to steer straight. She keeps swinging back and forth like a compass needle, searching for true north. Eventually, given time, she steadies out and finds her course.

Shooting Fish in a Stream

I'd loaded all our gear for the shoot. Jake was still inside the house. As far as I knew, he was still asleep in bed. But I wasn't about to go back in and get him. We'd already had a fight about it, and if I went back in we'd probably have a real fight. So I opened the back of our Chevy van and sat with my legs dangling off the bumper, and dozed there. In the yard next door our neighbours' kids – these two blonde kids, one of whom is mildly disabled in some way I've never been able to figure out – were running around and screaming, looking for eggs and chocolate. Apparently it was Easter, which I'd kind of forgotten about. In our family, now that we were older, Easter didn't mean much; it just meant a day off. Our dad was watching golf and our mom was writing letters to her relatives, and me and Jake were doing this shoot. Or we were supposed to be doing it.

Half an hour later, Jake appeared at the back door. He paused on the steps to spit in the bushes and light a cigarette. He'd taken up smoking again, at around this time. I waited as he shuffled casually down our drive, trailing smoke, and eased himself up against the van.

'Did you remember the spear?' he asked me.

That was it. He didn't thank me at all for loading the goddamn van. I mean, he was the one who was supposed to be running the show. It was his thing. But he's like that, Jake.

'The spear's with the fishing rod,' I said.

He cupped his hands to the window and peered into the back seat.

'I don't see it,' he said.

'It's inside the bag.'

'So long as it's there.'

I stood up and tossed the keys at him. They bounced off his chest and flopped onto the driveway, all spread out like a metal squid. He looked down at them, wrinkled his nose, and nudged them with his toe back towards me.

'You're driving,' I said.

'I'm too hungover to drive.'

'I loaded the van.'

He sighed and scooped up the keys. 'You little dinglehopper.'

To get to the stream where we intended to shoot, we had to drive halfway up Indian River Road. Neither of us had been out that way since Otis had died. It wasn't as if we'd been avoiding it; there'd just been no real reason to go, until now. The road starts at the base of Mount Seymour. From our house, first you have to get onto Deep Cove Road and follow that past Myrtle to the Raven and Dan's Kitchen and this place that used to be a gas station, until the pumps got closed and it became an auto repair shop. The sign says Central Motor Service but everybody just calls it Tony's, after the old guy who runs it. At Tony's you hang a right and head up Mount Seymour Parkway, to Parkgate Shopping Centre, where you take another right. Then you're just about there.

The van was low on gas, so we stopped off at Parkgate. We had to stop off anyway, for the fish. While Jake filled her up, I went into Safeway. At the fresh food counter near the back, they had all kinds of seafood laid out on a bed of ice: crab, shrimp, mussels, haddock, seabass, flounder, and lingcod. I saw all that but I couldn't see any salmon. When I asked the guy working the counter, he shook his head.

'Shipment's due in today.'

'None at all? I don't need sockeye or anything. Just pink.'

'Sorry.'

'Give me a couple of trout, then, I guess.'

He yawned at me, displaying molars riddled with silver.

'How many?'

'Two big ones.'

He scooped them up and slapped them down on his scales. It came to just under ten bucks, but I couldn't pay him there. I had to get in line at the front and pay the cashier.

When I came out, our van was parked in a disabled bay, its hazard lights on and its engine idling. Jake wasn't in the driver's seat. Then I saw him trotting across the parking lot, a six-pack dangling in one hand. The cans clicked and clanked against each other as he ran. We both climbed back in the van, and he dropped the beers between us on the floor.

I said, 'I didn't know the liquor store opened that early.'

'Apparently it does.' He put the van in gear and pulled out; as he drove, he reached back and tugged his seatbelt over one shoulder, wearing it casually without actually buckling it up. He was breathing hard. 'You get the fish?'

'I got trout.'

'Otis wanted salmon.'

'They didn't have salmon.'

'Hell.'

'We could go to Superstore.'

Jake stopped the van at the turn-off to Mount Seymour Road, and we sat there with the signal ticking. He was thinking. Superstore was another twenty minutes away.

'Do they look good?' he asked me.

'They're fresh.'

'Frozen would have been cheaper.'

'They wouldn't have thawed in time.'

'And these ones look good?'

'They look like fish.'

A car had come up behind us. The driver laid on his horn. Jake lazily flipped the guy the finger, and then took his foot off the brake. The van nosed forward.

'Fuck it,' he said. 'I guess it doesn't matter.'

The first part of Indian River Road zigzags past a series of cul-de-sacs and crescents. All the houses up there look identical, as if they've been pre-cut in a factory and shipped out here for assembly. Each one has a peaked, shingled roof, a single or double garage, lightly-coloured siding – beige or grey or baby blue, usually – and a driveway long enough to park a bus in. The yards are about the same size, with wide green lawns, and one or two are marked by the stump of a tree that had to be cut down. Sometimes the stumps can't be removed – the roots go too deep – so they just stay there, clinging to the ground like giant grey barnacles.

Hixton Place is the last cul-de-sac, and just after the turn-off for it we drove past these three signs. The first showed a set of lines coming together, signifying that the lanes ahead narrowed; the second had an arrow on it, snaking back and forth, and warned that the road was winding for the next five kilometres; the third just said, 'No Exit.' Beyond the three signs the houses gave way to forest, dense and dark and deep. The roadside was lined with shrubs and ferns that encroached on the shoulder, and massive Douglas fir trees rose up, leaning at eerie angles, creating a canopy that blotted out the sky. It was so dim and murky we could easily have been driving at twilight. The pavement was cracked and buckled and webbed with tar. We felt every bump through our seats because the shocks on the van were all shot to hell.

'This goddamn road,' Jake said.

'You'd think with all the money in this city, they could afford a better road.'

'They could at least build it straight, without so many hairpins.'

'It's a fucking deathtrap, all right.'

Jake sort of snorted at that.

'No shit,' he said.

As we approached the next corner, a logging truck appeared going the opposite way. It took the turn too wide and veered into our lane, so Jake had to swerve onto the shoulder to avoid it. The vacuum-effect of the truck's passing pulled at our van and rattled the windows. Jake leaned hard on his horn but by then the truck was already behind us, the logs on its flatbed rocking back and forth in their chains. Jake swore and steered us back onto the road.

We still had maybe three klicks to go.

Jake said, 'Hand me one of those beers, would you?'

'Not now.'

'Don't be such a bitch.'

Driving one-handed, he leaned over and felt around on the floor, searching for the six-pack. I hooked a finger under the plastic rings between the cans, and lifted the beers out of his reach. As I did he made a quick swipe at them. The whole car lurched with the motion, and he had to grab the wheel with both hands to keep her straight.

'You dildo,' he said.

'Wait till we get to the stream.'

'One beer never hurt anybody.'

'It definitely didn't hurt Otis.'

'That's the stupidest thing you ever said.'

I thought he might try again, so I sat bent forward, clutching the cans protectively on my lap, like a basket of eggs. Jake had bought Extra Old Stock, which was what Otis used to drink. I don't know if that was deliberate, on Jake's part. Maybe it was. The cans were cold and beaded with water and I could feel the chill on my thighs, through my jeans.

Then Jake said, 'As if you haven't done the same.'

It took me a second to figure out what he was talking about.

'Not like that. Not that drunk.'

'Sure. Like you weren't that drunk when you drove home after my birthday.'

'So what?'

'So it could have happened to any of us.'

'That's the point. That's why we can't do that no more.'

'I didn't realise we were making *The Last Boy Scout*, starring you.'

'You know what I mean.'

A kilometre further on we passed the shrine. I'd heard about it, so I knew what to expect. It was right on one of the hairpins. Jake slowed down as we approached, and I got a decent look at it. On the ground, in front of the tree, was a wooden cross, looking stark and white and strange against all that greenery. Around the base of the tree and cross there were bouquets of flowers and gifts and cards. There were also trinkets dangling from the branches, but I couldn't tell what they were. Weird hippy stuff, maybe. That was all I saw, and then Jake gunned the gas, accelerating around the corner so our rear wheels fishtailed off to the left.

'Take it easy,' I said.

'Did you see all that shit?'

'I saw it.'

We drove for a long time in silence. Then I told Jake that I'd heard Otis hadn't been wearing his seatbelt when it happened, and Jake said that he didn't care what I'd heard.

He'd known Otis a lot better than me.

We left the van at that strange tower you reach halfway down Indian River Road. It might be some kind of radio or television transmitter. I'm not sure. It's built like a miniature Eiffel Tower and surrounded by a chain-link fence. From there we hiked up an old logging road. We were both laden down with thirty or forty pounds of gear. We had straps criss-crossing our chests and bags hanging off our backs, and we trudged along together like a pair of pack mules. After half a kilometre that logging road reaches a fork, and hidden on the left is a hiking trail that not many people know about. We turned off onto the trail and kept going.

We took turns being on point because of the dew and spiderwebs. The sky was still overcast and beneath the canopy of pine trees it was cold – too cold for spring. Nobody else was on the path. At a certain point, maybe three or four kilometres along, we started looking for the stump. That's the place where you turn off the trail. It's easy to miss, and we didn't want to do the same while carrying all that gear. But Jake spotted it. Then it was a matter of thrashing our way through the underbrush for another few hundred yards. The ground was muddy from recent rains and covered in winter mulch that squelched under our shoes. The terrain dropped down gradually to the streambed. Up over the other side of the ravine was the spot where we'd gone camping a bunch of times, with Otis and some of the other guys, but today we weren't going that far – we were filming everything at the stream.

On the near side of it was a gravel bank where we dropped all our bags and sat down to catch our breath. Jake tugged two beers from the six-pack and passed one to me. As we sipped them we poked and prodded among the equipment, slowly unpacking.

'Goddamnit,' Jake said.

'What?'

'We forgot the tripod head.'

'It's attached to the camera from last time.'

He checked, and it was.

'That's something, at least.'

It had been six weeks since we'd filmed that scene, at Superstore. The story was supposed to be about a guy, this loser guy, who works in the grocery department stocking shelves and taking shit from everybody. Then one day he freaks out and decides to live in the woods, or imagines he does, or something. I was never quite clear on that. Jake and Otis had come up with the concept. I was just an actor, a prop. I just did what they told me. They'd filmed a few scenes of me at Superstore, and then another of me walking along a riverbank, slowly shedding my clothes, getting back to nature. All that had been preamble for today's scene, the climax. But a week before we were meant to film it, what had happened had happened, and we gave up. Now Jake had decided that we needed to finish it.

'Should I strip down?' I asked.

'Let's get the stock footage of the fish, first.'

While Jake prepared the camera and checked the lenses, I got out our two trout. The guy had folded them up in wax paper and bagged them for us. I unwrapped one of them. In my hands the fish felt slick and sticky, ready to slip free. I left it on a rock and went to get the fishing rod. It was a cheap Shakespeare rod and reel combo we'd picked up at Canadian Tire. There was already a hook tied to the end of the line. Prying open the fish's mouth, I worked the hook into its jaw – slipping the barb through its lower lip. Then I held the rod and used it to lift up the fish. It dangled there, looking dead. I jiggled it a bit, testing it out.

'What do you think?' I asked Jake.

He looked at it like I'd snagged a dead squirrel.

'It's pretty small.'

'It was the biggest they had.'

'I'm just saying.'

'It'll look bigger on camera.'

Using rocks as stepping stones, I picked my way to the centre of the stream. It was maybe ten feet across, and moving fairly fast because of the spring run-off. Jake took up position on the bank. He was shooting this bit handheld. Before we started rolling I tried a practice run: letting out some line and dangling the fish in the water. The current flowing past caught it and brought it around like a weathervane, so it faced upstream. I held the line steady while Jake worked the zoom on the camera.

'How's it look?' I asked.

'The line is in shot.'

'Try to frame it out.'

'Whatever. Rolling.'

I jerked the fish along, using it like a one-stringed marionette, trying to instill it with some sense of life. It wasn't easy. The hook kept bringing the nose up towards the surface, so it was bobbing at an odd and unnatural angle.

'Let her float downstream,' Jake said. 'Then reel it in horizontally. I'll track it.'

I thumbed the pick up to one side and spooled out more line, watching the trout as it drifted further away. When it was about twenty yards downstream, and barely visible from where we stood, I locked the reel and lowered the rod – so the tip was just above the surface of the water – and began reeling in. As I did I moved the rod back and forth to make it look as if the fish was fighting its way against the currents.

'That's better,' Jake said.

Jake tracked it from the bank, panning as the fish drew level with us. We popped off a few more takes like that, and then Jake went to check Otis's storyboards. The next shot was supposed to be of the fish jumping, so we moved upstream to a small cataract, where the water cascaded over a series of rocks. Above the rocks was a pool, which we planned to use later on, for the spear-hunting sequence. I stood beside the pool, and swung the fish out in a pendulum arc, plunking it down below the cascade. The water there frothed and burbled. Jake got right in close, checked his frame, and started rolling.

'Okay. Go for it.'

I tugged on the rod, which bent and then straightened out as the fish sprang free. It flew a few feet before flopping down, belly first, on the rocks. Then, caught in the currents, it sort of barrel-rolled back down into the froth. It looked ridiculous and pathetic and dead.

'I hope you got that,' I said.

'I got it all right.'

'This isn't going to work.'

'Do it again, but make it jump further.'

I straightened the fish in the froth, and waited until Jake gave me the signal. The second time I tugged harder, and the fish made it into the pool, but it still didn't look very convincing. The third time, I really reefed on it. The rod bent like a bow, and then whipped taut, but the fish didn't follow. The line had snapped.

'Fuck,' I said.

The fish was already floating away, lolling on its side as it drifted out of sight.

'Nice work,' Jake said.

'That's why I bought two.'

'You're lucky you did.'

'Well, I did.' I gathered in the loose line. Without the weight of the hook and fish it was light and flimsy as a cobweb. 'Want me to try again?'

'Forget it. It looked like shit. Let's just get you in the water.'

'Otis was never sure about this part.'

'Drink your beer and man up.'

While I stripped down it started to rain. The drops slapped loudly on the branches of the trees and pattered against the forest floor and drilled little bullseyes into the surface of the pool. Jake got out a plastic bag to cover the camera, changed the lens, and then set about mounting the camera on the tripod. That took a few minutes. As I waited I played around with the spear, which we'd carved out of an old walking stick. On the tip, using some garden twine, we'd lashed Jake's Swiss Army knife. It had a locking blade and looked like it would really do the trick. I paraded back and forth on the bank, practicing my spearing motions.

Jake caught me doing that and grinned.

'Okay, Brando – time to get wet.'

'Sure thing, Coppola.'

I was only wearing a pair of ginch. I'd asked if it could be boxers but Otis and Jake had insisted on ginch. I picked my way towards the pool. It was about four feet deep in the centre, and shallower around the edges. I stepped in cautiously. The water was meltwater, coming down from the winter snowcap up on Mount Seymour, and so cold that it burned.

'Jesus Christ,' I said. 'This better not take long.'

'I'll need at least twenty takes, maybe thirty.'

'Thirty my ass.'

I waded deeper, wobbling a bit on the rocks underfoot. When the water reached my groin, I gasped and took a series of rapid breaths, practically hyperventilating. It was that cold. There was already an ache in my thighs, knees, and shins – right in the bones. It felt like an icecream headache but all through my legs.

'Goddamn,' I said, my voice high and breathless, 'Oh goddamn this Jesus.'

Jake was already filming, recording my reactions, and trying not to laugh.

'Quit swearing. It's Easter, for Christ's sake.'

'Just say action, goddamnit.'

'Action, goddamnit.'

I stalked about the pool, holding my spear above my head. The rain had let up and the water was clear as a windowpane and I could see to the bottom, which was covered in stones and pebbles, all of them worn smooth and reddish in colour and rounded like eggs. I tried to think about a fish lurking beneath the surface, but all I could really think about was how cold I was.

'Can I stab, now?' I asked.

'Don't talk. But yeah.'

I stepped forward and lunged dramatically, punching the spear into the water. The impact kicked up a splash that soaked Jake's jeans and splattered the camera. The plastic bag protected it, but the lens still got covered.

'That was great,' Jake said, checking the camera, 'Otis would have loved that.'

'Shut up, man.'

'You covered the camera in water, you clown.'

'Well clean it off, then! I'm freezing, all right?'

Jake made a big deal about wiping off the wide angle lens with the corner of his shirt. He took his time finishing, too, which was just like him. As he did I waded over to the edge of the pool, where I'd left my beer balanced on a rock. I took a couple of long swigs, draining it, and dropped it into the water. It tumbled over the cataract and bobbled away in the same direction the fish had gone. Below the pool the stream was flat and grey as slate. It snaked back and forth through the trees, as tortuous and twisted as the road we'd driven in on.

Eventually Jake asked, 'Do you need a break or something?'

By then my feet and legs had gone numb. It wasn't exactly pleasant, but it made the cold more tolerable, like a natural anaesthetic.

I shook my head. 'If I get out, I'm not getting back in.'

'Okay – try it again, but don't soak the camera. Other than that it was good.'

We shot the same thing, multiple times, from various angles. The plan was to splice them all together in a little montage sequence, which was meant to give the scene a sense of energy. There was nothing quick or energetic about my movements, though. I plodded about the pool, raising and stabbing my spear in a series of mechanical thrusts. After each one I'd stop and look at Jake, waiting for him to adjust the frame and tell me to do it again. It wasn't working, and both of us knew it wasn't working, but neither of us admitted that. It was just a matter of getting through it, which we did. Eventually.

'We need the shot of you with the fish, now. Where is it?'

I pointed with my spear at our pile of gear. 'In that plastic bag.'

While he rooted through it, I stood and stared at the water. Beneath the surface my legs were white and bent outwards, splayed by refraction. They looked broken and mangled, as if I'd been in some kind of accident. I cupped a handful of water and let it trickle through my fingers. The cold wasn't too bad, by that point. Not as bad as it had been the day of the funeral, back in February. The service had been so crowded that we couldn't even fit in the church. We'd huddled outside and gotten slashed with sleet as we listened to the eulogies through these loudspeakers. Near the end we were let in to view the body, but it hadn't looked like Otis. They'd combed his hair – slicking it all over to one side – and Otis had never combed his hair. Somebody had said it was because of the accident, as a way of covering up the damage to his head, but just then I couldn't remember who had said that. It might have been Jake. It seemed like the kind of thing Jake would've said.

'Hey!' Jake called.

I looked up at him. He was cradling the other trout in his hands.

'You okay?'

'Sure. It's not even cold, now.'

'I was talking to you.'

'I didn't hear.'

'Bring the spear.'

Holding it across my shoulder, like a caveman, I waded towards where Jake stood on the bank. In the shallows the water only came up to my knees. I planted the spear, butt-first, in the gravel, and together we managed to shove the knife-tip into the fish – right behind the gills. The blade pushed the skin out on the other side of the fish, like a tent pole stretching canvas, before it sliced through. The trout hadn't been cleaned or gutted and blood trickled down over the knife handle. Jake shot a few close-ups of that, and then directed me back to the centre of the pool. He explained that I was going to hold the spear underwater, as if I'd just made a lunge, and then when he called action I'd lift it up, fish and all. We'd match the two shots so that it looked like I'd speared the fish.

'Does that make sense?'

'Sure.'

'You good to do it?'

'Uh-huh.'

He started rolling. I lowered my spear-tip. The water swirled around it and a ribbon of blood slithered away from the fish. I waited. I was in the moment. I thought maybe if we got this shot – just this one – and if it looked good, then it would have all been worth it and we would have accomplished something and Jake would be happy and we could go home. I heard him call action and I brought my spear up in a shower of water, and I sort of roared as I did it. I roared and I shook the spear. I shook it so hard the fish fell off the end and flopped into the pool, near the edge. I tried to save it. I still had the spear, so I could only reach one-handed. I touched the sleek body but my fingers wouldn't close and the trout slipped away, drawn down into the cataract by the currents, scooting right through the chute and sliding out into the stream below. The fish disappeared for a second, and then resurfaced, belly-up, bobbing amid the froth as it drifted away, and away, and away from us. I watched it go. I didn't want to look at Jake, but eventually I had to. He had sat down on the bank, beside the tripod. He had his head in his hands. It was quiet except for the sound of the water warbling.

'I'm sorry, man,' I said.

'It doesn't matter.'

'It just slipped off.'

'You might as well get out. You're turning white.'

I looked down. He was right. My torso was pale and waxy, like a corpse. A warmth had spread over my body, diffusing through my limbs, comforting me. Instead of getting out, I lingered in the water. It was nice in there. I found a large flat rock and perched on it, so the water came up to my neck. Jake picked up his beer and stood and sipped at it, ignoring me.

'You should come on in,' I said.

'Quit messing around.'

'I'm serious. It's like those guys in Norway. They go ice swimming.'

Jake shook his head and started packing up our gear. He tore the plastic bag off the camera, clipped on the lens cap, and removed the tripod mount from the underside. Then he fitted the mount back on the tripod head and put the camera in its carry case. I was aware of him doing these things, and moving about on the bank, but I didn't pay him much attention. I stayed where I was. I couldn't feel my body anymore. I couldn't feel much of anything. I wasn't thinking much of anything, either. But I had the vague impression that I'd become part of the water, that I was the water. I sat very still, like a fountain statue, with the spear across my knees, and I stared at the stones on the bottom of the pool and I wondered if this was what it was like to be dead. No feeling, no thoughts. Just this sensation of nothingness.

Then one of the stones seemed to shift. When I saw that, I thought I'd pushed it too far, and had started to hallucinate. I was hypothermic or braindead or something. But the stone moved again. It was long and solid, this tubular-shaped stone, and speckled red so that it blended in with the others. I had no idea where it had come from but it was there all right.

'Jake,' I said.

'Would you get out of the water, asshole?'

'Do you still have the camera?'

'I'm cleaning the lens.'

'There's a fish in here.'

'What?'

'There's a fucking fish right here in front of me.'

I didn't turn my head to look at him, but from the corner of my eye I saw him raise the camera, slowly. He removed the lens cap and opened the viewfinder. The red record light flashed on.

'Where?' he said.

'I'm looking right at it.'

It was about ten feet away, in the shallows near Jake's side of the pool.

'I see it,' he said, and I could hear the edge to his voice. 'Christ it really is a fish.'

'I told you.'

'I thought you'd lost it.'

'Me, too. I thought I was tripping out.'

We were both talking in whispers, as if worried the fish might hear us.

'You got to spear it, man,' he said. 'You got to.'

'Just keep rolling that camera,' I said.

I eased myself up to a crouch. I still had my spear. My hand was cramped in a claw around the shaft. I couldn't do much else but I could hold that spear. And I'd practiced this. I'd practiced it a bunch of times. I took one step forward, slowly, and another. On the third, the fish went still, as if it had sensed me. I could see its fins waving, like silk fans, to keep it balanced. If I went any closer I thought I'd spook it, but I was just within striking distance, now. So I raised my spear, drawing it upwards, arching my whole back with the movement, and then brought it forward in a single furious motion, as if swinging a giant hammer.

I knew right away that I'd hit the fish. I felt the pillow-punch of flesh followed by the impact as the spear-tip struck bottom, and then the shaft started to tremble and quiver in my grip. The fish was thrashing around down there and the water grew cloudy with mud and blood. I leaned on the spear, keeping the fish pinned against the bottom, grinding the knife blade in the pebbles. I started shouting that I'd got it, I'd got it, and Jake was shouting, too, but I was too scared to do anything except keep it pinned, because I figured if I moved the fish would fight its way free. Our spear wasn't meant for spearing. It didn't have a barb or anything. I was yelling that I didn't know what to do, and Jake was still filming and directing me from the bank, and it almost felt like a real film shoot. He kept repeating that I had to scoop the fish up and flip it out of the pond – all at once.

'It'll get free,' I said. 'It'll get away.'

'No, no – just go for it. Fucking go for it, man.'

I grabbed the spear with both hands and hefted up, like a guy digging with a spade, tossing a shovelful of dirt. Something silver and red came up with the spear and cleared the surface, then slipped free and flipped once in the air and landed in the shallow water at Jake's feet. It started to flap wildly, spraying scales and blood, skittering around and sloshing up mud. It was going so crazy it looked as if it was being electrocuted or fried alive. We were both shouting and hollering at one another and Jake dropped the camera and tackled the fish. He fell on it and grabbed it in a bear-hug, pinning it against his chest as it whipped its tail at him, and I threw my spear aside and sloshed over and dove down on top of him, holding him so the fish was sandwiched between us, trapped, and the whole time I was yelling, 'Don't let it go! Whatever you do don't let it go!'

Afterwards we laid the fish out on the bank and opened a couple more beers and sat staring at it. It was nearly two feet long and hefty, with a girth about the width of a fist. The body was torpedo-shaped, tapering to a wedge of a tail. Our spear had gone through its back and come out its belly, just behind the pelvic fin. Then there was the colouring. Its head had an olive-green hue, but the sides and back glistered a rich, ochre red – the red of fresh lipstick, or a wet tulip. I didn't know much about fish, but I knew I'd never seen a fish that red before.

'You figure it's a salmon?' I asked.

It was hard to get the words out. I was huddled in a towel, trying to warm up.

'Got to be – it's too big for anything else. Maybe a sockeye?'

'It's so red.'

'I think that happens, when they spawn. They go red and swim upstream.'

'It's nearly spring, I guess.'

'Unreal,' Jake said, shaking his head.

We were both covered in water and blood and scales that glistened against our skin like sequins. Jake had cuts all over his hands and forearms, from clutching at the fins, and being lashed by the tail as it whipped back and forth. He went over and squatted by the pool to rinse his wounds, wincing from the pain or the cold, or both. It was starting to rain again. I tilted my face up into the hot drizzle. Overhead, pine trees leaned at strange angles against the sky. My skull ached. When I closed my eyes, white spots floated like cottonwood seeds across my vision. I was getting some feeling back, now, and I couldn't stop shivering.

I heard the crunch of footsteps on gravel, and looked up. Jake was standing over me. He had our camera in his hand. It was covered in mud and dripping water. A jagged crack zigzagged like a lightning bolt across the lens.

'Well, this is fucked,' he said cheerfully.

'Maybe we can salvage the footage.'

'Maybe.' He shrugged and dropped it at my feet. 'Either way it was worth it.'

'Otis would never believe this.'

'I don't even believe it.'

He crouched down, placing one hand across the salmon's belly, as if checking to make sure it was solid, and real. Then he seemed to notice something. He scooped it up in both hands and studied the pale underbelly. The flesh was torn and bloody where my spear had come out. He poked a finger in there, pulling back a flap of skin.

'Check this out,' he said.

He brought the fish over and held it before me, upside down, like an offering. By bending the back, he exposed the wound and innards. Among the guts I could see all these tiny orange globs, hundreds of them, shining like miniature baubles. Each one had a black dot in the centre, barely the size of a pin-prick.

'Harsh, eh?' Jake said.

'Must have ruptured the egg sac.'

My teeth chattered as I said it. The trembling had shifted into shudders that coursed through my whole body. I couldn't stop them. They shook me in violent waves, as if I was having seizures.

Jake noticed. 'You okay, bro?'

'So cold, still.'

'Just sit tight and finish that brew and I'll pack up our junk.'

He traded me his jacket for my wet towel, and put the can of Old Stock in my hand. I could barely hold it – my fist felt stiff as stone – but I sat and sipped stupidly while Jake moved around me. The beer tasted warm and good, and I liked the fizzing sensation of the bubbles in my brain. A few minutes later he had everything ready and helped me to my feet.

On the hike back, Jake carried more of the load. I felt better once we were moving. It warmed me up a bit. I still couldn't feel my fingers or toes – not until we got back to the van. By then we were both soaked again from the rain, and once we climbed inside, the windows steamed up immediately from all that moisture. We cranked the heat, waiting for the defrost to kick in. Jake dropped the salmon on the floor between us; it was wrapped up in that same plastic bag we'd been given for the trout.

'What are we gonna do with it?' Jake asked.

We looked at it. Neither of us said anything. Not then.

I wasn't ready to drive so Jake did. I sat with my palms cupped in front of the vent, warming them as if before a fire. The rain was really coming down now, sloshing over the windshield and windows like water in a carwash. The sound of it drumming the roof and the pendulum movement of the wipers was calming, hypnotic.

When we came to the bend where it had happened, I asked Jake to pull over. I thought he might argue, but he didn't. There was space to park at the side of the road. He tugged on the brake and we both hopped out and walked back to the shrine. The branches of the tree created a natural canopy, and the ground was dry in a ten-foot radius around the trunk. It was a big Douglas fir, with a trunk maybe six feet across. The bark was all gouged up from where the car had slammed into it, and underneath the inner wood showed white as bone. It looked like an animal had been chewing at it. Other than that, though, the tree was fine.

The tree hadn't given an inch.

Then there was the cross, and the cards, and the flowers, and the gifts. They were all clustered and arranged around the base like presents under a Christmas tree. A few of them were even wrapped in cellophane, with bows, to protect them from the weather. Hanging from the branches were those little ornaments: angels and dream catchers and ribbons and prayer flags – exactly the kind of junk I'd imagined. We stood side by side and stared at all that for awhile. Then, without really thinking too hard about it, I kicked over the cross. The base cracked and splintered and it went down easily. Jake looked at me. He was surprised, but he was game. Jake always is. He laughed and tore down one of the dreamcatchers and said, 'Happy Easter, motherfuckers.' We trashed a bunch of the other stuff, too, stomping and kicking together, quite casually, like two kids wrecking a flower garden.

Before we left, I went back to the car to get our salmon. Using a little line from the fishing reel, and a hook, we strung the fish up from the tree, so it was just hanging there at about chest height. Anybody driving by would see it. The wound was still ripe, leaking blood and eggs. Some of that dripped onto the soil. It occurred to me that Otis's blood was probably in the soil, too. It had to be. And maybe also in the tree, taken up by the roots. I mentioned that to Jake and he said that it was true. We cracked open our last two brews and splashed a little beer around. Libations, Jake called it. Then we drained the rest, spiked the cans, and trotted back to the van. The keys were still in the ignition. I climbed into the driver's seat. As soon as Jake had settled in beside me, I released the brake, popped the clutch, and really opened her up. We both rolled down our windows, so the rain splashed in against our faces. Jake whooped and howled like a wolf. Neither of us was strapped in, and I was going too fast for that road, considering everything that had happened. But by that point I have to admit I didn't really care.

Sealskin

At the foot of Gore Avenue, Liam pulled up in the parking lot that overlooked the Western Fishing Company Plant. He turned off his car but did not get out and instead sat listening to the engine, which tinked intermittently like slow-cracking glass. The plant was a barn-like structure, at least a hundred yards long, with a peaked, shingled roof and red siding; it sat on a concrete wharf jutting out from shore. Above it a column of seagulls turned around and around in a sluggish tornado. They were attracted by the fetid reek of herring roe, which permeated the air all along the waterfront. It was a terrible smell and if there was such a thing as hell Liam thought it probably smelled a little like that. He waited and watched the clock on his dash: it was quarter to seven and their shift didn't start until seven. The other guys would already be inside having coffee, but Liam had stopped partaking in that ritual.

As he sat there a black Ford truck turned into the lot. It was Bill, their boss. He parked a few spots over and climbed out, dressed in the blue, one-piece coveralls that all the union guys wore. Some of them came and left like that and skipped the change room, as if they lived in their coveralls even when not at work. Bill noticed Liam and waved at him and asked him if he was coming in for coffee.

'Nah. I'm good.'

'You avoiding Rick?'

Liam shrugged. He still had both hands on the steering wheel, as if ready to drive away.

'Don't pay any attention to that asshole.'

'I'll be there in a bit.'

'Suit yourself.'

Bill locked his truck and headed off towards the plant.

Liam waited until six fifty-five before he got out and from the backseat took his own coveralls and workboots, which he carried with him across the lot. That morning the tide was low and around the perimeter of the harbour you could see the high water mark: the rocks above it were sun-bleached white, the ones below were sleek with seaweed. At this end of the plant was the gear locker and shipwrights' warehouse, which could be seen through a garage door. Next to it was a regular doorway that led to the lunchroom and office. Liam could hear the others in there and avoided them by going through the warehouse to get to the change room. All the lockers had names and union numbers on them except one, which was his. He kicked off his shoes and took off his clothes and stuffed these articles into the locker.

He'd left his coveralls sprawled on the floor like a deflated person. He had an old set that Bill had dug out of the gear locker for him; they were thin and threadbare and dull grey instead of blue. Liam picked them up and stepped into the legs one foot at a time and slipped into the sleeves one arm at a time and then zipped the front up from his crotch to his chin. Doing this always made him think of those sea creatures that could change from people to seals and back again; each morning he put on this grey skin and became somebody else, somebody owned, and after work he peeled it off and became himself again, or at least somebody closer to himself. Next he tied up his boots, which he'd found in the dumpster behind the plant, and which were a size too large for him. After that he checked his watch, waited another minute or so, and went to face the men in the lunchroom.

He had timed it right and the guys were all standing around the table, having just finished their morning coffees. Aside from Bill there were five others: Diego, Steve, Jimmy, Elmore, and Rick. Rick was big and pushing fifty, with a shaved head and saggy skin and the hefty, muscular build of an old bull walrus. As soon as he saw Liam he started in on him, calling him a scab and a lazy Newfie in a way that sounded like a joke but wasn't and they all knew it.

'Must be nice not punching the union clock,' Rick said. He was gnawing on a chunk of chew, his mouth full of black juices. 'Being able to wander in whenever you please.'

'It's seven by my watch,' Liam said.

'Seven my ass. What happened? Your mom forget to wake you?'

The only one who laughed was Elmore; he always laughed at Rick's jokes.

'Nah,' Liam said. 'But your mom did. I stayed over at her place last night.'

That got a laugh and Rick spat into his empty coffee cup, using it as a spittoon.

'You lippy little shit.'

Bill chuckled. 'Admit it, Rick. He got you good.'

'Like hell he got me. He couldn't get his own cock out to piss.'

There was some more snickering and Bill waited for it to settle down before handing out the worksheets for the day. The other guys accepted the sheets without looking at them and shuffled out, stretching and yawning. They all knew what jobs they were doing but Liam didn't. Bill used him as a utility man and his duties changed from day to day. He was given his sheet last. Bill passed it over with a small smile of apology and when Liam saw the task at the top of his list he knew why: it said he would be working on the *Western Kraken* today.

'Rick needs some help,' Bill explained.

'Doing what?'

'His precious decking.'

Rick had stayed behind the others; when Liam looked at him, the seam of his mouth split open – the lips peeling back to reveal teeth stained brown like rotten kernels of corn.

'Hear that, scab?' he said. 'You're mine today.'

They walked down the wharf together, with Rick a few steps ahead and Liam trudging behind like the prisoner of a one-man chain gang. The walkway was as wide as a road and ran the full length of the wharf, with a long drop to the water on the left, and the packing plant and cannery on the right. When they passed the open doors of the processing area Liam glanced inside at the rows of workers; they all wore lab coats and rubber gloves and face masks, and they were already at work sorting the slabs of yellow roe that looked like elongated banana slugs, rushing past on the conveyor belts. Even outside the stench was sweet and rancid, nearly overwhelming. Most of the workers were immigrants, from China or Korea.

'Know why them chinks wear those masks?' Rick asked.

'So they don't have to smell the roe.'

'No – so they don't have to smell each other.'

From the wharf they descended a gangplank that led to the docks and marina where the fishing boats were moored. Beneath the gangplank, near the crane, was the spot that his seal usually appeared. Liam checked but couldn't see it in the water at the base of the wharf.

Rick caught him looking and asked, 'You still feeding that fucking thing?'

'No.'

'Better not be.'

Near the northwest corner of the marina they came to the *Kraken*, a seventy-five-foot seiner. Like all the vessels in the Westco fleet the hull was painted black and the bridge was painted red and white. It was Rick's boat. He wasn't the skipper, but when the *Kraken* was in dock he worked on it, and when it went out during the salmon and herring seasons he was its engineer. Rick hopped onto a bollard, using it as a stepladder from which he could haul himself over the gunnel, and after him Liam did the same. Rick was waiting for him amidships; he had his can of chewing tobacco resting open in his palm.

'Finally finished the forward deck,' he said.

Liam came to stand beside him, being careful not to step on the deck, and studied it in the way Rick wanted him to: with appreciation. About half the planks had been replaced and the new ones looked odd and incongruous set amid the older Iroko wood that was more worn. The seams between the planking had been caulked and paid with tar.

'Took me damn near a month to get it done.'

Liam nodded. 'Looks good.'

'Course it looks good.'

He pinched a fingerful of chew; the clump of tobacco looked like a large hairy spider, which he stuffed in his mouth and chewed on lustily, an errant strand dangling from his lips. Rick motioned towards the bow, where he had piled all the excess scrap from his repair job: torn-up planking and rusty nails and carriage bolts and sawdust and woodchips and dried bits of tar that resembled deer turds.

'First job is to get all that off of here. Then we're gonna sand down this decking and oil it.'

'I'll go get my tug.'

'It ain't your tug.'

'I'll go get the tug, then.'

'Be quick about it.'

The tug was not a real tug but a ten foot aluminum skiff with a deep hull and a powerful engine and rubber fenders, made out of old tires. It was tied up in the same place that the seal usually appeared: near the gangplank that led from the wharf to the docks. The docks rose and fell with the water level; since it was low tide, the wharf stood twenty feet overhead on wooden pilings, many of them leaning at angles, all of them pockmarked with barnacles and draped in seaweed. In the shadows of the wharf the tug rocked idly in its berth.

Two tie lines held the tug in place, and Liam undid these before hopping aboard. The tug had a wheelhouse, with room to accommodate the wheel, the dashboard, and the driver. He turned the key in the ignition and pressed the starter button, and the engine fired up with a low, hoarse rumble, coughing several times in the process; the tug began to shake and diesel smoke belched out of the exhaust pipe above the wheelhouse. Liam let the engine idle for a minute before easing forward the lever that controlled the throttle. To steer he stood behind the large wheel and held it with both hands, feeling through them the rumble of the motor.

The marina was separated from Burrard Inlet by a jumble of rock and concrete that acted as a breakwater, and it was between the breakwater and docks that Liam piloted the tug towards the *Kraken*. The larger boat was moored with its bow towards shore and the starboard side facing the water. Liam could see Rick standing on deck, waiting for him and watching him, and so he made his approach carefully: he dropped the throttle into reverse, countering his momentum, and turned hard to port so that the tug drifted in at an angle. As the two vessels came together he stepped out of the wheelhouse to brace against the *Kraken*'s hull with his palms, softening the impact to a kiss. Rick didn't offer to take his tie lines so Liam went to the bow to gather the first one himself. Coiling it in three slack loops, he draped it over his shoulder and clambered aboard the *Kraken*.

Before he was able to tie off, a series of waves entered the marina from the inlet and rolled beneath the docks; since the tug was still drifting free it pivoted to port and ground its prow into the side of the *Kraken*. Liam yanked on the rope and held it taut, trying to steady the tug as it bucked up and down like a startled horse on the swells.

'Jesus Christ!' Rick shouted. 'Watch what the fuck you're doing!'

'It was an accident.'

'You scraped the shit out of my hull.'

The waves had settled. Liam tied the rope off as fast as he could, looping it in quick figure eights around the nearest cleat and then finishing with a half-hitch.

'It was those waves,' he said. 'You could have helped me tie her up.'

'I could help you wipe your ass, too. But I figured even a Newfie scab like you would be capable of doing something that simple.'

Liam leapt down onto the tug, picked up the aft tie line, and threw it on deck. Then he climbed back up and tied it off, too. Rick was leaning over the side with both hands on the gunnel, peering down to inspect the damage; there was a clear scrape in the paint of the hull where the orange primer now showed through.

'You better touch that up.'

'You want me to do that now?'

'Don't be an ass. Get rid of that goddamn scrap first.'

Rick continued to swear and curse about the damage as Liam pulled on his work gloves. Trudging to the bow, he seized one of the splintered planks with both hands and carried it to starboard. On the forward deck of his tug was a steel container they used as a garbage skip, and into it he tossed the plank before heading back for another. He had to step around Rick who was kneeling on the deck, using a rag dipped in turpentine to wipe away excess tar, which in places had bled from the seams into the edges of the planks. For a time they worked like this with neither of them talking to the other and the only sound that of waves slapping against the metal hull of the tug and the wooden hull of the seiner.

Then, without preamble, Rick began telling Liam about the *Kraken*. He said it was over a hundred years old and had been used to carry supplies across the Atlantic in the Allied convoys during the Second World War. He also said that it had survived three attacks by the Krauts when a lot of other boats hadn't. Liam continued working and every so often made an affirmative or noncommittal sound in the back of his throat.

'What do you think of that?' Rick asked.

'That's really something.'

'Damn straight it's something.'

Liam hefted another piece of plank, this one riddled with nails, and lifted it carefully over Rick, telling him to mind his head, and Rick told him to mind his own. As Liam stepped up to starboard, he saw in the water a bulbous head that shone wetly and had the same blue-grey sheen as the waves, as if part of the sea had simply taken shape. It was his seal and she was looking at him curiously. Liam set down the plank and made a shooing motion with his hands, and when that didn't work he picked up a crooked nail and tossed it in the water – not directly at the seal but near enough to startle her. The nail made a plopping sound and the animal dropped beneath the surface, leaving concentric ripples radiating in her absence.

Liam looked back at Rick; he hadn't noticed anything and was still rambling on about the boat. He was saying that the company didn't build wooden boats anymore because they were too cheap, but everybody knew wooden boats were better quality and lasted longer and handled more easily in the water. Rick sat back on his knees and waved his rag at the boat moored opposite, which was a modern packer with an aluminum hull, bridge, and cabin.

'Think that no-account tin can is gonna be around in a hundred years?'

'No,' Liam said.

'Fucking rights it won't.'

After that Rick stopped telling him about the boat and they worked in silence again. Liam cleared the remaining pieces of planking, some of which had to be sawed in half or quartered to fit in the skip; then he gathered up the smaller chunks of wood and metal in a bucket, which he lowered down to the deck of the tug; lastly he got out a broom and swept the slivers and splinters and woodchips and sawdust into piles, and with a dustpan shovelled these piles into black garbage bags. When he said he was finished Rick stood up to check over the work and muttered about Liam's uselessness without being able to find any faults.

'Get rid of that shit and come right back.'

'Bill might have some other jobs for me.'

'I said you come right back – and I better not catch you feeding no fucking seal.'

Liam undid his tie lines and tossed them onto the tug and then jumped down after them, his work boots ringing off the metal deck. The engine was warm now and in starting up did not cough or choke as it had that morning but rumbled smoothly to a full-throated roar. Liam put the throttle in reverse and spun the wheel as he glided away, pivoting the tug one hundred and eighty degrees, then threw it in gear and headed back towards the plant.

Halfway there the seal appeared again. She surfaced off to starboard and kept pace, floating alongside him all the way to the wharf, and as he docked and tied up she hovered about ten feet away. Turning off the engine, he looked around to make sure he was alone, and then leaned over the side of the tug and spoke softly to the seal, as you might to a pet. He chastised her for turning up when Rick was around. He asked if she was hungry again, and also if she was lonely, and if that was why she acted so friendly towards him. The seal gave no indication that she understood any of these questions, but simply stared at him. There were no whites to her eyes, or irises or pupils – just twin orbs that were the colour of water in a well and almost as fathomless.

'I'll be right back, girl,' Liam said. 'Just sit tight for a sec.'

He walked up the gangplank to the wharf. On this corner of it, just above where he had moored the tug, was the hydraulic crane they used to load supplies onto the boats. At the base of the crane was its control box; Liam positioned himself there and turned on the power and manipulated the controls to swivel the arm of the crane until it extended over his tug. He had to gauge it by sight, and when the angle looked about right he pressed the button that let out the cable. On the end of the cable was a steel hook and he lowered this to within two feet of the tug, then trotted down there to attach the hook to the lifting chains on either side of the skip. The seal was still waiting patiently and he spoke assurances to her before heading back up to the controls. He raised the crane until the cable tightened and the chains went taut and the skip left the ground, swinging in the air with a pendulous motion. Beside the crane was a wheeled cart onto which he lowered the skip. Detaching the lifting chains from the hook, he left it hanging there as he pushed the cart towards the dumpsters at the far end of the plant.

In passing the gear locker he spotted Bill, who stood just inside the entrance, studying the shelves lining the walls and making annotations on an inventory sheet. Liam let his cart roll to a halt and went in. When Bill heard him coming he looked up, pen poised to write.

'Problem, Liam?'

'Just thought I'd check to see if you had any other jobs need doing.'

'You and Rick done already?'

'Not really.'

Liam didn't explain but stood with his hands on his hips, hoping.

'Hmm.' Bill tucked the pen behind his ear and scratched his

jaw. 'Tell you what – Frank left some scrap on the *Seattle*. After lunch I'll send you over there to clean it up, eh?'

'Sounds good.'

'Give you a break from Rick, at least.'

Liam was already walking off. He called back, 'What I need is a clean break.'

'You got to have thick skin around that guy.'

'I know it.'

Behind the gear locker and their lunch room were the garbage dumpsters. That was where Liam emptied the skip, tossing the larger pieces of wood in one at a time and dumping the smaller scraps out using the plastic bucket. When it was done he left the cart and skip there and carried the bucket with him as he walked back along the wharf.

En route he stopped at the processing area. The stench was getting worse in the midday heat, and now had a physical, oppressive presence that made Liam retch, but the workers seemed oblivious: they continued to sort the passing roe with precise, repetitive motions, as if performing some important ritual. Just inside the entrance was a plastic tub filled with herring. After the roe was extricated, the gutted fish were sent to another part of the plant to be turned into feed and fertiliser, but the workers always kept a few here; on their breaks they liked to toss them to the seagulls and watch the ensuing fights and place bets on which bird would end up with the fish. He had never asked if it was okay for him to take a few fish, but they had never challenged him about it, either. He grabbed half a dozen herring, all sleek and shimmering and slippery, and dropped them in his bucket. When he walked out with his load several gulls descended on him, squawking and flapping, and he made fake kicking motions to keep them at bay as he carried the bucket away, back towards the crane and docks.

At the bottom of the gangplank the seal was still waiting for him; she knew what he was bringing her and she rolled over once, slow and lazy as a dog, to show her appreciation.

'Over here, girl,' he said. 'I got you a feast, today.'

He stepped between the tug and the pilings, into the shadows of the wharf, where he would be shielded from the rest of the marina. Crouching down, he reached into the bucket and scooped out one of the herring, which he tossed in the water. It landed with a slap and hung there suspended, trailing smoke-like streaks of blood across the surface. The seal moved in to take it, snapping it up and tilting her head back to let the herring slip down her gullet. She had teeth like a dog's and used her jaw the same way, but her snub nose and watery whiskers reminded him more of a cat. When she finished he tossed her the next fish, and the next. She was bold but not stupid and would only come within five or six feet, so he had to throw each one that far and then wait for her to finish it before giving her another.

'Good girl,' Liam said. 'Tasty, eh?'

Between portions she would weave back and forth in the water, and by studying the torpedo-shape of her body he had developed an understanding of the way she controlled it – using gentle movements of her fins, tilting and twisting them, elegant as the hands of a geisha. When she rotated the water rolled off her skin; it had a rubbery texture that looked thick and tough and impervious, and he wished he could touch it just to see what it felt like. It was grey like the sea on a cloudy day and glistened in the same way, as the sea glistens.

As he tossed her the last fish he heard footsteps coming down the gangplank; he stood up abruptly, hurried to the tug, and hid the bucket behind the gunnel. Then he began to undo his tie lines, moving casually and with what he hoped looked like nonchalance. He did not check to see who it was right away but waited until the person reached the dock: then he saw that it was Elmore, lumbering along with his arms dangling at his sides like a Neanderthal. But he wasn't looking in Liam's direction and didn't seem to have noticed Liam or the seal. She was still floating in the sheltered waters beneath the wharf and after Elmore had passed out of sight Liam told her that he had to get back to work, now. She twisted and rolled as if she understood, and continued showing off as he rinsed the blood from his gloves and fired up the tug and pushed off. Thinking she might follow him, he watched the water in his wake while navigating to the *Kraken*, but she seemed to have figured it out and did not reappear.

Before he'd had the chance to tie up Rick stuck his head over the gunnel and shouted down, 'Thought I told you to come right back.'

'I'm here, aren't I?'

He heaved himself aboard and brushed by Rick and began tying off.

'Where the hell you been?'

'I stopped in to see Bill.'

'If you been feeding that fucking seal...'

'I ain't been feeding it, all right?'

'Told you what I'd do if I caught you feeding that pest again.'

'Yeah, yeah.'

'I'll catch it and kill it, like we do when we're at sea. Skin the fucking thing.' Rick chuckled, as if imagining it. 'That's right. Skin it and make me a pair of sealskin boots.'

Liam had finished with the tie lines. He tugged on his gloves one at a time, twisting his wrists back and forth and flexing his fingers to fit them into the fingers of the gloves.

'What do you want me to do?' he asked.

'I want you to get to work instead of slacking off, scab.'

'I'm not a scab, okay?'

'What are you, then?'

'Just a worker.'

Rick bent to the toolbox he kept on deck, and began rooting through it. 'If you work here and you're not union you're a scab.'

'I tried to join the union and they wouldn't let me. I told you.'

'They probably thought you were too dumb.'

'They said I'm only temporary so that's why.'

'I don't give a shit what they said.' Rick stood up. He had a sanding block in one hand and a sheaf of sandpaper in the other. He tossed these at Liam's feet. 'Now would you quit yapping about it and get to work? I want this deck sanded by lunch so I can oil it later.'

'Aye aye, captain.'

Liam sat cross-legged on deck and fiddled with the sanding block and thought of all the other things he could have said and wanted to say but hadn't. He was sweating from heat and frustration and the sweat made his coveralls itch so he unzipped the top to his sternum, baring his chest. Taking a sheet of sandpaper, he folded it in thirds and tore off a strip along the first fold and fitted the strip into the sanding block. Rick watched him do this and also watched him as he knelt and began to sand, using both hands to pull the block up and down the first plank along the wood grain. The paper made a whispering sound and gave off small puffs of sawdust. Soon his gloves and forearms were sprinkled with it, like yellow powder.

He could feel the sun on his back through the coveralls like the weight of a hot iron, and he could feel Rick's eyes on him as he worked. Rick was drinking coffee and observing from beside the galley door, and as far as Liam could tell that was all he was doing. At one point he asked Rick if they could turn on the radio in the galley and Rick told him no because all they played these days was rap and nigger music and there was no point listening to that.

'It'll help pass the time.'

'Don't worry about the goddamn radio – worry about the goddamn decking. I want it smooth as a baby's ass before I oil it up later.'

Liam finished one plank and crawled on his knees up to the next. As he scrubbed at it Rick came to stand beside him and scrutinise what he was doing; every so often Rick would criticise some aspect of his sanding, telling him to go faster or slower or to go back and redo a particular patch. Eventually Liam straightened and sat on his knees and looked up at him. Rick loomed blimp-like above him and his shape was just a shadow with the sun behind it.

'Don't you have something to do?'

'Yeah – I got to make sure you don't fuck up my decking.'

'I won't fuck up your deck, all right? But I won't get much done with you standing there looking at my ass.'

'I ain't looking at your ass, you little queer.'

'Sure – I'm the queer.'

The shadow stood motionless for a few seconds. Then Liam felt something wet sprinkle in his hair and he smelled the bitterness of coffee beans.

'What the hell was that?'

'An accident – like you.'

Rick walked away snickering; Liam bent to the deck and sanded as if he were trying to erase something or scrub out a stain, and as he knelt and worked like that, lathered in his own sweat, he could see the long summer of slavery that stretched before him, and it seemed to be endless and indefinite and eternal, each day melting into the next and Rick the only constant.

At noon the union men gathered in the lunchroom next to the gear locker. They sat together around a rectangular table and undid the top halves of their coveralls, which they allowed to hang down from the backs of the chairs so that the sleeves just brushed the floor. To Liam it looked as if they had sloughed off part of the skin that they worked in, making them more human, but he knew this was deceptive since below the table they still wore their uniforms.

As the men ate their sandwiches and drank their coffee they talked about Elmore's new Harley, and how to repair a broken compressor on a fridge, and the strip club near the shipyards they occasionally went to after work. Liam listened to all of this and said nothing. Originally he had tried to take part in these conversations, but anything he said had left him open to some barb or rebuttal from Rick, and he'd learned instead to sit and eat and wait for lunch to end. He'd grown so accustomed to doing this and tuning out their talk that it startled him when he heard his name mentioned; he looked up, still chewing a mouthful of macaroni. Elmore was telling them all how he'd seen Liam feeding the seal.

Liam swallowed his food and said, 'No I weren't.'

'What do you mean you weren't?' Elmore said. 'I saw you.'

Then he looked over at Rick, as if anticipating how he'd react.

'You little liar,' Rick said. 'You little fucking liar.'

'It was only a couple of herring.'

'Those things are a goddamn pest. If you'd ever been on a

real fishing boat you'd know that. Tear holes in nets and eat the catch. Just giant rats is all they are.' He sat back and crossed his arms and chuckled. 'Looks like I'm gonna go a-seal-hunting this afternoon, boys. Catch me a seal and do it in like them Eskimos – bash in its little head.'

Liam put down his fork, then picked it up again. 'Yeah, right,' he said.

'Don't think I would?'

'You better not.'

'Or what?' Rick said. 'What you gonna do, scab?'

Liam didn't answer and they stared at each other in silence. Then Bill burped, long and low, in a deliberate way meant to make all the guys laugh, which it did.

'Take it easy, Rick,' Bill said.

'You on his side, boss?'

'I'm not on anybody's side – I'm just saying take it easy.'

'I'll take it easy when this scab starts doing his job, not feeding no fucking seal.'

'That reminds me,' Bill said, scratching his jaw, 'there's a bit of a mess on the *Seattle*, from Frank's rebuild. It needs clearing and I figured Liam could tackle it this afternoon.'

'No problem,' Liam said.

'Like hell,' Rick said. 'You're oiling up my deck this afternoon.'

Bill shook his head. 'Sorry, Rick – the *Seattle*'s skipper is coming down tomorrow to check her out, so I want her looking slick. You might have to finish the deck on your own.'

Rick looked from Bill to Liam as if he suspected the plot they'd concocted. Without saying anything, he stood up and went over to the sink and flicked his coffee into the basin. He rinsed the cup thoroughly and deliberately, using his fingers to wipe out the dregs, and placed it upside down on the counter next to the taps. The men all watched him do this. Then, still without saying anything, he went out, and Elmore went out after him.

Later Liam would remember all that, and the way it had happened.

To reach the *Seattle* Liam had to pilot his tug by the gap in the breakwater that gave access to Burrard Inlet, and through which the fishing boats passed during the herring and salmon seasons. Out there the water was choppy and surging with whitecaps; he could see sailboats skimming the surface and cargo freighters lying flat like toppled skyscrapers, and beyond them he could see the North Shore, where he lived, with its beaches and condos and wooded slopes, and its mountains that rose up in grey swells still topped by snow, like larger versions of the whitecapped waves. The sense of space was vast and captivating and, as always when heading that way, he imagined momentously turning the wheel, hand over hand, and steering out through the gap into the uncharted waters beyond, and, as always, he didn't do this or even seriously consider it but instead stayed on course and continued towards his destination.

The *Seattle* was as old as the *Kraken* and just as imposing. Frank was the contractor who had been hired to rebuild the cabin, on behalf of the Native owners, after the end of last herring season back in March. Frank was younger than the union guys and had treated Liam differently to them. For some days, especially when Frank had been replacing the strakes in the hull, Liam had worked alongside him, but the job was done now and so was Frank.

In the galley Frank had left the old cupboards that he'd removed, as well as a series of rusty two-inch pipes that looked like they'd been part of the boat's freshwater supply system. Sprinkled on the surrounding linoleum were wood chips, sawdust, and flakes of rust, and all that mess needed cleaning. With a crowbar Liam broke the cupboards into individual panels; beneath the fake oak laminate they were made from cheap plyboard that cracked easily. The counter was thicker and stronger and had to be cut down with a handsaw. He carried the pieces out one at a time, followed by the piping, and laid it all down on deck near the bow. Next he set to work on the debris, which he swept slowly into piles, then re-swept for no real reason except to waste time. With a dustpan he transferred the rust, wood, and sawdust into a black garbage bag that had turned hot and tacky in the heat. Then he walked around deck, carrying the bag and hoping he looked busy and trying to think of something else to do.

The new counters in the galley were still dusty so he wiped those down, smearing the dust into grey streaks and then wiping the surface a second time. He did the same to the table and when he finished he sat at it, twisting the damp cloth back and forth in his palms and feeling the easy, listing rhythm of the boat beneath him. He checked his watch and knew it was time to go but still he did not move. As he sat there he glanced out the galley porthole; across the marina he noticed two, blue-clad figures, tiny as toys, standing by his tug in the shadow of the wharf. It was the same spot that he usually fed the seal.

He went outside and clambered onto the starboard gunnel and perched there, bracing one hand against the cabin roof for balance. He shielded his eyes from the sun to peer at the two men and tried to make them out. It looked like Rick and Elmore. He couldn't tell what they were doing but they were hunched over something on the dock. He felt it then: a sense of anticipation and foreboding, a kind of sickness, curdling in his stomach.

'Son of a bitch.'

From the gunnel he jumped down to the dock and landed hard, tumbling forward onto his hands and knees. Then he was scrambling upright, sprinting full-tilt through the marina; his boots pounded on the wooden docks, which swayed and rocked underfoot like the floor in a funhouse. At one of the gaps between sections of dock he tripped and stumbled and caught himself and kept running. As he drew near the gangplank he slowed down. The men were there, in the shadows of the wharf. It was Rick and Elmore like he'd thought and they were hoisting something off the dock, using a rope they'd looped over one of the crossbeams that supported the underside of the wharf. He could tell by the tubular shape that it was a seal, his seal, but at first he didn't know what they had done to her; she was no longer grey and speckled like the sea but bright crimson as if they'd dipped her in red paint and made a piñata out of her. Then he saw the blood drizzling from her tail, and he saw the bare muscles and tendons, and he saw the way she hung there all skinless and garish and shining like some nightmarish vision of hell.

He saw all that and the men saw him at the same time. Rick was squatting down and tying off the rope they'd used to string up the seal and Elmore was standing at his side. They turned to face Liam and for a brief moment seemed uncertain how to behave. Spread at their feet were the tools they'd used to catch and kill her: a bucket of herring, a fishing gaff, some netting, a claw hammer, a serrated six-inch knife. There was also something grey and reddish and rubbery that looked like a jellyfish. Rick bent down to pick it up, clenching it in his fists, and lifted it so it unfolded to reveal itself. It was the seal's skin.

189

The side Rick displayed was red as a matador's cape, and like a matador Rick shook it to taunt him.

'I warned you, didn't I? I told you what I'd do.'

Liam said nothing but only stood there. He had started to cry and when they saw that they made sad and sympathetic and mocking faces; they joked about killing his little pet and snickered at the jokes for each other's benefit. Standing there laughing, with their tools strewn about them and the skinned body hung behind them and their coveralls spattered in red, they looked less like men and more like demons or some malevolent imitation of men.

Liam made an outraged, animal sound that wasn't a word and wasn't a scream but something in-between, and then ran at Rick and grabbed him and started hitting him. They wrestled and clawed and punched at each other until Liam felt something connect with the side of his head and then he was on the dock. He pushed himself up and rushed at Rick again and got hit again and went down again, and this time he stayed down as they stood over him and kicked him a few times – quick and vicious toe-punts – in the ribs, the back, the kidneys.

He had closed his eyes and when the blows stopped he opened them and saw the two men looming over him. They told him that he was crazy and that he had brought this on himself and that he had got what he deserved. Then they were gone and he was alone on the dock staring up at a blue sky. The seagulls were circling up there; they'd already caught the scent of fresh blood and meat and flesh. A few swooped down and settled on the dock; they eyed Liam and eyed the hanging seal as if trying to decide which one was dead. When he moved they fluttered back out of reach, and began croaking indignantly as he rolled over and pushed up onto his hands and knees and eased himself to his feet. He felt as if he had been in a car accident: not quite sure how it had happened but knowing that it was bad and knowing also that it was partly his fault. He was still crying but not sobbing, just weeping steadily from the pain, the tears blending with the blood on his cheeks as if his eyes were bleeding.

He shuffled over to the rope they'd used to hang the seal. It was lashed to a cleat on the dock with a clove-hitch. He undid the knot and held the rope, struggling with the weight of the seal, which was surprisingly heavy – probably a hundred pounds or more. He allowed the rope to slither through his hands, the nylon threads scouring his palms, and in this way lowered the seal down to the dock. A puddle of blood had formed beneath her, and in it she landed wetly and heavily, her body folding upon itself before flopping to one side.

She looked as if she had been turned inside out and he didn't understand how her innards could hold together like that without spilling everywhere. She did not resemble his seal any more but he recognised her by the eyes: they were still dark and doe-like and gazed up from the depths of death as if she recognised him and understood the role he had played in her fate. There were cracks in her bare skull where they had hit her, and they'd used the end of the gaff as a makeshift meat hook, shoved up underneath her shoulder blades to hoist her. He gripped the hook and yanked it down and it came out with a soft sucking sound, like a spade shearing turf. Laying it aside he knelt with her and petted her muscled back, so tender and vulnerable without the tough hide, and spoke to her in the friendly tones he had used while feeding her. The seagulls created a circle around him like the attendants at a funeral, waiting for him to finish his mourning so they could enjoy the after-service feast.

To prevent that, he slid his hands beneath the seal and rolled her towards the edge of the dock and off into the sea. She landed with a splash and bobbed back up, before the head dipped under and dragged the rest of the body down, dropping as still and silent as a scuttled ship. As he stood the gulls squawked bitterly and hopped forward to inspect the place where the seal had lain. Others approached the skin Rick had left on the dock and began to peck at it. Liam swatted them away and picked up the skin, clutching it protectively. He stroked it. One side felt just like he expected it to feel: sleek and smooth as human skin, but thicker and stronger and more resilient. The other side, the inside, was tender and had a wet, gelatinous quality, softened by fat and blubber. He held it draped over one arm and carried it with him up the gangplank. He was limping badly; one of their kicks had given him a charley horse in his thigh and the muscle spasmed at each step.

Outside the processing area two workers stood with their face masks pulled down around their throats like the breathing sacs on frogs. The workers were smoking and they stopped smoking to watch Liam as he walked by carrying the sealskin. He knew he was bleeding because he could feel the warmth of the blood on his chin and taste it in his mouth, and because red drops splashed onto the concrete every few steps, but he didn't know how bad it was until he got to their warehouse and went into the washroom and turned on the lights and looked in the mirror.

His lip was split wide and his nose was bleeding and swollen and probably broken; one of his bottom left molars felt loose and he could wriggle it with his tongue, like a kid about to lose a primary tooth. He draped the sealskin over the nearest sink and then ran the tap in the sink next to it and splashed water on his face. The water was cold but each handful seemed to burn. As he washed away the blood more continued to drizzle from his nose. It hurt too much to pinch the bridge so from one of the stalls he tore off pieces of toilet paper, which he twisted into plugs that he stuffed up his nostrils to stem the flow of blood. He had just finished doing this when Bill appeared in the doorway. Seeing Liam, he stopped in mid-stride, and then came another few steps forwards. Liam didn't turn around but gazed at Bill in the mirror and waited for him to speak. Without quite meeting his eyes Bill told him that he had heard what they'd done and that it was a shitty thing and that he was sorry. He didn't say exactly what he'd heard, but the sealskin was right there in the sink and Bill glanced at it uneasily without commenting on it, so it seemed as if he knew everything.

'They worked you over good, eh?'

Liam acknowledged that they had.

'I'll make sure they get written up for it. It's almost impossible to touch these union guys but they'll get a warning, at least.' Bill scratched at his beard in that nervous way of his and twisted his left boot back and forth on the linoleum floor, making it squeak. The tap was still running and Liam stood over it with his hands braced on either side of the sink.

'Tell you what,' Bill said. 'Why don't you take the rest of the day off? Take a couple days off if you want. Don't come back until you're ready.'

Liam said that he'd do that and thanked him and waited some more. Bill said he was sorry again and eventually, finally, he left. The twisted tissues that Liam had jammed in his nostrils had bled through. He plucked them out and discarded them and replaced them with fresh ones. Afterwards he looked at himself in the mirror for several minutes as he thought about what had happened and then thought about what had to happen now because of it.

*

His trolley cart and garbage skip were still where he had left them that morning by the dumpsters. He folded the sealskin and laid it carefully inside the skip before returning to the warehouse. From the low shelves just inside the entrance he got down three cans of marine paint in the primary colours and three cans of primer. At the back of the warehouse was the gear locker where they stored all of their tools, and from one of the cabinets he took a rivet punch and a hammer and that was all he needed. He put the paint cans and tools in the skip and pushed the cart down the dock, moving as slowly and painfully as Sisyphus pushing his rock. The workers were no longer on their smoke break and nobody noticed him. The tide was higher now and the marina water getting choppier as afternoon wore on. The gulls still circled ceaselessly, endlessly, indifferently.

As before he used the crane to manoeuvre the skip, this time angling it over the tug and lowering it directly onto the deck. He walked down the gangplank without hurrying and detached the skip from the crane. Only once did he look at the place where the seal had been; its blood was already going dark and tacky in the sun, like treacle. He turned away and gazed across the marina. From the tug he could see the *Western Kraken* and he could also see Rick plodding back and forth on deck, mindless and purposeful as a golem. Liam watched him for a few minutes, and then hobbled over towards the boat, deliberately accentuating his limp. Rick saw him approaching and stopped what he was doing and came to stand at the stern, facing the dock. In one hand Rick had a paint brush and in the other he had a pot of decking oil.

'What the fuck do you want?'

'Bill asked to see you.'

'You ratted on me, you little scab.'

'No. But he knows. I guess somebody saw. He called me in to tell my side of it and now he wants to hear your side.'

'I got shit to do,' Rick said, and spat a gob of black goo onto the dock at Liam's feet.

'Whatever. I'm just saying what Bill said.'

Liam turned and limped away, hoping he looked weak and defeated, and took shelter on his tug. In the wheelhouse he hunkered down to wait, feeling the burn in his back and side where he'd been beaten. From his position he was fairly well-hidden but he had a good view of the gangplank and wharf above. A few minutes later he heard the sound of boots on the dock, and then saw Rick lumbering up the gangplank. After he'd passed, Liam counted to ten before he untied the tug, fired it up, and piloted it directly to the north end of the marina. This time at the *Kraken* he docked with deliberate carelessness: grinding the prow right into the hull and scouring out a two-foot gouge. He lashed one tieline loosely to a cleat on deck and lifted the cans of paint and primer one at a time, placing them on the portside gunnel, and once they were all lined up he climbed aboard with the hammer and rivet punch.

The forward deck gleamed in the sun with the fresh coat of oil Rick had given it. Now that the new teak planks were stained they blended in better with the older ones, but the contrast was still evident and always would be. The pot of oil was sitting on the deck; Liam kicked it over casually and got down to work. He took the first can of paint – the red can – and rested it upside-down on the portside gunnel. Placing the rivet punch against the bottom, he brought the hammer down on the punch and drove it through the tin. As he worked the punch back and forth to free it, red paint started leaking out like the first evidence of a wound. He picked up the can and, holding it between his palms by the lid and base, shook it like an odd musical instrument as he walked methodically around the deck. The red paint splashed and spattered across the newly oiled planks, leaving coloured arcs like slashes of blood, as well as blotches of various sizes, from large spots down to tiny speckles. When the spurts of red dwindled to a trickle he let the can drop and started on the next. This one was blue and the brightness of the hue created an unreal contrast against the red. The red alone had looked like a mistake; two colours made it more meaningful and more like art. He added the blue judiciously, using the entire deck as his canvas. The paint had a chemical smell that reminded him of the model paints he'd used as a child, only stronger. He breathed it in as he worked and the heady odour made him giddy and dizzy and high. Then the last of the blue sputtered out, so he punted the can towards the prow and reached for the can of yellow.

The result was becoming more beautiful with each coat, and he grew so engrossed in his project that he paid no attention to who might have noticed, or whether Rick could be coming back, until he heard a shout from the direction of the wharf. He looked up and saw the big man rumbling down the gangplank, his whole body rolling with the motion like a bull on the rampage. Liam dropped the half-finished can of yellow and left it to spill across the deck. In quick succession he punched holes in the remaining three cans of primer, knocking one overboard in his hurry. He left one of the others dribbling over the gunnel and bulwark and hull, and the last he lobbed like a grenade into the galley, where it landed with a clunk and began emptying across the floor.

Rick's footsteps were pounding on the docks, closer now, and Liam moved to undo his tie line. As he did he shoulder-checked and saw Rick's hands appear at the portside gunnel, followed by his head, rising up like a baleful moon, his expression full of rage and hate and something worse, something murderous. Holding the rope in one hand Liam leapt down to the tug. Rick was screaming and rushing at him and Liam knew that he didn't have time to start the engine so instead he just shoved hard with his hands against the hull of the *Kraken*, pushing away from the larger vessel. As he did he felt something brush his scalp and looked up and saw Rick leaning out over the water, having lunged for him and missed.

'You son of a bitch,' Rick was screaming, 'you son of a bitch!'

His face had gone almost purple and he continued shouting and screaming at him, telling him he was going to kill him and calling him a faggot and a cocksucker and a Newfie scab bastard, but all these insults sounded meaningless and empty over the five feet of water between them. Liam stood and stared at him like you might stare at a dog barking on the far side of a fence, and continued to stare as Rick shrieked and shook his fists and stomped up and down the deck, going rabid, working himself into a frenzy. Behind him, on the wharf, an audience had gathered. Rows of packing plant workers stood gazing down, in their white lab coats and face masks, observing the display like medical students who had come to witness some kind of strange human experiment.

Rick was still ranting when Liam fired up the tug, drowning the noise out. He did not say anything and did not look back as he pushed the throttle forward and manoeuvred the tug around the northwest corner of the marina. He headed for the gap in the breakwater that he had always dreamed of passing through, and it felt like a dream as he did so for the first and last time. Burrard Inlet opened up before him and the vista of North Vancouver lay behind it. To the west he could see the upright supports of the Lionsgate Bridge, and between them the strands of the suspension cables were strung like spiderwebs that glistened in the sun.

He cranked the throttle further, as far as it would go, and the tug lumbered forward, moving steadily and resolutely into the oncoming waves, which broke across its bow and crashed against its hull. He felt the concussions vibrating up through the deck, and each wave exploded in a shower of white spray, cool and light as snowflakes, that he felt flecking his face. In the distance were a few windsurfers slicing through the water like small fins, as well as trawlers and cruisers, but none of those were near him. Four or five miles out, when he was midway between the North Shore in front of him and the shipyards behind, he cut the motor and let the tug drift, rocking like a cradle on the waves.

He went to stand on deck. It was mid-afternoon and the height of the day's heat, and in his coveralls he was broiling. He unzipped the front carefully, removing first one sleeve and then the other, having to peel the sweaty garment off like the skin he'd always imagined it to be. He lowered it down to his waist and pushed it further, to his knees, and then kicked off his boots so he could step out of it. From there it seemed only natural to peel off his tank top, too, and his boxers and socks, until he was naked beneath sun. Out there he could no longer smell the stench of rotten herring, only the richness of the sea air, which he inhaled in long and grateful lungfuls – as if he'd just emerged after holding his breath in a swamp.

The sealskin was still lying on deck. He picked it up and held it out at arm's length, studying it. It was a complete hide. They had slit the seal's belly and opened her up to her throat, leaving the back intact. The scalp, too, was intact, with its empty eye sockets and flaps to the left and right that would have formed part of the jaw. He turned the skin around and draped it across his shoulders, cupping the scalp over his head and letting the tail hang down his back. It reached to just below his knees. He let go and found he could wear the hide like that without having to hold it in place. On his back it felt tough and comforting, a kind of armour, and he imagined himself as an Inuit or bushman, inhabiting the hide of his animal totem. Dressed like that, he went to perch at the prow, with one leg on deck and the other propped on the gunnel, supporting his elbow, in the pose of a thinker. He studied the downtown shoreline and could just make out the shipyards he'd left behind. There was no sign of any boat coming from there and he guessed that meant they'd decided not to follow him but instead would wait for him to come back.

'I'm not going back,' he said.

It felt good to say the words aloud. After he did, as if in answer, he heard an odd, deep sound like a dog barking. He looked around. At first he saw nothing and thought he had imagined it. Then, off to the starboard side, he spotted a small, bulbous head. It made that unmistakeable dog-like sound again, and he made the same sound back at it, or his best imitation of it. At that the seal fell silent. It seemed to be regarding him with scepticism, as if it sensed he was an imposter but wasn't quite sure.

Then the moment passed; the seal lost interest in him and dipped beneath the waves and didn't resurface. Liam got back behind the wheel and fired up the engine. Instead of turning around and heading for the shipyards, he kept going towards the North Shore, his home, wearing nothing except his sealskin cape, feeling aloof and alone and untouchable.

Reaching Out

I was halfway down the mountain when I saw this kid thumbing for a ride. Generally I got no qualms about picking up a hitcher, but I don't do it much anymore on account of people being scared of me. They see so much crap on the news and in the papers that they're about ready to piss themselves when a man in a plaid jacket and a hunting cap offers them a lift. Most of them don't want to get in with me, and the ones that do are jumpy as jackrabbits.

This kid seemed decent enough, though. He was wearing hiking boots and a green rain slicker and had a backpack slung over one shoulder – just a regular sort of kid. He was standing near the parking lot at the entrance to Old Buck trail. Out of season there aren't as many people up the mountain, and it could have been a while before anybody else picked him up. It wasn't raining, but it had been for most of the morning and looked ready to start again at any time. So I pulled over and rolled down my window.

'Where you headed?'

The kid blinked at me. 'Just down the mountain.'

'I'm going down if you want.'

He thought about it, fiddling with a clasp on his backpack. But I'd been cutting brush all day and didn't much feel like sitting there while he hummed and hawed. I put the truck back in gear. 'Look, your majesty – you want a ride or not?'

That decided him. He slipped into the cab, placing the bag on the floor, and shut the door. But he kept a hold of the handle, as if he was ready to jump back out. These goddamn people. I tell you.

I said, 'Hold on to your horses.'

And I popped the clutch and floored it. I drive the road up Seymour every day. It's as familiar to me as my own driveway, and I can hug the curves blindfolded. The kid didn't know that, though. He was fiddling with his seatbelt, trying to get the tongue to click, but the buckle on the passenger side is broken. When he figured that out, he didn't mention it. What he did was sort of drape the seatbelt over one shoulder, like a sash, and clutch at the grab-handle – the one attached to the roof of the cab.

'You drive pretty fast.'

'That's the only way.'

Rounding the next corner we fishtailed onto the shoulder. Gravel spit from under my wheels into the pines lining the ditch, drilling against the trunks like buckshot. The kid had actually closed his eyes, as if he was expecting to die, and I figured I'd made my point. After that, I dropped back down to fifty. I felt around in my pocket for a cancer-stick, and hung it in my mouth.

'You got a match, kid?'

'I don't smoke.'

'Crap.'

I'd used my last one, and the damn lighter in my truck was busted. But I felt foolish putting the cigarette back, so I let it hang there, limp as a dick. Every once in awhile I even took a drag on it. And as I was doing that, puffing away on air, I noticed this smell. It had infiltrated the cab – a rotten-meat type smell. At first, I figured the kid had farted.

'You let one rip, kid?'

'No. Sorry.'

'You don't have to be sorry. Just thought I smelled something funny is all.'

I shut my trap for a bit. Ever since what happened to Robbie, I haven't had much of a way with people. I'd just rather not talk, is all. I would have left it at that, but the smell got worse. It got so much worse that I would have assumed the kid had stepped in a pile of dog shit – except it wasn't quite that type of stink.

'Christ it reeks in here.'

'Yeah, man.'

'You smell it?'

'Yeah – I smell it too, now.'

'Maybe it's outside.'

I rolled down my window all the way and leaned out, clutching my hunting cap to my scalp so I didn't lose it in the blast of wind. I breathed in deep through my nose. The air out there was mountain-cold and tasted of autumn and pine and the recent rain.

'Nah,' I shouted. 'Ain't outside.'

When I pulled my head back in, the stench hit me all over again. It triggered a memory, in that way smells can, of the time I'd been fixing the support beams beneath our porch, and found a raccoon that had crawled under there to die.

I slowed the truck down, and stared at the kid, who was staring at me.

'Smells like a dead animal,' I said.

He didn't say anything for a while. With one hand, he took hold of the carry-strap on his backpack, which sat nestled in the wheel well, between his feet. It was a blue nylon day-pack, old and worn. The kind anybody would have.

'I don't feel so good, man,' he said. 'Maybe you better let me out.'

I kept coasting along at fifty, glancing between him and road.

'What's in the bag, kid?'

He looked down at the bag, frowning, almost as if he didn't know what was inside.

'Christ – how long you been out in the woods?'

Without taking his eyes from the bag, he said, 'Just today.'

'You went for a hike or something?'

'That's when I found it. On the hike.'

'Jesus. Why in the hell did you put it in there?'

'I didn't want to carry it.' He was still staring at the bag, and still holding onto it real tight. 'It was hard enough touching it once.'

'I mean, why not just leave it be?'

'I couldn't do that.' He finally looked up. 'I might not be able to remember where it was.'

'Right,' I replied, as if that explained it. As if that explained everything about this kid with a rotting animal in his bag. I asked him to at least roll down his window. Having both windows open made it more tolerable. The kid sat and watched the trees strafing past, and I kept studying the bag. The shape didn't give anything away. All I had to go on was the size. A raccoon would have been too big. A squirrel would have been too small.

'An owl, eh?'

'What?'

'In the bag. An owl.'

'It's not an owl, man.'

That stumped me. An owl had seemed a good bet. I sat there sucking on my unlit cigarette, trying to figure out what else it could be, but before I asked the kid again, he said, 'Do you work up here?'

He said it as if it was just part of the conversation. The next logical step. It took me a moment to answer. My head had to sort of shift gears.

'Sure,' I said, 'I cut trail for the forestry department.'

'Like your job?'

'I guess. Don't have to deal with any people. No boss breathing down my neck.' I hesitated, then thought I should maybe ask him something. 'What do you do, kid?'

'I work in Wendy's. Flipping patties.'

'That sounds okay.'

'We get free food, but my boss is a dickhead.'

'I had my share of those. Dickhead bosses, I mean.'

I took a long drag on my smoke, tasting the faintest hint of nicotine. All that talking was getting to me. I don't talk much with anybody except my wife, and that's different since I always know pretty much what she has to say. But the kid seemed intent on hashing it out.

'I like going hiking on my own,' the kid said. 'I like the sounds of nature. It's a lot quieter than a city, but noisier in its own way too. After the first hour or so your ears start to adjust, like they're tuning into a totally different station, you know?'

I grunted, to sort of signify that I did.

'You start picking up on things. The wind rustling the trees. The sound of a stream running. And all the animals – woodpeckers, chipmunks, whatever. I don't know. Maybe this sounds stupid. But it gets so you can even hear the silence, ringing in your ears.'

He paused, as if he expected me to say something. I cleared my throat. 'It's like that sometimes for me, when I'm cutting trail. It goes all quiet and pure like that.'

'That's it. That's exactly it. It's pure. There's no people around. People ruin everything. Wherever they go, they bring... they bring...'

But he didn't finish his sentence, and I couldn't think of a way to finish it for him. I took the smoke from my mouth, and did something funny: I tapped it to ash it, even though there was no ash. I was tapping imaginary ash, as it were.

'Anyways,' the kid said, 'that's what I think.'

'I hear you.'

From the way he'd been talking I figured he was a kid with a lot of ideas in his head, and that was all right by me. He was bright, but not real snotty or arrogant like some of the kids I've picked up. All told I guess I wouldn't have minded Robbie ending up like that. I tried to imagine what Robbie would have looked like at this kid's age. I took the face that was so familiar to me and changed the features, broadening his jaw and lengthening his nose and stretching him up into manhood. He would have been handsome – a real lady killer.

'I had a boy, once.'

'You mean you had a son?'

'Sure did. Robbie. He'd be about your age by now.'

I rested one elbow on the windowsill of the driver's side door, feeling my sleeve snap and ripple in the cold air rushing past, and waited for the kid to ask what he was going to ask.

'What happened to him?'

'He got sick. He got real sick and died.'

'Oh, man. I'm sorry.'

'Yeah. He was a good kid. Real smart, real talented. Would've made a better man than me, I can tell you that much.'

'That must have broke you.'

'Almost killed me. Probably would have, except for my wife. She's a real woman.' That didn't make much sense, so I added, 'She's just really strong is all.'

'My mom's like that, too. When my dad left she was only nineteen, and waitressing in bars. She had to put three kids through school and still managed to go to night classes. She's a teacher now.'

'You should be goddamned proud of her.'

'If I ever see my old man I'll tell him we were better off without him.'

I nodded. One thing I could never understand is a father that walks away from his children. A relationship is one thing. That's between two adults. Even a marriage – fine. Sometimes it doesn't work out. But to walk away from your kids. That just don't make any sense to me.

'Are you okay, man?'

'Sure. Why?'

'You just started driving a bit fast again.'

'Sorry.'

I slowed down. My knuckles on the steering wheel were white. I took breaths of clean air, in and out. The stink hadn't gone away despite all our gabbing. The butt of the cigarette in my mouth was all gummed and soggy by that point. I flicked it out the window. Probably the longest cigarette I ever smoked – and I hadn't even smoked it.

When I looked over, the kid was staring at the bag again. I waited. I wanted him to come to the decision on his own, without any prodding from me. We had something between us, now. We had some water under the bridge.

'Could you pull over?' he asked.

I pumped the brakes and eased us onto the shoulder. There was a solid wind blowing and the pines at the roadside swayed back and forth, all together, like mourners at a funeral.

'I've got to take a leak.'

Very deliberately, the kid lifted his bag and put it beside him on the seat, within arm's reach, before he got out of the truck. I watched as he made his way a few yards into the bush and stood with his back to me as he started watering the plants. I looked at the bag.

Now that I'd stopped, the stench should have been unbearable. But it was almost as if my nostrils had adapted and grown kind of accustomed to it.

I didn't move the bag. It was a fifteen or twenty litre pack, with two compartments and a small front pocket. It was all zipped up. With my right hand, I reached over and pinched the zipper of the main compartment between my thumb and forefinger. Then I coaxed it up, opening a slit in the side of the bag. I saw something that looked like clay, or plaster – grayish white and very smooth. I widened the slit. For a moment, I thought the thing actually was clay, sculpted into that stiff pose, with one finger extended and the others curled in upon themselves. It looked as if it was reaching out, or asking to be touched. So I did. I touched it. It was real, all right. The nails had gone bluish-grey and were rimmed with grime. I didn't see the base, but it couldn't have been the full arm. It must have started at the elbow. It was small, too. A lot smaller than mine, anyway.

When the kid got back in the car, the bag was zipped up again. He cradled it protectively on his lap, like a basket of eggs, as

I pulled out into the road. We didn't talk the rest of the way down. There wasn't much else to say, really. When we got to the base of the mountain, by Northlands golf course, I asked him, 'Maybe I should take you to the police station.'

'I guess so.'

'You want to go to Lonsdale, or downtown?'

'I live on Commercial, so downtown's closer.'

I took Mount Seymour Parkway to the Second Narrows, and crossed over the bridge. Underneath us the inlet was sloshing about, whipped up by winds. I came off at Nanaimo and hung a right on Hastings Street. After the calm of being up the mountain the city was a madhouse: long lines of traffic, drivers jockeying from lane to lane, horns honking, stereos blasting, people shouting. The sun had split the clouds, and the light flickered in shop fronts and flared off car windscreens. The pavement was still wet and glistened like the surface of a lake, blinding me to the point of tears.

The police station is this giant concrete block squatting on Cordova and Main, right in the worst area of the city, like a fortress surrounded by junkies and dealers and bag ladies. I couldn't find any parking out front, so I just had to flick on my hazard lights and pull over to drop off the kid. He hopped out, taking the bag with him, and then reached back through the window to shake my hand, real firm. His eyes were rimmed with red, as if he'd been crying, or was about to.

'Thanks for the ride, man.'

'Sure, man. No problem.'

Then he shut the door. I watched him trudge up the steps towards the station. As he reached the top, I leaned over and shouted at him through the passenger side window.

'Hey kid! How in the hell you gonna get home?'

He turned back and looked at me and didn't answer.

'Tell you what. I'm gonna go park up, get me some matches. I'll have a smoke and wait out here a spell. Then I can give you a lift back, later.'

'You don't have to do that.'

'I know I don't.'

He raised his arm, in thanks or acknowledgement, then went on in.

I parked up the street. On the corner of Cordova was a little minimart where I picked up some matches. Then I walked back and sat on the station steps, which were covered in gobs of spit and polka-dots of smashed gum. The cops going in and out of the doors ignored me. I was still aware of that smell, clinging to my clothes and lingering in my nostrils. The cigarette helped, some. I sat and smoked and tried to imagine how the kid would do it – how he'd show them that child's arm. He'd probably just walk in, put the bag on the counter, open it up, and reach inside. It was too late to worry about fingerprints. He must have touched it a bunch already. And if the cops had any sense then it wouldn't matter a whit.

Any idiot could see that he was innocent.

Scalped

Today is my last day on the barge, and I've been consigned to the ice bins. Roger's got me oiling the chains that pull the rakes. I'm spraying them down with an industrial-strength lubricant. What I do is this: I shake up the can, making the widget clack, and hose down a series of links. Then I wait while the lube leeches in, foaming and sputtering and creating a kind of lather, stained brown by rust and grease. Afterwards, I slot the end of my crowbar into each link and bend it back and forth, back and forth, slowly freeing up the pins. Every herring season the salt air causes the chain-links to rust, and every year we go through this ritual to loosen them and prevent them from seizing up. I've started with the starboard bin. All the ice has been cleared out – we did that a few weeks back – but in here it's still cold and damp as the bottom of a well, and the leftover moisture is oozing down the walls and pooling on the fiberglass floor. The power has to be shut off, for safety reasons, so my main light source is a halogen work lamp, strung in on an extension cord from the lower deck.

Roger and I were supposed to be doing this together, but last night he got a call from our supplier. The new alternator for the motor in one of our ice-making machines was ready, and he had to go pick it up – way the hell out in Delta. That was his reasoning, anyway. But I figure it's also partly my punishment for telling him that I'm leaving, for abandoning ship.

He seemed to take a certain satisfaction in explaining my duties to me.

'You'll be on your own in the bins, greenhorn,' he said.

'I can handle it.'

We were up in the lounge: me on the sofa and him sitting in his big reclining chair – his captain's chair. Doreen had already gone to bed. In the evenings she likes to retire early, as she calls it.

'I'll be back later on. Until then, you're in charge.'

'Captain for a day, eh?'

'That's right. Just watch yourself on them rakes.'

'I'll be careful.'

To do this work, the chains and rakes have to be at head height. The rakes are metal girders that span the whole width of the bin. Each one is studded with two-inch steel spikes, for combing and flaking the ice. I am very wary of these spikes, hovering at the edge of my vision, glinting in the half-light like the claws of a hawk. I've always had a thing about the rakes. Now that we're back in dock the nightmares have settled, but I won't fully relax until I'm safely ashore, and have put some distance between me and them. For now, for today, I move very carefully: ducking and stooping and lurching about with a hunch-backed gait.

At around two o'clock I run out of oil. We have more canisters up top, in the storage cupboard in the breezeway. Leaving my crowbar on the floor, I crab-walk sideways towards the door of the ice bin – keeping my head tilted at an angle, bending low beneath each rake. I've left the door open for the extra light it affords, and the entrance is a pale square in the dark, like the far end of a tunnel. Against it, the rows of rakes stand out in stark silhouette.

At the last rake, right near the door, I misjudge my step – or maybe the rakes lurch a bit, making a sudden movement just as I duck under. The tension in the chains causes them to do this, occasionally, and in this case it's as if they're reaching out for me. Something connects with my head and my neck crackles and then I am on the floor. I am on the floor and there is this searing, scalding pain in my scalp, right atop my skull. I clutch at the spot, twisting and squirming and arching my back as if the pain is electrocuting me, coursing through my whole body. I don't cry out – there's nobody to hear me cry – but what I do is make these soft whimpering noises, almost childish. And for a moment, in my pain-addled panic, I have the crazy thought that what I've always feared is actually happening: the rakes are coming for me, lurching into life and slowly descending, to break me and mangle me before I can get off the barge for good.

I'm so convinced of this that I open my eyes to check. But the rakes aren't moving – they just hang there, glistening like obsidian. Eventually the scalding pain dulls to something more tolerable: a kind of scorched feeling, like when you've burnt your hand on the stove. I sit up slowly, testing my neck. It's kinked, and I can feel the tendons creaking, but it seems okay. Then I shake off my work gloves and feel my head. The hair is wet and matted and when I inspect my fingers they are sticky-slick with red. The sight makes me think of a phrase Roger is fond of using: *bleeding like a stuck pig*. I'm bleeding like a stuck pig.

'Hell,' I say, and the word bounces around me in the darkness. 'Aw, hell.'

Eventually I pick myself up. Just outside the ice-bin doors, on the lower deck of the barge, there's a bathroom that we use while we're on shift – delivering ice or servicing boats. I stagger in there and splash cold water over my head, then scrunch-up some toilet paper and press it to my scalp, trying to staunch the bleeding. It stings like acid. I perch on the toilet and have a bit of a think, trying to decide just how in the hell I'm gonna explain all this to Doreen.

When I come into the galley, Doreen is standing at the counter with her back to me. She's got potatoes bubbling on the stove and I can smell something – a crumble, probably – baking in the oven. On the countertop she's kneading a mound of dough the size of a bowling ball, massaging it with her small, firm fingers. She hears the door and greets me without looking back. She knows it's me since we're the only two on the barge today.

Then she says, 'Thought I'd make us some bread to go with your meal tonight.'

That's how we're referring to it: my meal. Not the last meal, or the goodbye meal. It's just easier all around, I guess.

'That's great,' I say. I hover in the doorway, fiddling with my work gloves – bending the empty fingers back and forth. Then I clear my throat and say, 'Uh, Doreen?'

Finally she looks my way, and her expression changes when she sees the blood on my shirt, my dripping hair, the ball of scrunched-up tissue stuck to my head like a wilted flower. I start explaining that I had a mishap, just a little mishap, down in the ice bin. A bit of an accident. But she can see that. She smacks her palms together, striking them in an up-down motion once, twice, to dust the flour off, and puts her hands on her hips in a schoolmarm pose.

'What did you do?'

I explain about the rake, about misjudging my step. I don't tell her I think the rake might have moved because that would sound odd, paranoid, maybe even a little insane. But Doreen, she's real understanding. She reaches down for her glasses, which hang from a cord around her neck, and puts them on before motioning me over. She's nearly a foot shorter than me, and I have to kneel down in front of her, like a penitant, so she can take a look. She peels away the padded tissue – the sting making me stiffen – and then I feel her exploring up there, pushing my hair to one side. She makes a slight sound of affirmation in her throat.

'That's a war wound, all right.'

'Is it bad?'

'It's not good.'

'Will it need stitches?'

'Come and see.'

She makes an elevating gesture with her hand, palm-up, and leads me from the galley into her and Roger's bathroom, which is at the back of the cabin. During season, Doreen doesn't like the deckhands using it. She's always saying, 'You grease monkeys have your own toilets to dirty up.' It's got square floor tiles, a shortened bathtub, and a vanity mirror above the sink. She gets me to crouch in front of the mirror. Fresh blood is leaking from the cut, not just in my hair but over my face: a single streak has snaked down my cheekbone and jaw like warpaint. Doreen takes up position behind me. She's holding a small make-up mirror – the kind in a clamshell case, that snaps open. I can't read her expression.

It's almost sly, as if she's about to share a secret. She asks me if I'm ready, and holds the mirror up behind my head, so I can see the damage to my scalp in the double-reflection.

'Right along here,' she says, pointing with a forefinger.

The gash is about five inches long, and half an inch across. The skin on one side of the cut is buckled and peeled back in a flap, like when you slice the tip of your finger while chopping vegetables. Underneath, in the crevasse, I see something smooth and pink, which is either a layer of fat, or maybe my skull. Seeing all this, I make a small meeping sound, like a mouse or a baby bird. That's all that comes out.

'Yep,' Doreen says cheerfully, 'I'd say you'll need some stitches.'

I still don't say anything. My face has gone very white, like porcelain.

'But don't you worry – we can see to that right here.'

I look at her, in the mirror. 'Shouldn't we go to the hospital?'

'What for?' She's frowning, now. 'I was a nurse for twenty-odd years before joining Roger on the boats. I'm not just the cook around these parts – I'm the First Aid Officer, too.'

'It looks pretty serious.'

'Don't be a nervous nelly. Nothing to it.'

I turn my head – feeling the tendons clicking in my neck – so I'm looking up at her, face-to-face, rather than at her reflection in the mirror. She's got her arms crossed, and peers down her nose at me from underneath her spectacles, waiting while I decide.

'But if you'd rather I drive you down to A and E, and make a big deal about it...'

'No, no,' I say. 'It's okay. Let's do it.'

She beams and pats my shoulders. I can still smell the flour on her – that comforting scent of cooking and home and wholesomeness. 'That a boy. Now the first thing we have to do is get this cleaned out properly.'

She tells me to take off my blood-spattered workshirt, and directs me to kneel beside their tub. There are two bath balls next to the taps, and the tub smells of lavender and Epsom salts. The shower head is the kind attached to a metal hose. She removes the nozzle from its holder and turns on the cold tap. Then she instructs me to lean forward and lower my head. I kneel like that, as if I'm praying, with my chest pressed to the edge of the tub, and wait. In a moment I feel the cold water wash over my scalp, making the cut sting.

'That's it,' Doreen says, 'You're okay, there.'

The water spattering into the basin and swirling down the drain is pinkish. Doreen lets the shower run for several minutes, until my scalp goes numb from the cold and the water clears. She twists off the tap, straightens me up, and pads my hair dry with a face cloth.

'You hold that there,' she says, guiding my hand up to the cloth to replace hers, 'and apply pressure, while I fetch the field kit.'

She leaves me perched on the toilet seat. Beneath the cloth, the cut begins to throb again as the blood returns to it. There is a fan in the ceiling – tucked away behind a vent – and I can hear it rattling around and around. I feel dizzy, dazed. I'm staring at a spot on the tiled floor, worrying about this whole scheme with the stitches, these do-it-yourself stitches. It's the kind of thing you hear about going horribly wrong. The wound gets infected, and turns septic, and then some poor bastard gets blood poisoning and dies, just like that. Or at the very best, the stitches are a botched job, and you end up with a hideous, zigzag scar.

It's not really the kind of predicament I ever thought I'd find myself in.

When Doreen comes back, she's carrying the big green First Aid kit that we keep on the barge. It's the size of a fishing tackle box, and built in the same way: with a flip-up lid and plastic fasteners to snap it shut. Doreen stands in the doorway, surveying the bathroom critically. She tells me there isn't enough room in here – there's not much counter around the sink – and that to do this right, to do this proper, we'll have to go into her and Roger's bedroom, across the hall.

I follow her over there. I've glimpsed their room in passing before but I've never entered it. All of us deckhands sleep in the bunkhouse across the breezeway. Their room is bigger and more spacious, with a proper double bed and furnishings. Like everything else on the barge, it's functional, tidy, and well maintained. The bedclothes are tucked in and pulled taut as a trampoline. Next to the headboard is a small table and on the table sits a lamp, an alarm clock, and the King James Bible. Against the far wall, adjacent to the window, stands a dressing table. That's where Doreen sits me down. Atop it there's another mirror – the oval kind you can swivel around. This time when I look in the glass I see a young, frightened face.

'Sorry about this, Doreen,' I say.

She plonks the First Aid kit down on the dresser. 'You didn't do it on purpose.'

'No,' I say, thinking back, 'I reckon not.'

'Then you got nothing to apologise for.'

'Feel like a damned fool, is all.'

I don't know when I began talking like this: saying things

like 'I reckon' and 'damned fool'. It's happened sometime during these three seasons I've spent with them. It's as if their words and phrases have been slowly sinking into my brain, becoming part of my vocabulary.

'Wasting your time, is what I'm doing.'

'I'm still getting paid, aren't I?' She thumbs open the clasps on the kit, flips back the lid, and starts rooting around inside for whatever it is she needs. 'It's no skin off my nose if I'm patching you up instead of cooking and cleaning and tending to the barge.'

'No – it's just skin off my scalp.'

We both laugh about that. I stop laughing when she begins taking out her equipment. She lays down a hand towel first, then places each item on it in a well-spaced row: a bottle of betadine, a pair of scissors, some tweezers – which she refers to as the pick-ups – and another tool that's shaped like a set of forceps.

'What's that?' I ask.

'The needle holders.'

Next to the needle holders she puts a small plastic package, about the size of a sugar sachet, labelled 4-0 nylon black monofilament. Then she continues poking about in the box.

'Wow-ee,' she says, 'lookie here.'

She holds up a green flask. It's a small bottle of Napolean brandy – about half the size of a regular mickey. The label is faded and peeling, the glass filmed over with grease.

'Roger would flip,' I say.

'He must have forgotten about it.'

Roger keeps a dry barge, and has for years. I don't know if it's because of some accident back in the day, or if it's to do with their religion, or if it's just his policy. But he's fond of saying that alcohol and water don't mix – and enforces it whether we're docked or at sea. The deckhands all grumble about it, but not in front of Roger.

'Could come in handy,' Doreen says, placing it to one side.

But she's still after something else. She keeps digging for another few minutes, and eventually shakes her head. 'Gosh darn it,' she says, which is as close as she gets to cursing.

'What's missing?'

'The needle. Can't suture a laceration without a needle.'

'Darn, eh?' I say. 'Guess it'll be the hospital after all.'

'Don't be silly. I got plenty of needles in my sewing kit.'

'Sewing needles?'

'Yup.'

She's already headed for the door. I call after her, 'Don't you need a different type of needle for, uh, suturing?' I don't know much about stitching wounds, but I know that much.

'It's not that different,' she shouts back.

I can hear her opening drawers in the lounge.

'But doesn't it have to be sterilised or whatever?'

'I'll boil it.'

She says it as if we're talking about cooking dinner. An egg or a potato, maybe. I'll boil it. It's that simple. And maybe it is. But it's not making me feel any better about this whole operation of ours. I sit tense and still, listening to her and trying to deduce what she's doing. I hear the kettle whistle, followed by the pouring of water – into a pot, I'm guessing – and then Doreen returns to get the needle holders and pick-ups, which apparently have to be sterilised, too. She putters around for a few minutes out there, and when she reappears she's got a bottle of Tylenol in one hand, and a mortar and pestle cupped in the other. She tells me it'll only take a few minutes to sterilise the needle, and while we wait she's going to fix me up something to take the edge off. That's the phrase she uses: to take the edge off.

'Do I need that?'

'In the hospital, they'd give you local anaesthetic – but we got to make our own.'

'Makeshift anaesthetic, eh?'

'Worked for Roger when he lost his finger.'

'Great.'

'That reminds me – I need him to pick up some salad for your dinner.'

She fishes her cellphone out of her purse. It's a pink brick, a Nokia, with those big, easy-touch buttons. I helped her pick it out at the start of season, when we were shopping for barge supplies. She told me she didn't want anything fancy – no bells or whistles, she said – just a phone that could make calls, so a basic Nokia seemed like a safe bet.

'Let me just see here,' she says.

She tips her head to peer over her glasses at the display, punching in the number slowly and deliberately, with her forefinger, in the way older people do. She always dials, even though I've added Roger's number to her contacts. Then her phone is ringing, quite loudly since she has the volume turned up, and I can hear Roger answer it. She reminds him about the salad, and then starts telling him about my little run-in with the rakes. As she does, I stare at myself in the mirror. I'm still holding the cloth on my head like some kind of pantomime clown.

'That's right,' she says. 'I'm gonna patch him up here.'

I hear Roger ask something, but I can't make out the words. In response, Doreen says, 'He's holding up all right. He ain't blubbing, anyway.' She pauses, and adds, 'Yep – he scalped himself good.'

I can hear Roger howl at that, and I kind of chuckle, too. The way she says it makes me think of the Westerns Roger reads while we're at sea, and which he's got me reading: Max Brand and Louis L'amour and Zane Gray. In them, the Apaches are always scalping people, or collecting scalps. When a brave gets his first scalp, it's a real big thing, apparently. Like he's become a man. I don't think it counts if you accidentally scalp yourself, though.

'Tell him I'll finish the rakes before dinner,' I say.

'You heard that?' Doreen asks Roger. There's another pause, and then, 'Uh-huh. I will. Just you make sure you remember the things for my salad. And we'll see you later.'

She puts down the phone and catches my eye in the mirror.

'Alternator's been delayed, but he'll be back for dinner. He said to make sure we check you've had your tetanus shot, because of the rust on them rakes.'

'What happens if I haven't?'

'Then we'll get you one.'

'At the hospital?'

'Or the clinic.'

'So we'll be going in anyway?'

'Don't worry about that, now.'

She checks her watch. Apparently there's still five minutes to go. In the meantime, she starts preparing her anaesthetic. She taps three Tylenol into the mortar – the pills rattling like chips of ceramic – and begins grinding them up with the pestle. Outside the window to my left, a passenger plane is streaking slowly across the sky, leaving a stream of vapour. It's headed towards Vancouver airport, over in Richmond, where I'll be flying out from in a month or so. I track its progress, trying to imagine that. The whole thing doesn't seem real just yet.

'There goes a plane,' I say, just to be saying something.

Doreen glances at it, grunts, and asks, 'You all set for this big trip of yours?'

'I got my work visa, and my ticket booked.'

'No backing out, now.'

'No ma'am.'

'And this girl you're going to see – you're sure about her?'

'I'm sure I like her well enough.'

I haven't told her and Roger that we'll be living together. To them that would amount to a kind of marriage, a real commitment, and I'm trying not to think about it like that. We're just feeling things out, is all. Seeing how it goes.

'What's she do, this girl?' Doreen asks.

'She does what they call Theatre in Education.'

Doreen frowns. 'Like some kind of actress?'

She says it suspiciously, as if it might be improper, somehow.

'More like a teacher. Working with kids, and doing drama.'

'Well, I sure hope it turns out for you. The thing to ask yourself is whether or not she would stand by you. That's all that matters, when it comes down to it. The rest is just...' She makes a waving motion, as if brushing away a fly.

I think about that. The plane has disappeared, leaving a line that divides the sky.

'I reckon she would,' I say.

'Let's hope so,' Doreen says, and checks her watch again.

To adapt her sewing needle into a suturing needle, Doreen has bent it with a pair of pliers – curling it into a kind of crooked, thumbnail shape. It's sitting in the bottom of the pan of steaming water, alongside the pick-ups and needle holders, and also a turkey baster, which looks like a giant eye dropper made out of metal. Doreen puts the pan on a coaster so it doesn't burn the dresser. The steam fogs up the mirror, obscuring my face.

'Time to operate,' she says. 'How's it feeling?'

'It still stings something fierce.'

'I'll bet. And it's gonna get worse.'

Before we start, she dumps the powdered Tylenol into a glass tumbler, splashes in a few ounces of the brandy, and stirs it around with a teaspoon. She puts the glass in my hand.

'Go slow – there's fifteen hundred milligrams of Tylenol in there.'

'Is that a lot?'

'It's enough.'

I take a sip, tentatively. It has the usual burnt-fruit taste of brandy, but with a bitter afterbite, almost salty, from the Tylenol. Doreen tears open the pack of latex gloves, shakes them out, and snaps them on. With her fingers, she smooths my hair away from the wound, so the strands won't get tangled in the stitches. She's humming to herself as she does it – one of her country tunes, I think – and you can tell how much she's enjoying this whole thing.

'The good news,' she says, 'is that the tough part comes first.'

'That's the good news, eh?'

'We got to flush the wound.'

She picks up the turkey baster and squeezes the bulbous end. Then, while dipping the tip in the steaming water, she releases the bulb to fill up the baster.

'This is salt water,' she explains, 'a makeshift saline.'

'Seems like a lot of this operation is makeshift.'

'Shush, you. Brace yourself – it's gonna smart like heck.'

Using her left hand, she parts the gash in my head and peels back the flap of skin. I watch this curiously through the fogged-up mirror. Raising the baster, she squirts the warm saline into the cut in a steady stream. I jerk in my chair, slopping a bit of brandy on my chest, and make a faint, feeble sound – as if I've been stung by a bee.

'There you go,' Doreen says, patting the area dry. 'Not so bad, was it?'

'If you say so.'

She's already moving on, reaching for the bottle of betadine. She splashes a little of the ochre-coloured liquid on a cotton pad, dabs this on the area surrounding the cut – but not in it – and then fishes the pick-ups, needle holders, and needle out of the pan. It takes her a few tries to thread the monofilament through the eye of the needle. When she's managed it, and tied it off, she takes up the needle holders and I get to see how they work. They act as a set of tongs, pinching the needle. Holding it like that, she gets into position behind me. She asks if I'd like her to turn the mirror around, but I tell her no, it's okay – I want to see this.

'So long as you don't faint on me,' she says.

I raise my glass obediently. I've knocked back an ounce or so, now, on an empty belly, and I can feel the slow smoulder of the liquor spreading through my limbs. Doreen leans over me, holding the pick-ups in her left hand and gripping the needle holders in the right. The line of thread dangles down against my cheek like a cobweb.

'I need you to sit still, now,' Doreen says, in the same matter-of-fact tone she uses to explain one of her cooking recipes. 'What I'm going to do is stitch this left to right, using a simple running stich. Do you know what that is?'

I tell her I don't.

'It'll save us time.' She places the tip of the pick-ups near the wound, to steady the skin, and then moves in with the needle. I feel the first prick as it pierces my scalp, and I wince instinctively. Doreen waits for me to get myself together before working the needle deeper, hooking it under the skin with a twisting motion of her wrist, talking calmly to me all the while. 'An interrupted stitch goes sideways across the cut, like railway tracks, but you have to tie off each suture, which is a real pain in the petutty.'

'I hear you.'

'A running stitch crosses the wound at an angle, which means you can keep stitching continuously until you're done, and only have to tie it off at the beginning, and the end.'

I can't see the site of the wound too well, or what she's doing, but I see my scalp lift up under the pressure of the needle, before it breaks the skin and pokes back out the other side. It's an odd sight, seeing that steel crescent emerging from my scalp. I can feel it tickling, but it doesn't hurt much. She releases it, holds it in place with the pick-ups, and pinches it again with the needle holders to pull it all the way through, trailing a tail of thread. To finish the first stitch, she loops the thread around the tips of the needle holders, making some kind of knot. She snugs that up against my scalp, and ties it off twice more for good measure.

'If you want to get fancy,' Doreen says, aiming the needle again, 'if you want to get highfalutin, you can do what we call a running subcuticular, where the stitching is all under the skin – to make it less noticeable – or a vertical mattress technique, for deeper wounds.'

The needle slips in and out, and she plucks at it with the pick-ups. I tip my glass back and forth, sloshing the liquid around. 'Sounds like you sure know your stuff, nurse Doreen.'

'You didn't believe me, did you?'

'No ma'am.'

As she works, she keeps talking to me. I know it's her way of keeping me distracted, putting me at ease, but that doesn't make it any less effective. I watch her face in the mirror. She's frowning slightly, and each time she sticks the needle into my scalp her eyebrows raise and her mouth parts, in a look of hopeful concentration. Her hands are steady and assured, a nurse's hands, and now that I'm able to sit still the stitching motion is smooth: a piercing and plucking, entering and exiting, as the needle goes in, hooks under, and rises up.

This goes on for several minutes, while Doreen maintains her running commentary. She tells me that the line has to be snug, to hold the skin together, but that it's also important not to make it too tight. 'Choking the dog, they call that,' she says, and chuckles. She also tells me about the various other injuries she's had to deal with on the boats: Roger's severed fingertip, the deckhand who mangled his arm in the ice-making machines, the fisherman who tried to leap from his boat onto the barge and got his foot crushed between the hull and the gunnel. I've heard most of them before. They're the war stories of the barge, which are always recounted with a certain relish. The worse and more gruesome the injury, the better.

'Compared to some,' I say, 'I guess I got off easy.'

'This here cut of yours ain't nothing to sniff at.'

'No?'

'No sir.'

'How many stitches you putting in, anyway?'

'Eleven and counting.'

Eleven. It seems like a lot. It seems like something you

might hear about, rather than something that had happened to you. He needed a dozen stitches, people would say. He cut himself wide open. He bled like a stuck pig.

'How you holding up?' she asks.

'I'm fine, Dorie,' I say, even though I've never called her that. It's what Roger calls her, sometimes. 'I'm fine, Nurse Dorie. You just keep on putting in those stitches. Slap in as many as you like – as many as you see fit.'

Her mouth twitches, like she's trying not to smile.

'Okay, Chief,' she says. 'Now go easy on that firewater, you hear?'

'It's going down easy, all right.'

'I can see that.'

My tumbler's nearly empty, now. I sit with it resting on my belly as she finishes up. She's found a rhythm, and executes each stitch with an expert flick, almost a flourish. She puts in two more stitches – thirteen in total – and then begins tying the thread off. She does this in the same way as before: looping the thread around the needle holders, pulling the end through, and tightening the knot. She repeats this ritual three times. To finish, she puts the needle holders aside, takes up the scissors, and snips off the thread right close to my scalp.

'All done, Chief,' she says.

She drops the needle, pick-ups, and needle holders back in the pan – the metal rasping on metal, making that whisking sound – and holds up the compact mirror again so I can see. She tilts the mirror back and forth to show various angles, like a barber displaying a finished haircut. The crescent wound is stitched with a diagonal series of sutures, each one about a centimetre apart. The surrounding skin is still stained by betadine, but the laceration looks smaller now that it's been closed up. The fierce, fiery burn has faded to a dull smoulder.

'Thanks, nurse Dorie,' I say, knocking back the last of my brandy. 'You did a hell of a job on that.'

'Language.'

'Heck of a job, I mean. Heck of a job.' I plonk the tumbler down on the dresser and stand up, feeling nice and loose, gangly as a rag doll. 'Well, I better get back down there, eh? Back to the front line, right? As Roger would say, those rakes ain't gonna oil themselves.'

'Somebody's had a bit too much anaesthetic.'

'No ma'am.'

'You come with me, now.'

I keep protesting, but she takes my hand and leads me into the lounge, where she sits me down on the chair – the big reclining chair that's usually reserved for Roger. It's a plush chair, soft and padded, with plaid patterns on the upholstery. I sink right into it like a dream.

'Now you sit tight, Chief,' Doreen says, 'I got us a meal to fix.'

'And I got me a job to do.'

'Your job is to sit in that chair, young man.'

She's pretending to be cross with me, but I can tell she's getting a kick out of it.

'That's no job,' I say.

'You're on watch, like when we're at sea.'

She leaves me sitting there and begins puttering about in the kitchen. Roger's recliner has one of those levers – like the handbrake on a car – that you crank to raise a footrest and lower the chairback. I do this and lie down in it and gaze out the window. Not the one on the port side, which overlooks shore, but the aft window, which has a view of Burrard Inlet.

The tide is high, the harbour swollen with water: oily and dark and roiling against the breakwater. I imagine what Roger must feel, sitting here at the helm of the *Arctic King*, buoyed up by the confidence of his experience, an entire life on the boats, on the sea. It's a good feeling.

'How's it looking out there, Chief?' Doreen asks from the kitchen.

'It's looking mighty fine, Doreen.'

My scalp is tingling again. I reach up to touch it, spider-walking my fingers around the stitches, which feel odd and knobby and foreign.

'Say, nurse,' I say. 'These sutures are starting to hurt again. I think that potion of yours is wearing off.'

She comes to stand in the doorway, arms crossed, looking stern. She's got her apron on again. 'You can't have any more Tylenol, Alex. Not for a few hours, at least.'

I wince and palm my head, as if it's really killing me. 'Maybe just another ounce of that brandy, then. Just something to take the edge off.'

Doreen shakes her head, and I figure that's it, but she surprises me by going into their bedroom, where we've left the First Aid kit, to fetch the brandy. I clap my hands and stand up and perform a wobbly-kneed pirouette. There's a stereo above the TV in the lounge, with a stack of Roger and Doreen's music next to it: Willie Nelson, Johnny Cash, Emmylou Harris. I put on *Luxury Liner* and settle back into Roger's seat, feeling just peachy, while I wait for Doreen. She's taken the brandy into the kitchen. I hear her getting out a glass.

'Say,' I call, 'why don't you have a little yourself, Dorie? Just to take the edge off.'

'Edge off what?'

'Off our goodbye. I'm leaving, for God's sake.'

'Language!'

'For gosh sake.'

I hear her chuckle. 'I haven't had a drink in eight weeks.'

'That's eight weeks too long.'

'Maybe just the one.'

'That's right. Just the one.'

I hear the fridge door open and close, the crack of ice in the ice tray, and the clink of cubes hitting glass. When she comes in, she's got a pair of highball tumblers, filled to the brim with liquid. She hands one to me, and I sniff at it suspiciously. It smells like lemons.

'What's this?' I ask.

'Brandy sour. Figured you needed something to slow you down, Chief.'

'Well, I'll be. Who would have thought you weren't just a cook, and a nurse, but a bartender.'

She laughs and pats her hair, in a gesture I've only scene in old films – a kind of retro puffing of her perm. Then she takes a seat on the sofa across from me, and raises her glass.

'Just don't tell Roger,' she says.

'Alcohol and water don't mix.'

'A dry barge is a safe barge.'

'Good old Roger.'

We both laugh, affectionately, and then settle into silence. Out on the inlet there's a tugboat chugging by, and on the stereo Emmylou is singing about some guy named Poncho who got shot in Mexico.

'What do you think he'll do?' I ask. 'About the barge, I mean.'

Doreen sips her cocktail and considers this.

'We got a couple more years left in us, before we retire.'

'Before you retire from your retirement.'

'That's right. And of course Roger's been looking for somebody to take this old girl over after that.' She glances at me, and then her eyes slide away, over towards the window, as if this person might be out there instead of in here. 'But that's the company's problem, really. They'll find somebody who wants the job. It's good, honest work. Man's work.'

'I know it.'

She looks at me, and smiles, and it's a tough thing to see – so sad and understanding.

'What about you, Alex?' she asks. 'Is this trip for good?'

'I wish I could tell you, Doreen.'

'You sure are giving up a lot.' She gestures with her free hand – a sweeping gesture that seems to take in not just the barge, but the city and landscape outside the window. 'But we all got to make our own way, I guess.'

'I'll be back now and again.'

'And this girl of yours – does she ever come out to visit you?'

The way she says it implies that any girl wouldn't be worth much if she didn't.

'She sure does.'

'Well, maybe next time you could bring her out to the barge. Have lunch with us, and show her around.'

'That'd be something.'

The oven timer goes in the kitchen. Ding.

'That's your bread,' Doreen says, but doesn't make a move to get it.

We're still sitting there, stirring the pot, when Roger gets back.

We hear him on the stairs first – the iron rungs ringing out, anvil-like, beneath his steel-toed workboots. Then comes the familiar, beer-keg rumble of his footsteps rolling down the breezeway. Me and Doreen stand up, like soldiers coming to attention. Roger has that effect on you. Nobody – even his wife – likes to be caught by Roger doing nothing. Being idle, he calls it. She slides into the kitchen and I hear the sound of her dumping her ice into the sink, then the tap running as she rinses her glass. My own brandy sour is only half-finished. I debate leaving it like that, then down the rest and tuck the glass behind the lamp on the side table, out of sight. Just before he arrives, I turn down the stereo and pick up a book – one of Roger's westerns – and go to sit with it on the sofa, taking Doreen's spot.

The door opens in the kitchen, and Roger bellows, 'Something sure smells good.'

'Dinner's almost ready,' Doreen tells him. 'You got my salad?'

'I got it. Where's Alex?'

'Our invalid's recuperating in the lounge.'

He comes on through without taking off his boots, and pauses in the doorframe. It looks too small for him, that doorframe. At sixty-seven he's still big and strong as an old boar. In one hand he's gripping a paper bag, the top rolled down to form a handle. I smile and stand up, clasping the western in front of me like a prayer book.

'Well, greenhorn,' he says, 'let's see this scrape of yours.'

He stomps over to me and I bow my head for him to inspect. I realise I'm going to be doing this a lot, in the weeks to come: for friends, for family, for total strangers. Displaying my scar like a new tattoo.

Roger takes my head in his hands. His fingers are thick

and powerful and it feels as if he could crush my skull like a walnut. I'm holding my breath, hoping he won't catch a whiff of the brandy. He whistles, long and low.

'That's a man's wound, Alex.'

'Didn't I tell you he scalped himself?' Doreen calls.

'He sure did.'

I laugh along with them at that. Roger lets go of my head, but he's still standing close to me. When I look up, his eyes are narrow, his jaw tight.

'You smell like booze, boy.'

'It's the anaesthetic,' I say. It's the only thing that occurs to me.

Doreen pokes her head in. 'I gave him a little nip of brandy to stop him squirming.'

Roger looks at her, hard, and something – maybe everything – seems to be hanging in the balance.

'Where'd you get brandy?' he asks.

'There's a flask in our First Aid kit. Must be as old as the barge itself.'

Roger glances once around the room. It's as if he senses something's amiss. His gaze lingers on his chair, which is still laid flat. I forgot to set it right. Then he turns back to me.

'I take it the rakes didn't get finished, either?'

'I figured we could do them together, tomorrow.'

'You're leaving tomorrow.'

It sounds harsh, the way he says it. Like I've committed a crime.

'Not until evening. We got the whole day, if we want it.'

'Hmmm,' he says. Then, raising his voice, he asks, 'So he was squirming, was he?'

He's talking to Doreen, but still peering at me.

'He went a little green around the gills when I started stitching.'

'It hurt like a son of a gun,' I say.

He grunts. 'I'll bet it did. I got you something by way of compensation. I guess it's a little redundant, now.'

He reaches into the paper bag. Doreen is still hovering in the doorway, looking as anxious as I feel. It's as if there could be anything in that bag. Anything at all. He unfurls the top, rolling it up real slow, and shoves one of his big bear-paws inside. Then he tugs the bag away from the bottom, like a magician performing a trick, and there in his hand is a six-pack of Labatt, in bottles. Doreen actually squeaks.

'Well, Roger Laramie. I never thought I'd see it.'

'It's the boy's last night, Dorie. And what with his head and all, I figured he could use a brew or two.' Then he scowls at me – part mocking, part serious. 'Didn't know he'd already gotten into the brandy, of course. I guess this ain't much compared to brandy.'

'No – that's great, Roger. That's really something.'

'Might even have one myself, if my old lady looks the other way.'

Doreen tuts with her tongue, playing the part he wants her to play. She comes over to take the beers from him, holding them protectively. 'I best be in charge of these.'

In passing the table, she deposits two beers – one at the head, where Roger will sit, and one off to the side, by my seat.

'You men take a load off, now,' she says, disappearing into the kitchen. 'It'll be awhile before dinner's ready. I got to put the steaks on and prepare the salad, yet.'

I shuffle over there. Roger takes the time to adjust his chair, raising the back, and puts a new CD on the stereo. He chooses Johnny Cash. Johnny one-note, he calls him. Good old Johnny one-note.

Once we sit down, Roger caps his bottle of Labatt, and passes me his Swiss Army knife so I can do the same. In the process, I tilt my head forward, and Roger starts chuckling. Without meaning to, I've shown him my stitches again.

'It's like your scalp is smiling at me,' he says. 'That's gonna scar, all right.'

'You think?'

'Does a chicken have lips?'

Through the door to the kitchen, I can see Doreen laying out steaks on a skillet. Each one hisses as it hits the pan, sending up a brief burst of grease-smoke. She glances over. 'Now he's got something to remember us by.'

'That's right,' Roger agrees. He waggles the stump of his finger at me. It got lopped off at the second knuckle. 'You got yourself a battle scar. Every fisherman needs one, see?'

'Even if I did it to myself.'

'That's mostly the case, unfortunately.'

He raises his beer, and I do the same. We don't clink bottles – we just raise them like that, in a kind of toast across the table.

'No matter where you go – Wales or wherever the heck it is – and no matter how big you get for your britches, you'll always have that there scar on your scalp. You're marked.'

'Yes sir,' I say, as if professing a vow, 'I guess I am.'

And once I've said it, I imagine I can feel the burning scar beginning to cool, like molten metal, settling into something more solid and more permanent.

Acknowledgements

Earlier versions of these stories first appeared in the following magazines and anthologies: *Ascent Aspirations* ('The Art of Shipbuilding'); *Brace*, by Comma Press ('Tokes From the Wild'); *CFUK* ('Edges'); *Cottonwood* ('Scalped'); *Dream Catcher* ('Fishhook'); *The Lampeter Review* ('Scrap Iron' and 'There's a War Coming'); *New Orphic Review* ('Sealskin'); *Nu: Fiction and Stuff*, by Parthian ('Carving Through Woods on a Snowy Evening'); and *Transmission* ('Shooting Fish in a Stream').

'Mangleface' won first prize in the annual Frome Festival Short Story Competition, and was subsequently published in the Parthian anthology, *Rarebit*. 'Reaching Out' won the Cinnamon Press Short Story Award, and was published in the winner's anthology of that title. 'Sealskin' was awarded the Writers' Trust of Canada/ McClelland & Stewart Journey Prize, and was republished in The Journey Prize Stories 26. 'Snares' was a finalist in the *Carve Magazine* Esoteric Short Story Contest, and an extract of the story appeared in *Cheval 6*.

Thanks are due to those editors and judges, as well as the various readers who have helped select and edit these stories along the way: Becky, Claire, Dave, Jim, Marilyn, Martin, Matty, Mike, Naomi, and Richard.

More short-story collections from...

Winner of the
Edge Hill Readers' Choice award

Rachel
Trezise

Edgy, finger-on-the-button prose...
Trezise very much speaks for and about
her generation; she is honest, funny,
perceptive and fresh... a first-class writer
The Short Review

GOLDFISH
MEMORY

MONIQUE
SCHWITTER

PARTHIAN

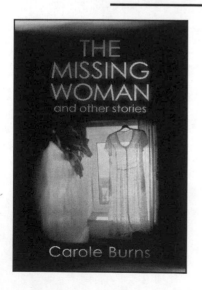

THE
MISSING
WOMAN
and other stories

Carole Burns

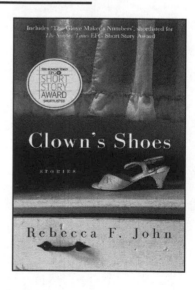

Includes 'The Glove Maker's Numbers', shortlisted for
The Sunday Times EFG Short Story Award

Clown's Shoes
STORIES

Rebecca F. John

www.parthianbooks.com